Fron

Please use with care and return...

2365 Rice Boulevard, Suite 202, Houston, Texas 77005

10 9 8 7 6 5 4 3 2 1

Library of Congress Cataloging-in Publication Data

White, Andrea, 1953-
Radiant Girl / by Andrea White.
p. cm.
Summary: In the aftermath of the 1986 Chernobyl nuclear power plant disaster, a Ukrainian girl named Katya comes to understand the things most important about her homeland, and in combining the mythological strength of her ancestors with a newly acquired comprehension of the scientific truth of the event, Katya fulfills a promise she made to herself many years before.

ISBN 978-1-933979-23-6 (jacketed hardcover : alk. paper)
1. Chernobyl Nuclear Accident, Chernobyl, Ukraine, 1986—Juvenile fiction.
[1. Chernobyl Nuclear Accident, Chernobyl, Ukraine, 1986—Fiction. 2. Nuclear power plants—Accidents—Fiction. 3. Disasters—Fiction. 4. Ukraine—Fiction.] I. Title.

PZ7.W58177Rad 2008
[Fic]—dc22

2008014633

Book and cover design by Cregan Design,
Ellen Peeples Cregan and Marla Garcia
Edited by Lucy Herring Chambers and Nora Krisch Shire
Illustrations by Elaine Atkinson
Photographs:
Pages 108,199, 202, 221, Copyright 2007, James B. Willard, http://brokenkites.com
Pages 95, 161, Copyright 2006, Igor Kostin/Corbis Corp., www.corbis.com
Page 247, Portrait of Katya, Courtesy of Tetyana Keeble

Printed in the U.S.A. by Ocean-graphics LLC

Andrea White

bright sky press

HOUSTON AND ALBANY, TEXAS

Dedicated to Alexander Volkovicher,
a wonderful father and man, and to the
countless other Chernobyl victims like him.

This is a fictional story based on the true events of the 1986 Chernobyl accident.
Any resemblance to any person living or dead is entirely coincidental.

Prologue, 1980

Пролог

WITH HER EYES CLOSED, Vera Dubko listened to the chorus of crickets outside her window. Spring was here. How many more springs would she see?

Not many...

"Granny?" a little voice called to her from the darkness.

Granny Vera rolled over in the direction of the voice and spotted a bump in the other bed in the room, the one nearer the window. A small person was lying underneath the green knitted blanket.

Her daughter?

No, her daughter was long dead, taken from her by the famine. Stalin's famine. How she hated that man.

"Granny!" the voice cried out, and this time she recognized it.

Katya. The daughter of her son, Ivan. Her son who was as strong as a bull and as stubborn. "Yes, *donechka*."

"Tell me a story," Katya pleaded.

Once everyone had many stories, but now her son and daughter-in-law had a car, a gas stove, and electric lights. "Have I ever told you about the day I saw our *domovyk*?" Granny Vera asked.

"No," Katya replied. "Papa told me that house elves don't exist."

"Your Papa doesn't know about him," Granny Vera said.

"Did you see the elf on the mirror?" Katya said.

"Yes. My grandfather carved the figure to remind me of him," Granny Vera said.

"What was his name?" Katya asked. Her voice was full of awe.

"We never found out his name," Granny Vera admitted.

"What was he doing?"

When Granny Vera squeezed her eyes shut, she could remember that morning long ago as though it were yesterday. "Now at the beginning…" She began her story using the opening her grandmother had relied on to set the tone. When she spoke these words, she felt connected with her grandmother, with all her ancestors. "My mother had baked a loaf of *paska*, Easter bread, in the wood oven, and she set it on the kitchen counter to cool."

"The same wooden counter in our cottage?"

"The same one," Granny Vera said. "As it was a beautiful day, we went out to the garden to collect some greens. When we returned with our arms full of sorrel and cabbage, a boy stood in our kitchen. He had his back to us.

"My mother called out, 'Oh, my!'

"I was too startled to say anything. I just watched as this boy, a little smaller than me, whisked away the loaf of bread."

"Was the *domovyk* a thief?" Katya asked.

"Noooo," Granny Vera said. "When he got hungry, sometimes, he took some bread. But he left our valuables alone."

"He only ate bread?"

"As far as we could tell," Granny Vera said. She dropped her voice. She tried to make it low and convincing as the boy's had been. "There's going to be a thunderstorm tonight,' the *domovyk* warned us.

"Maybe so, but leave us some of our bread," my mother scolded him. She started for the *domovyk*, but before she could catch him, he jumped out the open window with the loaf under his arm. When we stuck our heads out, all we saw were the cows grazing, the dog on his chain and a neighbor riding by in his horse-drawn cart."

"What did he look like?"

"He was dressed like a young boy, in brown pants and an embroidered shirt. At first, when we came into the room, I thought he was a villager, but then he turned, and I saw his profile. His blue eye was a little too round, almost like an owl's. His blond hair was low on his forehead, and there was much hair on the back of his hands. I knew he wasn't human."

"Was there a storm that night?" Katya asked.

"The worst," Granny Vera shuddered, thinking of the thunder and how the very earth had shaken—as though the lightning was going to split the world in two. "Mama was angry about the loss of the bread, but Papa was grateful for the warning. He was able to get the animals, which were our livelihood, safely sheltered."

"I want the *domovyk* to come see me, too, Granny," Katya said. "Now. Tonight."

"He doesn't come where he's not welcome," Granny Vera said, and her words hurt her. She would never forget when her son, Ivan, a boy of about seven and full of the patriotic talk fed to him by his schoolteacher, informed her that her creatures were superstitious myths. He had said, "Mama, for my country to make progress, we must forget the old ways." He had gazed squarely into her eyes before adding, "We must denounce them." Had Ivan been threatening her? In the old days, children were encouraged to tell the authorities about anyone, even parents, who weren't loyal to the Communist Party.

"Did I tell you about seeing the wood sprite?" Katya asked.

"You did," Granny Vera said.

"He looked just like a tall reed, but he didn't fool me. I spotted his face and his tiny little hands," Katya said.

"You didn't tell your father, did you?" Granny Vera said.

"You told me not to."

"Your father makes a good living." Granny Vera sighed. "We should be grateful. Now go to sleep."

"If you see a *domovyk,* will you tell me?" Katya asked.

"I will," Granny Vera said.

"You didn't finish the story," Katya said.

"What?" Granny Vera had already dropped back off into a dream about her wedding and the brown crockery plate that her new mother-in-law had given her. It had little glazed rabbits around the rim. "To symbolize our land, our hearts," Polina Dubko had said.

"You know what you always say," Katya reminded her.

Granny Vera did remember. "And so it shall be until the end of the world."

"Remember, Granny, how I used to get so sad when you said that?" Katya said.

Granny Vera laughed softly. "You would howl and scream, 'But the world's not going to end, is it, Granny?'" Her granddaughter's breathing was even now. When there was no response, she said, "Good night, child."

As Granny Vera snuggled back down under the covers to listen to the night's song, she whispered a prayer, "*Gospody*, father, she's so young. Let her remember me. My stories. Let them come alive for her."

PART I

YANOV, 1986

1986
Chapter One

Глава первая

WHEN I ARRIVED HOME FROM SCHOOL ON MY BIKE, I found my mother waiting on our front step. Our cottage was a three-room house made out of sturdy wood and painted white. Its bright blue shutters made our home look happy, almost grinning.

"Katya!" my mother called to me. She was a big-boned woman with cinnamon freckles on her shoulders. Her brown hair had reddish highlights that matched my own fiery red hair.

Every year, Mama spent thousands of hours sewing clothes for the wives of the men who ran the Chernobyl Nuclear Power Station nearby. Although she wore thick glasses, she had a deep tan from working in our garden, and that kept her looking young. "How was your day?"

"Good," I answered. Nina Ivanovna, my teacher, was kind. I wouldn't admit it to my parents for fear of seeming conceited, but I could tell I was the smartest girl in the class.

Mama pointed at the wooden hut she used for a kitchen in the summer to keep our house cooler. This hut, half the size of our regular kitchen, was behind the cottage next to a fenced garden and the outhouse. Nearby, a wooden table sat under an expansive old oak tree. The red barn and a chicken coop were on the other side of our yard.

"Your play clothes are in the hut," Mama said.

I looked at her, puzzled. Usually I changed in my room before I ate my snack.

Mama's quick smile reminded me. April 25, 1986, had finally arrived. My eleventh birthday. My parents had asked some relatives, neighbors and friends over for a birthday celebration tonight. "Your Papa and I have a few things to do, and we don't want you in the house," she said.

Recently, along with several unexplained trips to Kiev, my parents had peppered me with questions about my favorite color and my favorite flower. Several times my parents' conversations had stopped abruptly when I entered the room. One particular phrase I had overheard, "teen room," sent a tingle of delight up my spine.

Although my story begins five summers after my Granny Vera's death, I still slept in the room that she used to share with me, and from what I'd been told, it looked exactly as it had since long before I was born. Granny Vera's pot of geraniums still bloomed on the window. Her wooden wardrobe took up one wall. The old mirror, spotted with age, rested on top.

"After you've eaten, why don't you go play in the woods for a while?" my mother asked. Underneath her casual tone, I detected a current of excitement. She was letting me play in the woods on a school day! More proof that my parents' surprise this year was special.

"O.K., Mama." I worked to keep my voice equally indifferent. But the moment she disappeared through the carved frame, I pressed my ear to the splintery door.

"Go right," Papa ordered Mama. "No, a little bit left." The soft sound of my mother's tennis shoes chased the clunk of my father's boots. One of my chores was to clean those boots of Papa's. They were black and stopped at his mid-calf. Too often, they were caked with the rich mud of our country, the U.S.S.R.

"Ouch!" my mother shouted.

I closed my eyes and tried to imagine which pieces of furniture they were moving. Papa's big chair? Our small breakfast table? But no picture formed in my mind. I must have giggled because Mama called, "Katya, are you listening?"

Her footsteps pattered towards me. She called through the closed door, "Usually you're in a hurry to spend an afternoon in the woods."

Reluctantly, I stood up. My dog, Noisy, had been curled up beside me as I eavesdropped, and now my movement startled him. When he hopped off the front stoop onto the grass, he looked expectantly up at me. Noisy was a feisty terrier with flopped-over ears and a brown and white coat, but I especially loved his nose. It was blue-black and curious about every smell on this earth.

I walked to the summer kitchen with Noisy barking at my heels. Since my mother had a rule—*no animals inside*—I shut the door in the dog's face. He howled pitifully.

As always, strings of garlic and dried peppers dangled from the low ceiling. Their pungent odor was familiar, but new smells wafted from the pots bubbling on the iron stove and the stoneware dishes crowded on the counter. I spied a few favorite dishes, garlic buns and the crepes called *nalysnyky*, but my birthday cake was nowhere in sight.

As Mama had said, a pair of jeans and a sweatshirt lay on the rough wooden table. Gratefully, I slipped off my brown school uniform and dropped it in a pile on the floor.

My mother bustled into the room, stirring the flavors as she moved. "Katya, please, a little neatness," she scolded me.

I began clumsily folding my dress and the black apron I wore over it.

Mama ladled a bowl of sausage and cabbage soup and set it down in front of me. "How about some bread and hot chocolate?" she asked.

I shook my head and sat down. "No, thank you."

"You should eat more," my mother complained.

"I'm saving room for tonight," I explained. "Did you make a chocolate cake?"

"Did you ask me for a chocolate cake?"

"You know I did."

"Well, I don't know…." Her voice trailed off in a maddening way. She was probably teasing, but I couldn't be sure. "Mama…."

With a grin spread across her broad face, she headed for the door. "Now, go. I've got quite a bit of work to do," she said. "But be sure to be back well before dark."

I waited for her to leave before opening the door for Noisy.

He bounded in, his tail a whirl of motion. Barely had I set my half-full bowl down by the rough-hewn table leg before the dog greedily lapped up the soup. Without further thought, I placed the tongue-cleaned bowl on the counter like I always did and ran out the door.

On my way to the gate, I picked up a tan straw basket that leaned against the vine-covered garden fence. By June, the fields would be covered with poppies, daisies, forget-me-nots and cornflowers, but April was probably too early for wildflowers. Still, maybe I'd get lucky.

As I passed by my neighbors' wooden cottages, Noisy trotted at my side. Although each of them had its own personality, I thought of these homes collectively as the Ancients. Like our own cottage, they were squat structures, a few with thick straw roofs, most with peeling paint, all with a fenced area for cows, goats, chickens or pigs. Bicycles, motorcycles and scooters, alongside a few carts and horses, were parked nearby. On laundry lines, hand-washed shirts and patched trousers flapped in the breeze. Against the backdrop of the tall trees, the Ancients looked timeless.

When the lane dead-ended into the woods, I started down a dirt trail made by the elk and deer. Mama and I used these trails on our hunts for mushrooms and berries, and Papa and I followed them on our weekend hunting and fishing trips. Unless it was the dead of the Ukrainian winter, we counted it an unlucky Sunday when he didn't have boar, deer, rabbit, or trout for dinner along with seasonal gifts from the forest like mushrooms, wild strawberries and dandelions.

I don't know how to explain what always happened to me on my visits to the forest. I forgot all about the long division we were reviewing in school and about Sergei Rudko, a boy in my class, who had a newfound interest in me. Today, I forgot my excitement over my parents' surprise. I even forgot that it was my birthday.

My head filled with the chirping of the doves, magpies, and blackbirds, the swish of the wind, the swaying of the grass. My body grew lighter, my feet surer, my eyes quicker. A woven roof of tree branches covered my head, and the moist forest air enveloped me. By the time I rounded the first bend in the path, I had ceased to be Katya Dubko and had become a child of the forest. My playmates, the wood nymphs and water sprites, were creatures that no one but Granny Vera and I could ever see.

I stepped off the trail into a small clearing and began hunting for the fluffy dandelions that I liked to blow into the wind. Just as I had suspected, late April was too early. After a fruitless search, I returned to the path. A few hundred yards away, I spotted my magic boulder, a perfect gray egg, waiting for me.

I had discovered my boulder on a day much like this. I was probably no more than four or five. My neighbor, Boris Boiko, who was nine years older than me, was taking me fishing in the woods. I was riding on his shoulders. Even though I was too heavy for him, he was trotting like a pony. When Boris tripped, we had landed on the rough path.

"Are you all right?" Boris cried. His lashes quivered over dark eyes full of concern.

"Yes," I said. But I wasn't. My shin had hit a rock, and I had to bite my lip to keep from crying.

"Let's rest here." Boris picked me up and plopped me down next to the boulder. For a few minutes, we listened to the stream and watched the dragonflies. "Are you feeling better yet?"

I nodded. To keep from crying, I forced myself not to look at my leg. The bruise must already be turning purple.

Boris twisted around. "Look." He pointed underneath the boulder. "A hiding place."

Forgetting about my hurt leg, I crawled over to him. I stuck my hand inside the moist, dark space. "What would you put there?" I asked.

"Secret things," Boris whispered.

With these words, I forgot all about my hurt leg. "I don't have any secrets," I admitted.

"Sure you do. Everybody has secrets," Boris said.

"What's yours?" I asked.

"I can't tell. It wouldn't be a secret," Boris said.

When I got old enough to take trips into the woods by myself, I began hiding special things underneath this same rock. At first, I kept all I needed for a picnic with my forest creatures: an old worn-out green blanket that my mother had knitted, a bowl to make mud cakes and a blunt knife to cut the slices. As I got older, the contents of the hiding space grew more varied. Not only did I keep my fishing pole, lines, hooks and handmade bait, but just a few days ago, I had hidden a note from Sergei, the boy in my class.

As I walked towards the boulder, I thought about Sergei. He had handed me the note during recess. A few days earlier, we both had been the high scorers in the physical fitness competition and had received certificates from the principal. Since my best friend, Angelika, had a crush on Sergei, I expected the note to refer to her, to her bright smile and her brown eyes. I was speechless when I read, "Katya, let's go out together." Hoping that the boulder would somehow help me solve the problem of Sergei, I had hidden the note in my secret space.

Motorcycle World, a magazine, was another prized possession I kept underneath the boulder. Like most things slick and glossy, it was foreign. Maybe French. The motorcycles were all shiny and much too big for a ten-year-old to drive. My parents called me *the only girl in the whole Ukraine who liked fairies and motorcycles.* Despite their teasing, I had spent many peaceful hours leaning against the rock and studying the pages of *Motorcycle World.* When I was older, I hoped to own a bright red Yava with silver spokes and a curled handlebar.

This day, I set my basket for wildflowers next to the boulder and began searching the streambed for rocks to skip. I was examining a flat one, oddly shaped like a heart, when I heard a muffled sneeze.

The noise sounded as if it were coming from the far side of the boulder where the *ocheret* with its slim reeds and thick brown cattails grew tall and thick. At my side, Noisy was strangely silent.

I took a few cautious steps around the boulder.

At first, I saw nothing, only the *ocheret.* But then I spotted a boy—a small boy, with his body pressed close to the rock. His pants

were dark, and his off-white shirt was embroidered with an old-fashioned geometric pattern of red squares and black triangles. His bright blond hair, nearly as long as a girl's, was neatly combed and glowed almost white in the sunlight.

Most startling of all were his eyes. His eyes were blue, bluer than the *pisanki* eggs that Auntie Maria decorated. They were even bluer than the cornflowers that would soon bloom in droves in the fields around my cottage.

For a moment, as I looked into his eyes, I forgot about everything except a small memory of Granny Vera. Unlike most storytellers who started with, *Once upon a time*, she began her stories with, "*Now at the beginning…*" It was as if I could hear her saying this phrase, and I sensed that I was at the beginning of something new. Yet at the same time the feeling was familiar. For hadn't I felt this way when I had played with my forest creatures? Nothing obvious happened, maybe only a shift in the light. But suddenly, the air shone like glass, and my skin prickled with the awareness of another world just beyond my reach.

Noisy raced to the boy and sniffed his hand.

The boy ruffled the dog's hair with his long pale fingers. "You've come," he said simply to me. He looked to be about a foot shorter than me and so skinny that his features were all angles.

"Who are you?" I asked. I searched my memory for my Granny Vera's stories but found they had grown hazy in my mind. Granny Vera knew everything. She must have told me about a creature who looked like a human but who lived in the woods. How could I have forgotten?

A red squirrel dropped from a branch overhead onto the forest floor. In a flash, Noisy was chasing after the animal.

"Who do you think I am?" the boy said.

I sat down across from him and took a good look. His face appeared translucent, as if I could strain my eyes and see through him. That blond, shaggy hair curling over his ears also covered the back of his hands. It shone in the yellow light of the afternoon. And his eyes were so blue that they kept me from noticing anything else about them. "Are you a wood sprite?" I blurted out and immediately felt ridiculous. Since Granny Vera had died, even though I pretended otherwise, I had begun to suspect that my forest creatures weren't real.

The boy frowned as if insulted. "No."

"What's your name?"

"Vasyl," he said. "I know *your* name."

I was puzzled, though not yet afraid. "How could you know my name?" I asked.

Vasyl smiled brightly. "You are Katya."

I stared at him in wonder. Even though he denied being a wood sprite, he certainly seemed magical. "Can you tell fortunes, too?"

He laughed, but as young as I was, I understood that his laugh was hollow like the wind rushing past my cottage on a cold night.

Ignoring the haunting sound, I asked, "How do you know my name?"

"Today is your birthday, isn't it?"

"Yes. How did you know that?"

"You look radiant," Vasyl said, smiling. "Like a birthday girl should."

I blushed, pleased at the compliment. Then, I noticed that the sun had almost disappeared. The crickets were making a racket. The boulder had turned a deep gray. I was going to be late for my own party. As I stood up, I called, "Noisy!" I explained to Vasyl, "I have to go."

Vasyl held up his hand, saying, "Don't tell anyone that you've talked to me. Promise me—for your own good."

"I promise," I called over my shoulder in my haste to get home. "Noisy, let's go."

From out of the ferny depths beyond the boulder, the dog appeared at my side, his sides heaving.

"I need to see you again," Vasyl called. "Come back to the boulder."

I didn't bother answering but hurried down the path toward home, the empty basket bouncing against my side. This day in the woods, even the leaves were whispering to me, *Come back. Come back soon.*

Chapter Two

Глава вторая

IN MY VILLAGE, THE EARTH GLOWED AT SUNSET. But tonight as I headed home, I walked in the direction of a man-made brightness—the Chernobyl Nuclear Power Station.

Once when I was a lot younger, Papa had taken me by the station where he worked as a security guard. I remembered that it was constructed out of concrete and metal, larger than our whole village. But the station's physical layout held little interest for me. Because I believed the station was a magical factory that made energy out of nothing. I searched for men in white robes, beings who resembled angels. I imagined them gliding around the hallways, pushing buttons to create electricity, as I had heard they could do.[1]

Papa's job insured a good living for our family. Now that I was older, I understood in this sense the station truly was magical. We were all deeply grateful to the government for selecting our area as the site for the most up-to-date and modern power station that the Communist world had ever constructed. Since unlike conventional power plants, nuclear fission didn't create ugly clouds of black smoke, we assumed that our paradise would remain unspoiled.

In this half-golden, half-white light, my cottage with the blue shutters appeared in the distance. Noisy found his voice and began barking.

Because Papa worked at the station, our family qualified for a modern apartment in town, but my parents weren't interested in moving. Both had grown up in the country and loved living in the woods. Mama hated the thought of sharing walls with a neighbor. Papa claimed that he would never give up our garden or the fresh milk and eggs provided by our barn animals.

So long as the stars still burned brightly in the sky, I believed that my family would never leave our cottage in the woods.

I heard Mama's worried voice calling my name. Without being able to make out her face, I knew she was frowning.

For the second time that day, Mama was waiting for me on our front step. "There you are, Katya. Late on your own birthday."

I started to tell her the remarkable story of the boy in the woods. "Mama, you wouldn't believe…" Then I remembered. My promise felt as warm as a fresh brown egg that I had just slipped out from under my best chicken, Princess, in the henhouse. I hesitated, unsure what to do.

Sometimes, my tardiness caused Papa to get out his switch. Although I knew he wouldn't spank me on my birthday, I searched for an excuse to blunt my mother's disapproval. My basket was empty. I couldn't claim that I had been collecting wildflowers, mushrooms or berries.

Seeing that I was at a loss for words, Mama sighed. "I know. You were with your imaginary friends again and lost track of time."

I nodded, grateful for her suggestion. "One of them knew that it was my birthday." As I offered this, I had a vision of Vasyl with his white-gold hair and blue eyes. *"I need to see you again," Vasyl called. "Come back to the boulder."*

Who was he? What did he want from me?

"I was about to send your father for you," Mama whispered in my ear. "There are wolves in those woods." She ran her fingers through my hair, dark auburn now from sweat. "You know you're supposed to be home well before sundown."

"Yes, Mama," I said. Although her soft smile told me that I was forgiven, I was quick to change the subject. "When is everyone coming?"

"Soon," Mama said. "But first, your father and I have something to show you."

Just as the events of the afternoon had driven the birthday surprise out of my thoughts, now as I followed Mama into the cottage, I forgot the mysterious boy as completely as if I had never met him. Dreams of a teen room filled my mind.

"Ivan, your daughter is home," Mama called.

Papa appeared in the kitchen. I don't think I've mentioned what a strong man my father was. He was the strongest man in the whole area. Once, on a bet, his friend, Victor Kaletnik, borrowed an ancient ox wagon and filled it with rocks. Papa dragged the heavy load across an entire field. Family lore held that he would have trained for the Olympics in wrestling, if one of the party bosses hadn't quarreled with my grandfather and blocked his chance. I loved him more than anyone in the whole world. If there was a God, as Granny Vera had claimed, I knew that He had to be strong, kind and wise, exactly like my father.

"Happy birthday, my darling." Papa smiled at me. "We have a surprise for you, Katya."

Eagerly, my eyes searched the main room of our familiar cottage for the surprise. My gaze passed over the large *pechka*, a stove which stretched from floor to ceiling, and turned to an oak cabinet displaying my mother's finest dishes. I recognized all of them. Then I glanced at the photos of my parents, their parents and me hanging against the wall, many decked with artificial flowers. I had seen each of them one thousand times. No great gift was displayed on the small dining table covered in a white embroidered tablecloth, which took up the center of the room. Everything was the same. I turned to Papa, my eyes demanding an explanation.

"Not in here," Papa said, smiling at my confusion. He began heading back towards my room. Through the open door, I barely noticed the old furniture—two beds and a large wooden wardrobe—

because spring seemed to have bloomed inside.

A new divan was pushed against the wall. It was covered in a print almost as beautiful as a field of wild flowers. A matching green leatherette chair stood next to it, and a small desk for studying and playing.

No one I knew owned furniture so beautiful.

"Papa," I cried and ran to hug him. He was so huge that my arms were barely able to touch both sides of his hard middle. "Thank you!"

"Nothing is too good for my Katya," my father said. "But you need to thank your Mama. She is the favored seamstress of the manager at the furniture store. The manager put us at the top of the list to buy the furniture." In those days, it took special pull to get goods that the Western world took for granted.

I realized I had probably hurt my mother's feelings. She had been standing next to me, and I hadn't said anything to her. "Mama, thank you!"

"Happy birthday, my little one," my mother said. "I am sewing curtains for your room, too. With all the orders lately, I haven't been able to finish them in time."

"You are the best parents in all of the Ukraine," I said, and I meant it.

Papa and Mama burst out laughing.

"Hello," I heard a boy's voice call.

I recognized the voice of my neighbor, Boris. I immediately had one thought: *Boris drives a Yava.*

"We're in here," Mama said.

"Papa, can Boris take me on his motorcycle?" I added many beseeching *'bud'laskas'* even though I knew the extra pleases were unnecessary. My father would let me do anything that I wanted on my birthday. "When I was a girl, I did not ride on motorcycles," Mama said with mock sternness to Papa.

"We're in here, Boris," Papa called out in his booming voice. "And Katya knows what she wants from you for her birthday."

Boris stuck his head in the room. He was a handsome boy of around twenty. Although I liked Boris' voice most—it was deep, slow and methodical—I was also fascinated by his hands. They were expert at so many things, like milking cows, hooking worms, fixing tractors, and starting car motors. Although his fingers were thick, they were sure and never hesitated.

"I came straight from the Fire Station. Am I the first to arrive?" Boris asked. Since he had become a fireman, I hadn't seen much of him. It was such an important job, he always seemed to be at work or at school.

"Everyone should be here in a minute," Mama said.

"Look at Katya's new room," Papa said.

Boris whistled. "It's beautiful." He held his wool cap in his hand. His hair, combed back from his face, was only a little darker than his brown eyes.

My pride in my room didn't make me forget what would make

this day perfect. "Will you take me for a ride on your Yava, Boris?" I asked. "Papa says it's all right."

Papa nodded.

"Sure," Boris said. "Now, Natasha Dubko?" he asked Mama.

Mama smiled at me. "We have a few minutes before the party starts."

"Let's go," Boris said, and started out the door.

I wondered if happiness could be a kind of balloon, floating to the heavens and carrying me along with it.

Boris and I were heading past the vegetable garden on a shortcut to the lane when the Kaletniks drove up in their old black Volga. The Kaletniks were my parents' closest friends. Like my parents, they were the children of peasants, who had graduated from high school. But while my Papa went into the army, Uncle Victor attended college. He was now an assistant engineer at Chernobyl Nuclear Power Station.

Victor Kaletnik stuck his head out the window. Unlike Papa, he was already losing his hair.

I waved and called out, "Uncle Victor."

"I know you just turned eleven, Katya. But even in a country as modern as the Soviet Union, don't you think you are a little young to have a boyfriend?" he teased me.

Boris and I had reached the red Yava with silver spokes. I blushed as I swung my leg up behind him. Embracing Boris's waist, I thought how wonderful it would be if Boris were my boyfriend. I liked him much more than Sergei Rudko. While Boris had always been purposeful in his activities and interests, an expert in everything he attempted, Sergei was a dreamy boy who seemed restless with the requirements of school.

"Ready?" Boris called.

"Yes," I said, but my answer was drowned out by the roar of the motorcycle.

I knew I would never forget the engine's power surging through my body, or the wind rushing through my hair that night. The ride felt mysterious, as if we were setting out on an adventure. Looking into the sky, the stars reminded me of the boy in the woods; the constellations overhead burned as brightly as his blue eyes.

That boy had known my name! He had known it was my birthday. Did he know my mother's and father's names, too? Could he say how many chickens we had? My full heart answered the most important question of all: Did I trust him?

On my eleventh birthday, I trusted life. This was the only answer.

Chapter Three

Глава третья

BORIS AND I SPED DOWN OUR LANE past the Ancients and turned onto the highway.

Ahead of us, I spotted the bold concrete sign for Pripyat. Although this modern city was less than a half-mile from our sleepy village, I never ceased to be amazed at the differences between them.

Unlike Yanov, which was basically a collection of a few homes, Pripyat had wide streets, a hospital, tall office buildings and apartments, public statues, manicured flower gardens and many schools, including my own Pripyat Primary School #2.

As we drew closer, I longed to go down Lenin Street. I wanted to pass Angelika Galkina's apartment and have her look out the window and spot me roaring by on a red Yava. Since both of Angelika's parents were scientists at the power station, her family lived in the newest apartment complex in town, with an indoor bathroom and an electric oven, not gas. But since Angelika was probably on her way to my party, I wasn't too disappointed when Boris turned around and headed back.

My hair was windblown, and my skin tingled with excitement when we pulled up in front of my cottage a few minutes later. The Kaletniks' car was still the only car parked on the lane. This wasn't surprising as the guests were mostly our neighbors and a few relatives, all of whom were walking. Peering towards town, I searched in vain for Vitaly Galkina's car.

Angelika Galkina was the prettiest girl in my class, but only the second smartest. We had been best friends since kindergarten, but ever since Sergei had passed me the note, I had been nervous in her company. The truth was that, as much as I wanted to be her friend, I had never been relaxed around her. Like my practical parents, Angelika had no patience with my make-believe world in the forest.

I jumped off and thanked Boris.

"*Laskavo prosimo*," he said. "You're welcome."

Watching Boris remove a cylinder from the satchel that was strapped to the back of his motorcycle, I stood there mesmerized. As I followed him up to the front door, my eyes stayed fixed on the gift-wrapped object, trying to guess its contents.

Boris opened the door, and the party exploded into greetings:

"Happy Birthday, Katya!"

"*S dnem narodzhennya!*"

"Here's our birthday girl!"

My gaze passed over the group, and I spotted the many dear faces of people I had known all my life. As I stepped into the room, my great-aunt and uncle, the Krykos, raised their glasses. They were toasting me with *horilka*, a strong spicy vodka common in our village.

Uncle Pavel Kryko, a war veteran and our family jokester, had a peg leg and used a walking stick. His red nose had earned him the nickname, 'Father Frost.' Aunt Maria Kryko had the biggest breasts that I had ever seen, and her apron always smelled of boiled cabbage.

The next few minutes of hugs, kisses and endearments were a blur, as the happiest times usually are. I do remember that I got my ears pulled so many times that they felt as if they had dropped to my chin. In the Ukraine, it's our custom to pull a birthday girl's ears the number of years that she has been alive, and—as if this weren't enough—one to grow on.

Finally, I wrenched my aching earlobes away from Aunt Maria's tight grasp. When I turned around, I found myself facing Sasha Boiko, Boris' younger sister and my babysitter. She had tied her honey-colored hair back in a big green bow. She was handing my mother a jar of the Boikos' strawberry jam. As strawberry season was months away, I knew my mother would prize this gift.

Aunt Olga Pushko, my mother's cousin, bumped into me. She wore thick glasses that exaggerated her watery eyes. I didn't notice if her husband, Uncle Alexander, was standing in a corner somewhere. His wife always overshadowed him. She had a reputation for never staying still and, in fact, she was carrying a tray of food outside to the table and benches set up next to the summer kitchen.

"Katya, could you go see what mischief Yuri is up to?" Aunt Olga pleaded with me over her shoulder.

Aunt Olga's three little girls were quietly playing dolls on our kitchen floor. Next to them, her son, Yuri, an active six-year-old, was being scolded by my ancient neighbor, Oksana Evtushenko. Yuri was always catching bugs or trying to ride on Noisy's back. In our family, we referred to him as *chertneya,* or the little devil—not always kindly. As Granny Vera liked to say, "Boys will be boys." Or sometimes if a piece of mischief was particularly bad, "The snake was always in the garden." By the time I reached them, though, Yuri had slipped away. Oksana Evtushenko wanted to complain to me about her new cow. "Katya, she's the most stubborn animal that I've ever known."

In the entranceway, I noticed Galina Galkina. Standing stiffly and still clutching her large, square purse, she was the only woman in the whole room who was wearing the fitted suit of an office worker, rather than the loose skirts and blouses of Yanov. Angelika Galkina gripped her mother's hand.

Angelika wore a brown smocked dress that matched her eyes and was so beautiful that, for a moment, I was surprised that she was my best friend. I ran to greet her.

After the guests each accepted a glass of *horilka,* and the children collected cups of *kompot,* homemade juice, the party began to move outside. I touched Angelika's hand. "Do you want to see my room?" I whispered. I hoped that she liked my new furniture as much as I did.

Angelika nodded. Although she usually wore her blonde hair loose on her shoulders, tonight her mother had plaited it into pigtails and tied neat brown ribbons at the ends. With china-doll features and big brown eyes, I thought she was a pretty girl, but Mama disagreed. I had never noticed her small, slightly crooked teeth until Mama, who didn't like her, pointed out how unattractive they were.

I thought her uneven grin enhanced her personality.

I shouldn't have worried about Angelika's reaction to my room. At the doorway, her hands flew to her cheeks in astonishment.

"It's beautiful!" Angelika cried.

It would not have been modest for me to agree with her, but my divan was the finest piece of furniture I had ever seen. Although ordinary in size and shape, the couch was covered in a green fabric dotted with fields of daisies and daffodils, unusual for those dreary days of Soviet grays and dark blues.

I took Mishko, my teddy bear, who Papa had brought back from Moscow, and arranged him so he was lounging on the divan. Both Angelika and I giggled. We were still bending the teddy bear into comical positions when Aunt Olga stuck her head in my room.

"I heard that you got some new furniture," she said.

"Do you like it?" I asked.

"Very attractive," Aunt Olga said. Always practical, she added, "That divan looks like a foldout."

Immediately, Angelika and I began trying to figure out how to pull out the bed.

"You're right!" I told Aunt Olga when we had opened it. "Now I can have two people over to spend the night at the same time."

"Lyudmila and I," Angelika suggested. Lyudmila Pikalova was another girl in our class. Angelika liked her more than I did. Since Lyudmila flattered Angelika constantly, I always suspected that Lyudmila's mother encouraged their friendship. The Galinkos were such important people.

Although I had reservations about having Lyudmila over, I couldn't deny Angelika anything. "I'll ask my mother," I promised.

"Katya, come outside and get supper," my mother called.

I hated to leave my new furniture even momentarily. With a backward glance, I tried to soak up my room's cheerful modernity— the new divan, chair, and small desk, side by side with the older pieces, the oak wardrobe and the ancient mirror.

Outside, the moonlight lent the supper the allure of a fairy feast. Huge sticks of salami, *domashnyaya kolbasa* (that delicious, home-made garlicky-pork sausage), beet-root salad, pickled mushrooms, cabbage rolls stuffed with meat and rice, fried fish, and sweet pies crowded the table. The tablecloth's *kleyonka* (plastic cover) didn't dim the greens and yellows of its border. My mother had hand-stitched the cloth with her favorite pattern, nightingale's eye. Most wonder-ful of all, a chocolate birthday cake towered over one end. White candles, waiting to be illuminated, formed the number eleven.

"Birthday girl first," my mother said, as she handed me an empty plate.

Even though my stomach was already so full of excitement that I didn't know how I'd manage even a bite, I loaded up with cabbage rolls and beet-root salad and plopped down on the grass.

I spotted Uncle Victor Kaletnik heading towards me. He was about as slight as I was, and I had the feeling that if I wanted, I could pick him up and carry him on my shoulders. When he leaned over me, I quickly covered my ears, but he wasn't reaching to tug on them.

"How about a game of checkers soon with an old man?" Uncle Victor asked.

"I want to learn chess," I told him.

"Chess!" he responded, and called to my father, "Very strange, Ivan. Your daughter is an intellectual."

"Why is that strange, Victor?" my father responded.

"She wants to use her brain to think, unlike her father, who just uses his to recite patriotic cant." Uncle Victor laughed.

My father and his oldest friend were always joking, but my father's voice sounded weary when he answered. "Not tonight. I don't want to argue about politics tonight."

Angelika settled down next to me, her plate overflowing.

"Why couldn't your father come?" I asked her between bites.

"He's at the station," Angelika answered. Comrade Galkin was the assistant operator of reactor number four.

"Papa swapped shifts so he could be at my party," I explained. "He starts work at midnight."

Just then Boris walked up.

I felt my face flush as red as my ears with my newfound love for him, and I was grateful for the darkness. From behind his back, Boris pulled out the gift-wrapped cylinder that I had noticed earlier.

"What's this?" I asked, and hoped my shaky voice didn't give me away.

He smiled at me. "Your real birthday present."

I couldn't help imagining our great future together. Boris and I would live with my parents until we were able to find a cottage of our own. Inna Boiko would teach me how to make her famous strawberry jam. Perhaps, after Angelika and Sergei married, they would move into a cottage close by.

"I need to give you your gift early, because I have to go pick up my girlfriend," Boris said casually.

Girlfriend. My heart sank. Some days in the village, I had seen Marta Antropova riding on the back of Boris's motorcycle, but it had never occurred to me that she could be his girlfriend. I couldn't help thinking that if the situation were reversed, and I were twenty and Boris was eleven, I would have waited for him forever.

"Go on." Boris nudged me gently.

I must have been gaping at him. I tore off the paper and opened the cylinder. When I had unrolled the poster, I saw that it featured a red Yava. The newest model. "Oh, Boris, thank you!" I cried.

"You're the only girl I know who likes motorcycles," Angelika said disapprovingly, but I could tell that she was envious of my relationship with an older boy like Boris.

"I'm going to hang it up in my new room," I promised Boris. For the moment, I carefully rolled the poster back up and slipped it into the cylinder to keep it from getting wrinkled. When I looked up, Boris was gone.

The pain of losing Boris didn't stay with me for long, because Angelika said, "I want you to open my gift."

Out of nowhere, Aunt Olga appeared with a canvas cloth which she laid on the ground. I scooted onto it, and soon the cloth was piled high with presents in all shapes, sizes and colors. Angelika gave me a Barbie doll. Although she accepted my thanks with a modest "It's nothing," both of us knew that only someone with her father's connections could have brought me such a rare Western gift. Aunt Olga gave me a new bookcase; the Kalitniks, a book of fairy tales and a new teddy bear; my aunt, a set of marble eggs; and my uncle, a *matryoshka*, a wooden doll with smaller dolls nested inside.

I slipped the *matryoshka* out of its box. Granny Vera always said, "*Matryoshkas* are built like the human heart: Mysteries within mysteries." It was true that you never knew how many dolls a *matryoshka* contained. Most *matryoshkas* had five, and many had seven. Another mystery was whether the smaller dolls matched the outer one or exhibited a completely different pattern.

Eager to find out, I studied the biggest doll. She was a young woman wearing an embroidered shirt and skirt. She had big brown eyes, a round stomach, no hands and a red scarf on her head. In the moonlight, I squinted to see her better. Her scarf failed to conceal her red hair.

I held up the doll. "Thank you, Uncle," I called.

He was busy drinking and didn't hear me.

"Let me see it. Let me see it," Angelika said.

"Just a second," I answered.

I unscrewed the lid and found that the second doll was younger than the outer one. Like me, she was a redheaded schoolgirl. She had on the same brown dress and the white apron that I wore on ceremonial occasions.

Impatiently, Angelika made a move as if to grab the *matryoshka* from me.

I quickly unscrewed the schoolgirl's lid and was disappointed to find only one more doll. I held in my hands a baby, with no hair at all, wrapped in a white blanket.

Angelika bent over me. "Only three dolls, huh?"

I nodded.

"Can I open the Barbie?" she asked, having lost interest in the *matryoshka*.

"Sure," I said.

"Comrades." My Uncle Pavel Kryko held up his glass of *horilka*. Mama always said that Pavel Kryko's peg leg shouldn't give him an excuse to drink too much. Then Papa always said for Pavel Kryko, any excuse would do.

As Uncle Pavel repeated one of the jokes that he favored, his nose shone particularly bright. "Someone asked me," my uncle said, "'What do you do if vodka is interfering with your job?' I said, 'You quit your job.'" He began guffawing so hard that he bent over.

"Cake," my mother called out quickly, probably to draw attention away from Pavel Kryko's drunkenness. "It's time for the cake."

As if by magic, Aunt Olga appeared next to me. She was holding the chocolate cake now ablaze with candles.

I didn't have time to reassemble the *matryoshka*, so I scooped the bigger pieces into the box. Afraid I'd lose the baby, I slipped it into my pocket before standing up and hurrying over to the outdoor table.

Until the moment that I faced the lighted cake, I hadn't given any thought to my wish.

Without a pause, Papa's deep voice, Mama's soothing one, Uncle Pavel's slurred bass and Aunt Olga's soprano all united in calling out to me, "S *dnem narodzhennya*."

A wish. I had to make a wish.

Earlier that evening, I had dreamed of marrying Boris, but he already had a girlfriend.

Sergei was cute, but Angelika liked him, and I didn't want to lose my best friend. Of course, I longed for a Yava, but a motorcycle of my own was an impossible dream. I heard my name. My loved ones were growing impatient.

With the stars shining down on us, I gazed at the candles. The flames twisted red and yellow in the night breeze.

"You have so much," Angelika whispered. "What do you have to wish for?"

This was the hint that I needed. I shoved my hands deep into my pocket and felt the little *matryoshka*. I sucked in a deep breath and blew with all my strength. All the while, I fixed my mind on one true thought: *Thank you*, I thought, *whoever you are*. I did have so much: my parents, my friends, my motorcycle ride, my forest and the mighty Soviet Union. *I wish for these things never to change.*

Many of the candles flickered and went out, but two stubbornly continued to burn brightly. In our family, a birthday girl's wish comes true only if she is able to blow out all the candles in a single breath, and I stared resentfully at the holdouts. Although my wish wasn't for anything new, I still felt let down.

Encouraged by my little cousins' laughter, Uncle Pavel was attempting to balance his carved wooden cane on his nose. He tripped and stumbled into a corner of the table. A crockery plate bounced on a bench and shattered, spewing cucumber salad. I remembered the plate had been special to Granny Vera, but I wasn't sure why.

"Oh, my goodness," Uncle Pavel said, fumbling to collect himself and his cane.

Not again, I thought. Mama is going to be angry.

Aunt Olga rushed past holding a dustpan.

In all the commotion, I saw the fine spray of Yuri's spit raining on the cake. My little cousin had blown out my two remaining birthday candles. "Yuri!" I called. But the little demon disappeared underneath the table before I could scold him. A few moments later, I caught sight of a small figure running towards the garden.

My father walked over to my mother and me. He whispered, "I'm taking the Krykos home." His voice was heavy with scorn. He used this tone when he discussed the "weak ones": alcoholics, men who were out of shape or who couldn't take care of their families. "I'll go straight from town to work," he finished.

I knew that Mama was both disappointed Papa wasn't going to stay for the birthday cake and relieved to say goodbye to Uncle Pavel. She was anxious for him to leave before he told more bad jokes or caused more damage.

"Happy birthday, little one," Papa said.

"Thanks, Papa," I answered. "I wish you could stay."

Papa rumpled my hair. "You know I don't eat dessert anyway." He set off to collect Uncle Pavel.

What Papa said was true. He was the healthiest man in the whole village. He called *horilka* 'poison' and avoided sweets, even *kutia*, the traditional Christmas dish Mama made with poppy seeds, wheat nuts and honey.

Not me! Mama cut me a perfect piece of chocolate cake, the corner with extra icing. Even though I had been too full to finish a whole cabbage roll, I was suddenly starving and was able to finish my slice in a few bites.

A few minutes later, Angelika squeezed my hand. "Mama says we have to go." She shrugged. "School night."

I thanked her again. "I love the Barbie doll." The writing on the pink box was in English, which I couldn't read. But I was excited to comb the Barbie's hair. The bobbed-blonde style looked so Western.

After walking Angelika and her mother to their car, I returned to the cottage. The smell of coffee now filled our home. Aunt Olga and a neighbor were carrying a huge stack of dishes to the sink. Since I wouldn't be expected to help in the kitchen on my birthday, I began gathering my gifts from the ground outside and transporting them to my room. Inna Boiko cried out, "Have you seen my coat?"

"Katya, where are you? The Boikos are leaving," my mother called.

I walked back into the main room where my ears were pulled all over again, too many times to count. Out of the corner of my eye, I noticed a few pieces of Granny Vera's plate gleaming on the counter. Without comment, Mama scooped up the shards and dumped them in the trash.

The June bugs and gnats beat themselves against the light on the porch as Mama and I waved goodbye to the last of the guests. When we reentered the house, only a sweet, meaty smell lingered as proof that the gathering had taken place at all.

"I'm glad you had a good time," she said. As she stroked my hair, her eyes sought out the cuckoo clock.

I sighed and leaned into her strong arms. "It was perfect."

Chapter Four

Глава четвертая

SLEEP WAS IMPOSSIBLE. I lay on my narrow bed and gazed through the open window at the lights of the power station shining in the distance.

Although I had recently learned that science, not magic, ran the station, the process still didn't make sense to me. Papa had explained that the individual rods in a nuclear reactor's core contained atoms of nuclear fuel. As the fuel nuclei split, they produced energy. This heat energy boiled water to create steam. The steam turned generators to produce electricity.

But this explanation failed to answer my basic question: How could something invisible turn on my lights?

In a vain effort to find sleep, I had already counted chickens and recited my multiplication tables. I repeated my lines for the Young Pioneer ceremony. *I, Katya Dubko, becoming a member of the old union Lenin Pioneers, am taking an oath to live, study and struggle as it was told by Great Lenin.* But not even the oath made me the slightest bit sleepy.

I turned onto my other side and faced the new divan.

Too much had happened for me to fall asleep. So much, in fact, that I had forgotten the most amazing occurrence of all. The remembrance made me sit bolt-upright in bed.

The boy in the woods! And his curious words. "*I need to see you again,*" Vasyl had called. "*Come back to the boulder.*"

What did Vasyl want from me?

Sometimes when I heard the animals howling at night, not even my warm bed with the thick blankets Mama knitted provided enough comfort. Vasyl was probably cold and scared. I scolded myself for forgetting to tell the boy about the old blanket beneath the boulder.

And he must be hungry, too. Yet, ten feet away from me, our refrigerator was crammed with party food. The boy was so skinny; it seemed wrong for his stomach to be empty tonight. Often, I had to venture out into the night to use the outhouse. The boulder was just a little further.

My father wasn't due back until eight in the morning. My mother spent hours in our garden each day and always bragged that she slept like a peasant. Why shouldn't I offer Vasyl some food? I could be back in ten minutes.

I stepped onto the cold floor and moved silently towards my wardrobe. I slipped on a sweatshirt over the T-shirt that I had worn to bed and pulled on some trousers. I stuck the dirty sneakers I wore for gardening on my feet.

After I dressed, I tiptoed to my mother's prize appliance, our Oka refrigerator, and carefully opened the door. As I slipped a large sausage into one pocket and a hunk of cheese in the other, I heard a noise and froze, afraid that I had awakened Mama.

But it was only the clock. Although I couldn't see it in the dark, the brown cuckoo with the yellow chest must have burst out of her house to announce midnight. The bird's house was intricately carved. Papa liked to joke that the Dubkos' cuckoo lived in a bourgeois mansion.

My hands felt along the cool counter and touched the glass jar of *smaletz* (congealed lard) and the metal bowls holding dough and fragments of honeycomb before I found a rough napkin to wrap around the cheese.

I moved silently to the front door, which we never locked. Standing on the front step, I could make out the figure of my dog. Noisy was standing in the shadows underneath the oak tree, an area darker than the moonlit night. He looked wild. I guess I appeared forbidding to him, too, because when he saw me, he started barking. Thank goodness, Mama was such a sound sleeper.

I would have liked to take Noisy along for company and protection, but I decided against this plan. Without Noisy, in the unlikely event that I met someone in the woods, I could fade into the shadows.

I took a few steps towards him, and barking happily now that he had recognized me, Noisy followed me as far as his chain would allow.

"No way you're coming with me," I told Noisy, but he didn't believe me and threw himself against his chain. Taking pity on him,

I patted his head for a minute or so. When I began to move away, he whimpered. By the time I had reached the gate, he was crying pitifully, but I forced myself to ignore him. He could ruin everything.

I took a few steps along the path. During the daytime, I loved the way the forest muted the sun; but now, underneath the branches, the air was uncomfortably cold. The charcoal-gray woods surrounding me appeared dark and threatening. I hesitated, shivering. Although my parents turned to God rarely, only in emergencies, I knew Granny Vera always got strength from prayer. But I hadn't talked to God for a long time, not since she'd died. Maybe compromise was the solution. I whispered to myself, "Granny Vera, please keep me safe."

As gently as the stroke of my old granny's gnarled hand, the wind whooshed against my cheek. Overhead, the branches creaked and swayed. What more could I want for an answer? When I raced toward the boulder, I felt wrapped in Granny Vera's protection as surely as I felt the night air tingle on my skin.

As I moved deeper into the woods, my eyes adjusted. I found that the darkness had transformed the familiar landscape. Now, the tops of the trees disappeared into inky darkness. Spiderwebs sparkled like bright silver ladders. Patches of white moonlight checkered the otherwise black leaves. Against the noisy insect chorus, I heard the urgency of the rushing stream, and then something else.

Footsteps. And not a boy's, a man's. They were moving heavily through the trees. I didn't know who would be out this late at night, but fear, for myself and for Vasyl, came over me. I ducked into the thick bushes bordering the path. Crunching into dead leaves, I lay down to wait.

Stomp. Stomp. Not one but two pairs of feet approached. A pair of brown work boots and a pair of dull-gray waitress shoes. Whispered voices drew closer.

The couple, holding hands, was only a few steps away when I recognized Boris and Marta Antropova. In the dim light, I couldn't see Marta's hair, once red like mine, but now bleached like dried wheat straw or her gold tooth, but I recognized the shape of her legs.

How could Boris like her? I wondered. She has such thick calves.

When I was younger, one of my favorite games with Boris had been hide-and-go-seek. He was so much older than me that I could never find him in the woods unless he wanted me to. But he was wise enough to know that a long game would frustrate me. To help me succeed, he would stand behind a tree with his arms and legs visible. I would think I was so sly and smart when I found him. "You're it!" I would cry.

Now, I fought the temptation to jump out of the woods and surprise him.

"I'm getting a raise next month," Boris announced proudly. "You know what that means, Marta, don't you?"

Boris and Marta had stopped walking. They were so close that I could have reached out and touched them.

"We can finally get married," Marta answered.

I felt a stab of pain.

"Married? Who said anything about getting married?" Boris asked. I could tell by his playful tone that he was teasing her.

In the glow of the moonlight, I saw Marta lift her eyes to take in his face. Her hand reached out, and she touched his cheek.

"You're my own," Marta said. "And I will love you always and forever."

Boris slipped his hand over Marta's hand and kissed her fingers. "Yes. Forever."

In a ray of moonlight, I glimpsed Boris' red lips pressed to hers. His thick fingers, so competent with the engine of his Yava, brushed gently against Marta's face.

That kiss should have been mine!

Despite my jealousy, there was a romance to the scene different than anything that I had ever witnessed or felt before. I wanted to see more, learn more about what they were doing, when Boris began pulling Marta further into the forest.

"No, Boris. Not now," Marta protested.

"Come on, sweetheart, *kohana*," Boris soothed. He threw his arm around her. Whispers and giggles punctuated their disappearance into the dense foliage.

Where were Boris and Marta going? The heart of the woods was a dark, scary place. My parents and Granny Vera had always told me never to go too deep into the woods. That's where the wolves were. Lying on my stomach in the dark, I felt afraid, bewildered and, most of all, shut out. Whatever their business was, it seemed to break the rules.

As their voices faded, my thoughts drifted to how seldom I had seen Boris lately. How long it had been since we had been fishing together. How quickly he had left my birthday party. Then I thought of Sergei's note, and I remembered that a boy my own age liked me.

But Sergei was my height, rode a bicycle rather than a motorcycle, and didn't seem to have anything he could teach me. If only Sergei were more like Boris.

I briefly considered tracking Boris, but then I remembered that I had my own adventure—yet another boy to find. I brushed the dirt off my pants and sweatshirt and hurried down the path. I was rewarded when I caught sight of the gigantic rock, gleaming in the moonlight.

The boulder stood in front of me, but no boy. Look again, I reassured myself. Perhaps his dark clothes had camouflaged him. With a sausage sticking out of one pocket and cheese bulging from the other, I felt foolish, as if I had just dreamed of meeting him. Yet somehow, I mustered the faith to whisper, "Vasyl?"

I heard a rustling sound as though an invisible curtain were being pulled back—more likely an animal crunching the leaves. At the very edge of the forest, I could see shadows dancing, re-forming and shifting.

"Granny Vera," I reminded her. "You promised. Watch over me." As a backup, I gripped the sausage and cheese, ready to hurl them if an animal should charge.

Then, out of the darkness, a small figure emerged.

As I looked at the boy gliding towards me, I wasn't afraid. I felt sorry for him. Just a boy, he was alone in the woods. But also, once again, I was overwhelmed by the sensation that he was a magical being.

I noticed that he was wearing my old green blanket loosely around his shoulders. My mother had let me take it when she finished knitting another one exactly like it for my bed. It was my second surprise of the night, but not a good one. Forest creatures were supposed to join me when I invited them to my picnics, not barge into my hiding place and steal my things.

He pulled *my* blanket around his thin shoulders. "Hello, Katya." He didn't seem the least flustered to see me.

"You found my hiding place," I accused him.

"I was cold," he said simply. In the darkness, he looked and sounded older than he had during the day.

It was my blanket, after all, and he had taken it without asking— but I reminded myself that I had wanted to tell him about it anyway. And I didn't want to scare him away. I wanted to know more. "Here," I said, offering the food.

Vasyl was so thin. I expected him to eat the food ravenously like an animal. Instead, he shook his head.

"What's wrong? Aren't you hungry?" I asked.

"Not for that," Vasyl said.

I walked over and placed my offering on the top of the boulder. "You can eat it for breakfast."

Vasyl nodded and squatted next to the boulder. I sat cross-legged in front of him, shoving my hands into my pockets for warmth. I felt the baby *matryoshka* and pulled her out to show Vasyl. "Look," I said, "for my birthday."

Vasyl reached out for her and held her gently in his pale hand. "But where are her mothers?" he asked. "She is so tiny without them." He turned her in the moonlight.

"I forgot she was in my pocket," I admitted. "I'll take her home."

Watching him admire her, I wondered where Vasyl's home was.

He seemed comfortable in the woods.

When Vasyl set the *matryoshka* baby on the ground next to us, I felt like we had a threesome. My doll could join in the conversation. Amused, I left her in the dirt facing me. "So you live here?" I asked.

Vasyl rolled his eyes. "Now I do. I'm not welcome where I used to live."

This boy did live in the woods. Like Boris and Marta venturing too deeply into the trees, this too seemed wrong. "Where are your parents?" I asked him.

"Dead. For many years," he said.

Although his answer didn't seem to make him sad, I felt so badly for him that for a few minutes I didn't say anything at all. When I had recovered, I asked my most important question. "Why did you want me to come back?"

Vasyl turned his eyes to the night sky. "I have some bad news for you," he said. His voice held an edge that made me shiver in a way that was different from the chill of night air. I felt a jolt, also a deep longing to know.

"Bad news?" I asked quietly, dreading, yet wanting to hear what he would say.

Vasyl faced me, and the moonlight fell on only one-half of his face, leaving the other side cloaked in deep shadow. This peculiar sight fueled my growing nervousness, and I scooted away. "Tell me!"

"Our world," he paused, "what's left of it, is going to be destroyed."

I gazed beyond Vasyl into the forest. As a cloud passed over the moon, the shadows assumed new shapes. One grew the jagged edges of a fire. The black flames swelled to my height, then surged until they seemed as tall as a haystack. My nose felt hot from the flames as I heard his last word through a cloud of smoke. "Tonight," he promised.

Before the acrid smoke cleared, I pictured the fierce blaze traveling down my lane and engulfing its ancient cottages. I imagined my own dear cottage exploding in a fire that soared to the heavens. I had the vague impression of frightened people and lines of metal buses shooting off into the darkness. I was certain that I couldn't return to my home. That world would no longer exist. I looked at Vasyl again.

"You know I've told you the truth," he said with calm certainty.

"No, I don't," I cried as I stood up. "You stole my blanket. I think you're a thief *and* a liar."

"Wait." Vasyl reached for me as if to stop me from leaving. "I'm trying to help you," he pleaded. "You need to know."

"Help me?" I asked wildly. I took a few steps backwards. "How will your lies help me?"

He gestured towards the boulder, and I was newly aware of his pale, translucent skin. His hands were smooth and fine. His dark shirt was clean and well-pressed. The boy didn't look like he lived in the woods—he looked like what my teachers would call a bourgeoisie, someone soft who liked his comforts in life, his home.

I should have told him that he was crazy but, instead, I began running wildly down the path, oblivious to the branches and brambles that slapped at my legs and stung my bare hands.

"You'll come back," he called after me. "You need to."

Chapter Five

Глава пятая

I GRIPPED MY GREEN BLANKET TIGHTLY OVER MY HEAD, but it didn't shield me from Mama's voice.

"Katya." Her strong hands shook me.

My eyes flickered open. I rubbed the sleep out of their corners.

"Wake up," Mama said. She was standing next to my bed with her arms crossed over her chest. She was wearing her durable farm clothes, dark pants and a sweatshirt. Soon, she and Petro Shamenko would be at the barn milking our cow.

Petro Shamenko was the paid herdsman who helped my mother tend the animals. I had known this simple-minded man all my life. He swept the barn and milked the cows, slowly and carefully, as if the fate of the world rested on the successful completion of these chores. Yet he had a sweet playful side. When I was little, he had helped me collect chicken feathers for the small pillows that I was fond of sewing for the fairies.

I struggled to sit up.

"That's my girl," Mama said.

As Mama returned to the kitchen, I managed to get out of bed and begin dressing. The delicious aroma of fried dough filled my room—she was making pancakes. I slipped my brown dress-uniform over my head.

"Katya," Mama called from the kitchen, her voice full of suspicion. "Did you raid the refrigerator last night?"

With this reminder, the night rushed back to me: the theft of the food, the moonbeam on the path, Boris' proposal to Marta, and, most terrible of all: Vasyl.

My mother stuck her head in the door. "Katya, why aren't you answering me?"

"I did get hungry last night and ate a few pieces of cheese. That's all," I finished lamely. I wasn't used to lying.

"And a sausage," Mama added.

"Yes, Mama," I agreed. Then it occurred to me that if I had eaten all that food, I couldn't possibly be hungry. "And I'm still stuffed," I said as I went to the bureau for my hairbrush.

As I looked into the mirror, I glanced at the figure of the *domovyk*. He had the same half-smile as always on his wooden lips, and remembered again the horrible impression that I had in the instant before Vasyl said, *Our world is going to be destroyed.*

"Katya," my mother called. "What are you doing in there?"

Her voice chased away the unsettling night memories, and I found myself once again standing in the half-light of dawn. I touched the *domovyk* and said, "Stop looking at me," before I hurried into the kitchen.

A pile of pancakes, a bowl of sour cream and strawberry jam waited for me on the counter. The butter dripping off the side of the pancakes had formed a luscious yellow pool. Sitting down, I gazed at the photos on the wall beyond.

For their wedding photo, Papa had worn a daisy in his lapel. Mama had on a hat with a frilly veil that covered her forehead. My parents looked stiff, like people in black and white shots always manage to do. A photo of a middle-aged Granny Vera hung next to my parents' wedding portrait. My grandmother had a pleasant face with eyes the color of acorns and red hair. In the photo, she wore the Ukrainian national costume—a white embroidered tunic wrapped by a scarlet skirt, covered by an apron and sashed by a belt of coarse woolen thread. Strings of red glass beads hung around her neck. I missed her more than I had for a long time. Granny Vera would have been able to tell me about Vasyl.

Forgetting that I was supposed to be full, I finished my pancakes in no time. Meanwhile, my gaze swept the cottage. Everything appeared normal—unharmed, but I was in a hurry to go outside. To see the sun shining— just like it had the day before.

"You wolfed down your breakfast," my mother scolded me. "I thought you weren't hungry."

"The pancakes were so delicious." I offered this lame excuse as I quickly rinsed my plate. "Excuse me, Mama, but I want to get my chores done. I have a lot to do at school." I set my plate on the counter and hurried to the door.

"You didn't drink your milk," my mother said.

"I'm sorry," I said.

As my hand gripped the knob, my mother called out, "What am I going to do with you, daughter?"

Did she know, I wondered, how naughty I had been? That I had talked to a boy in the woods at night and given him food?

When she turned back to the dishes, I realized she had believed my lie, and I felt even worse.

Outside, the sun peeked over the horizon, and the grass, the sky, and the trees were hazy with spring mist. Still, I could tell that it was going to be another typical day. The same as any other April day, only hotter. I was barely out the door and could already feel myself beginning to sweat.

Looking around at our beautiful yard, I began to calm down. Vasyl wasn't real. He was just a forest creature. And even if he was real, he obviously was mistaken. Still, there had been something so scary about that fire. I remembered touching my nose and finding it as hot as a brick left overnight near the stove.

After a brief stop by the outhouse, I went to our chicken coop where Pirate, our cross-eyed rooster, proudly ruled. Entering, I smelled moist, decaying hay. "Hello, everybody." They were making a ruckus. "Cluck. Cluck." I shooed the noisy chickens outside.

After scooping up a bucket of feed, I followed the chickens and tossed the yellow kernels on the hard ground in front of the henhouse. Returning to their nests, I collected seven warm eggs in my apron and headed for the cottage.

I was about to open the front door when I heard a car. As our lane didn't get much traffic, I turned to see who it could be. I was surprised to recognize my parents' white Lada weaving down the lane.

Papa was home early or, more likely, I was confused about his schedule. I hurried into the cottage to store the eggs before rushing back outside to greet him.

The door to the Lada was open, but Papa hadn't gotten out. As I drew closer, I was shocked to see that he was slumped over the wheel. I ran toward him yelling, "Papa."

He reacted as if in slow motion. It took him a long minute to lift his head and look at me. His dark eyes were half-closed. His jaw hung slack. Most terrifying of all, he didn't seem to recognize me.

"Papa," I murmured. As I had done once with a wounded doe, I inched slowly toward him. When I was so close that I could see the stubble on his face, I got a whiff of the strangest smell. My Papa smelled just like the earth after a thunderstorm.[2]

"Step back, Katya," Papa ordered me.

I gave him room and watched as he slowly climbed out of the car. When he started off in the direction of our cottage, he was stumbling like Uncle Kryko. I wondered: Could Papa be drunk?

As I had seen him help my uncle, I ran up next to him so he could lean on me. When he threw his heavy arm around my shoulder, I staggered under his weight. He tripped, and we both collapsed into the grass, still wet with cold dew.

Mama turned the corner. When she saw us, she threw back her head and began laughing. Yet when she caught my gaze, her laughter stopped abruptly. Except for the sound of Noisy barking and Papa's snarly breath, it was quiet, so quiet again.

I was still lying on the wet grass with Papa's arm weighting my

[2] *The Truth About Chernobyl* By Grigori Medvedev, page 99, 1991 Perseus Books Group, New York

middle, when I noticed something unusual. In the direction of the station, a black plume of smoke twisted and curled against the dawning sky. It looked small and insignificant. I wanted to believe that it had nothing to do with me. But I had seen it before, and Vasyl's words ran through my mind. *Our world is going to be destroyed.*

Mama rushed towards us. "What's wrong?"

I felt tears sting my eyes. "I don't know."

"An explosion and a fire," Papa sputtered. "At the station…. Reactor Number Four."

Upon hearing these words, I remembered the change in the moonlight that preceded Vasyl's explosion and fire. Had my nose actually burned with the heat? Yet a glance at my cottage with its blue shutters reassured me. Maybe Vasyl's warning held some truth. Maybe the station, which I didn't really care about, was damaged. But my world, my cottage, was intact!

"They were running a safety test," I overheard Papa say when I was able to focus on the conversation again.

Papa struggled to sit up. "I feel so tired," he complained.

"Here. Ivan, let me help you," Mama said.

I jumped up and joined her. We each took an arm. Together, we pulled. It was like moving a lazy cow. Somehow, we steered Papa down the path and through the front door. His wooden chair groaned when he collapsed into it.

"Now, Ivan," Mama said. "Tell us what happened."

"You didn't hear the explosion?" Papa asked.

Mama and I shook our heads.

"Sound sleepers," Papa mumbled before closing his eyes. His head fell back. "I feel…" At the sound of his voice trailing off into a long, slow moan, my heart flung itself against my rib cage.

My mother must have noticed my stricken face. "Katya, your father will be fine. Remember how he carries on when he has a cold."

I knew that Mama was right. Papa hardly ever got sick, but when he did, he always acted grouchy and pessimistic.

Mama's gaze was steady. "Busy hands, calm heart. Now take off your father's boots," she ordered me.

Papa will be fine, I repeated to myself as I knelt down on the wooden floor. Everything is fine. As I unlaced my father's work boots, I enjoyed the ordinary sight of the curtains fluttering in the light breeze. I noticed that the photos of my parents and of Granny Vera hung in the exact places that they always had on the wall. I listened to the familiar sound of Noisy barking in the yard. Everything will stay exactly the same, I promised myself.

I tugged, and Papa's boot popped off. Instead of that stinky, father-foot smell, I was puzzled when I smelled another thunderstorm. To try to discover the boot's awful secret, I stared into the well, but it merely looked dark and worn.

"Stop playing with Papa's boot," Mama snapped.

"Yes, Mama." I guiltily set the boot aside.

"We'll help you to the bedroom," Mama suggested to Papa.

"I'm tired but not sleepy," Papa mumbled.

"Tired but not sleepy." Mama repeated the phrase as though it were one of my math problems that she couldn't understand.

"That's right," Papa said irritably. "Natasha, why don't you and Katya leave me alone?"

Mama cast her worried eyes toward the door. "Katya, go on to school."

I didn't argue with her. I didn't like watching my big, strong father act like an invalid.

As I ran out the door, Mama called, "Papa didn't get any sleep, and he probably just inhaled a lot of smoke. Don't worry, O.K.?"

"O.K.," I lied.

In the front yard, I knelt next to Noisy. "See you after school," I promised him.

On my bicycle, I glanced back once more at my cottage. Through the blue-shuttered front window, I could see Papa with his eyes closed, sitting in his chair.

Mama knelt before him.

Chapter Six

Глава шестая

I PUSHED MY BICYCLE WITH ONE HAND as Angelika and I strolled down Lenin Street. Angelika's apartment was on my route to school.

"Did you hear about the fire at the station?" I asked her. I wanted her to tell me that nothing was wrong.

"Father called this morning," Angelika said. "He said that we have a good fire department. Everything will be all right."

I was glad that Angelika didn't appear to be worried.

"My Papa came home early. He wasn't feeling well. Mother said it was the smoke," Katya said.

"Or maybe the flu," Angelika said. "My aunt was sick last week-end."

"That could be it," I said. I cheered up, thinking about this very normal possibility.

"I hope he gets better soon," Angelika said.

"He will be," I said, although I still felt uneasy.

Above us, a banner for the upcoming May Day Parade flapped in the wind. *Workers of all countries, unite. Long live May 1.* An amusement park was scheduled to open for the first time on May 1, the day of the parade, and when we turned the corner, we found ourselves facing it.

The Ferris wheel formed a yellow ring against the sky. Very few people from our area had traveled in an airplane. Even the adults were excited to get a view of our city from on high. My parents had promised me that I could ride in it.

Six more days until the amusement park opened, and I would be sitting in a booth on that Ferris wheel. I could hardly wait for May 1st. Before then, I promised myself I would figure out a way to tell Angelika I might ride with Sergei. When I thought about it, I decided that she must have noticed his recent special attentions. Twice when our class was playing soccer, Sergei had kicked the ball straight to me.

My mind wandered off into a daydream. Wouldn't it be great if I could ride the Ferris wheel with Sergei? We could sit side by side. Just the two of us. Why, our booth might even stall at the top. A fog might blanket the city that day, and we might find ourselves riding through the clouds.

"Carousels are for babies," Angelika was saying, gazing at the merry-go-round, which with the electric cars and the Ferris wheel made up the whole amusement park. "Of course, if Sergei were with me...."

Suddenly, I remembered I had a new problem, more serious than how to tell Angelika about Sergei's note. As my thoughts turned away from Sergei, I murmured a polite, "That would be fun."

"Do you think Sergei will ask me to ride with him?" Angelika asked in the gayest of tones.

The contrast between her total happiness and my nervous anxiety made me feel so lonely that I blurted out, "Do you think anyone can see into the future?"

"No," Angelika said. "Of course not."

I was too ashamed to tell even Angelika the whole story about the boy, but I was too worried not to share a part of it. I said simply, "Yesterday, I met a boy in the woods." I knew better than to tell Angelika that he seemed magical, like some kind of spirit. "The boy warned me that there was going to be an explosion and a fire." I pointed in the direction of the station, at the plume in the sky. "And this morning the fire happened."

Angelika's pretty lip curled in derision. I could see the gums above her small crooked teeth. "What could a boy know about that fire?"

"He might live in the woods," I explained. "Maybe he's not a regular boy."

Angelika's brown eyes flew open with alarm. "Have you told your parents about him?"

"Not yet," I said.

"You should tell your parents," she insisted. "That boy sounds dangerous. They need to send police to look for him."

I was starting to wish that I had never mentioned Vasyl to her. "I'm afraid they'll get angry with me," I sputtered.

"I'm sure they will," Angelika scolded me. "Because you know you shouldn't be with strange boys in the woods."

"You're right." How could I have been so foolish as to spill my wild story to Angelika? She might decide that I was odd and not be my friend. Vasyl was right about one thing. I needed to keep the secret of his existence to myself.

A vendor on the street cried, "Lemonade! Get your delicious, cold lemonade!" A few boys were kicking a soccer ball on the sidewalk.

I looked into my friend's happy face and tried to reassure myself. Angelika and the lemonade vendor were real. The boy in the woods was… His hair was too blond. His eyes were too blue. He seemed like he belonged to another world. Maybe he was some type of forest creature. Or maybe he was a nightmare.

As I looked at Angelika, her eyes searched out mine. She held my gaze a little too long, before turning towards Pripyat Primary School #2.

Chapter Seven

Глава седьмая

THE SCHOOL HALLWAY WAS CROWDED WITH KIDS. Angelika had left me to get a drink of water. Ahead of me, I spotted Sergei Rudko and Andriy Osadchiy walking to class. They each had on a school boy's uniform—a dark suit and light shirt. I followed close behind, hoping that Sergei would notice me. This morning, he looked more handsome than usual. I couldn't help admiring his tanned skin and blond hair.

Over his shoulder, Sergei caught a glimpse of me. My heart skipped a beat when he stopped and smiled.

I smiled back. Every girl in my school would say that with his light hair and ruddy cheeks, Sergei was cuter than Boris. But not me. Still I reminded myself that Boris was taken. Sergei crooked his finger towards me and took a step towards the lockers, leaving Andriy behind.

My heart pounding, I followed him. It felt so good to be chosen over all the other girls in my class.

"Katya," Sergei said. He was grinning as if a relationship between us was the most natural thing in the world. The next words out of his mouth made me feel as if I were dreaming. "Do you want to ride the Ferris wheel with me?"

"I think my mother will let me." I remembered Angelika only after I'd accepted.

"See you then," Sergei said. He turned and rejoined Andriy.

Watching the two boys saunter off, I promised myself to tell Angelika. But now that I had an actual date with Sergei, it would be even harder. Boys complicated things, I decided. Oh, how I hoped Mama would let me go.

When I entered the classroom, the last student to arrive, I saw the date written on the blackboard: April 26, 1986. I was never this late to class but Lydia Rybalka, my last year's teacher, had stopped me in the hallway and asked me to take a note to the office for her.

Although our classroom held about thirty students, my gaze immediately searched out Sergei Rudko. As I headed to my seat, Sergei looked frankly at me. His dark eyes stayed with me as if they were magnetized. When I returned his smile, a sensation of pleasure shot up through my chest from deep in my core.

I sat down at my desk against the wall.

Nina Ivanovna, a tall woman with an erect bearing, was furiously scribbling on the blackboard. She always seemed to want to cram as much into our heads as possible. Today her chalk hammered across the board with a vengeance. I kept waiting for her to mention the accident, but she never did.

After the bell rang announcing the start of class, Nina Ivanovna turned to face us. "Please begin the long division problems that I have written on the blackboard."

"Yes, Nina Ivanovna," we all recited.

Normally, math and science were my two best subjects. My father praised me, saying, "Science is the path to a good job." But today, as I stared at the equations, all I could think about were boys. To the right of me, Sergei made me think of my need to talk to Angelika. When I tried to forget about him, my head filled with thoughts of Vasyl. And then I wondered about Boris and Marta in the woods. And the woods took me back to Vasyl.

I should have known better than to talk to Vasyl or to carry him

food in the middle of the night. And although I still had no idea what he really knew, now that the station had experienced a fire, my actions seemed those of a criminal. I worried that I needed to tell my parents the full story, but I struggled to find the courage. I vainly plied myself with false reassurances like, *after all, when I met Vasyl in the woods, I didn't know he was a horrible person, a thief and a liar.*

"Papa," I would say. Before I could even begin practicing my confession, I could hear him shouting, "You did *what*!?"

I would have rather given back all my birthday presents than disappoint my father. I would rather go a month without food. I would rather…

My gaze happened upon the poster of Vladimir Ilyich Lenin

hanging on the wall next to me. He was a loving son and good brother, the best grammar school student, a revolutionary who devoted his whole life to making poor people's lives better. We all considered Lenin, the founder of the Communist Party, to be a caring father figure.

I looked at his familiar face which was drawn on the May Day banners and represented by a bust in the library. I implored him, Grandpa Lenin, What would you do?

Grandpa Lenin's yellow eyes just stared blankly back at me.

Chapter Eight

Глава восьмая

FOR AN HOUR OR SO, I STRUGGLED TO FOCUS my whirling thoughts on my studies. I tried to pay attention to Nina Ivanovna's lecture about the solar system. I should be memorizing the drawing of the planets on the blackboard, I told myself. She had just finished her crude drawing when a policeman appeared at the door.

"Students, remain silent," she barked, and she went to see what the man wanted.

From what I could tell from my desk, the policeman spoke calmly. Although most of the students started whispering among themselves, sharing their May Day plans, I knew the policeman was here because of my encounter with Vasyl, and I couldn't keep my eyes off the pair.

The policeman wore a gray rain jacket over his blue uniform. It wasn't a normal policeman's uniform, though, because I caught a glimpse of a gold star above his pocket.

Eventually, the policeman nodded, dismissing Nina Ivanovna, and he marched off. But my relief was short-lived. As if she were a madwoman, my teacher began rushing around and closing all the windows.

When Nina Ivanovna had finished, she rapped her ruler on the blackboard. The class stopped talking. "You students are being sent home," she said. The tone she used implied we were all bad kids.

Along with the other students, I waited for Nina Ivanovna to provide an explanation for her actions, one that made sense. Alone, I waited for her to single me out for punishment. "The outdoors is dangerous," Nina Ivanovna warned us. "Go straight home."

But her instruction was contradictory. If the outdoors were dangerous, why were we all walking home?

"I'll see you next week," Nina Ivanovna said, and turned her back to the class.

Watching my teacher clear off her desk, I knew nothing more in the way of an explanation was forthcoming. The school closing must be related to the accident at the station, but how? Nothing added up. Yet since adults' rules often confused me, I wasn't overly alarmed. Besides, like every schoolgirl since the beginning of time, I was excited about the unexpected holiday. Along with the rest of my classmates, I rushed out into the hall, already crowded with students, to find a holiday atmosphere. The whole school was being sent home. Not just our grade.

Waiting for Angelika outside the classroom, I caught bits of other students' conversations:

"They've never shut down school before."

"My dad says there was a fire and an explosion."

"What does the station have to do with our school?"

"The radiation, stupid."

Angelika appeared at my side.

Since her parents were both scientists, I thought she might understand the term better than I did. "What's radiation?" I asked her.

Angelika smiled a superior smile. "Energy that comes in waves."

I didn't admit this, but her explanation sounded fantastical to me. And this from a girl who mocked my tales about my forest creatures. "Can you see radiation?" I asked.

"Of course, not. It's invisible," Angelika said, as if she were answering a child.

When Angelika and I passed through the door into the brilliant sunlight, Nina Ivanovna's error was obvious. If the outdoors were dangerous, hailstones would be pummeling us. A tornado cone like the one I had seen in my science book would be swirling around the Ministry of Culture. Or at the very least, lightning bolts would be crisscrossing a dark sky.

Instead, the day was still beautiful. The sky's blue color was almost as unreal as the eyes of the boy in the woods. But thinking about the boy made me uneasy, and I pushed the memory aside.

I collected my bicycle, and we began walking to Angelika's apartment.

In front of us, a baby in a stroller started crying. The mother stooped to comfort the child. A sweaty jogger hurried past us. His feet pounded the pavement.

In the distance, I heard the wail of a fire truck, and I thought of Boris. He was probably on his way to the station, and this thought calmed me. Boris would know how to put out the fire.

"Hey, girls!" Andriy and Sergei called, floating by us on their bikes. With his blond hair flowing in the breeze, Sergei looked careless and happy, as if he were off to go fishing or to play soccer. "We're going to the station."

"Hey, Sergei," Angelika shouted after them.

Thinking I had called him, Sergei turned back to glance at me. I shook my head, tried to warn him with my eyes, *No. Don't say it.*

"See you soon, Katya," Sergei called.

When Angelika turned towards me, her expression was perplexed. "What did Sergei mean, Katya?" she asked.

A few yards from us, Sergei and Andriy had stopped to cross the street.

Even though the whole town seemed to be out enjoying the sunny day, suddenly biking to the station and breathing in that black smoke seemed like a bad idea. "Sergei, Andriy, you should go home," I yelled after them.

"Are you kidding? It's a holiday," Sergei answered. The light changed, and Sergei and Andriy pedaled off in the direction of the station to watch the fire like many others.

We had reached Angelika's apartment complex. It was a gray concrete building with a green leatherette door and a lone poplar tree in front.

"What did Sergei mean, Katya?" Angelika repeated.

The truth was bad, horrible. Especially when I had gotten caught like this and hadn't told Angelika in advance as I had planned. What could I do now but tell her? "Sergei asked me to ride the Ferris wheel with him," I confessed.

Angelika's face darkened. "Thanks for stealing my boyfriend, Katya." She turned her back on me and started towards her door.

"I was going to tell you. I promise," I called after her.

"You don't even like Sergei." Angelika glared over her shoulder at me. "You're just doing this to hurt me."

Was this true? I felt both guilty and confused.

Without saying goodbye, Angelika slammed the door and disappeared inside.

Standing on Lenin Street, holding my blue bicycle, I understood that everything was my fault. I was responsible for Angelika's pain, for the accident, for all that was going wrong. Although I knew Angelika liked Sergei, I had sought his attentions anyway. And didn't lots of young girls live in the area? Yet Vasyl had chosen me to hear his secret. Why would he do that unless he knew I was a bad person? Angelika was right to get away from me. I didn't deserve friends. Certainly not nice girls like her. Those boys wanted me because they knew I was bad, a daydreamer who made up lies about fairies and would go into the woods at night.

A fire truck barreled past and startled me. It raced toward the station. Was that Boris clinging onto a ladder on its side? "Boris!" I screamed.

The fireman tipped his hat. Only it wasn't Boris. The dark-haired man was a stranger.

I needed to go to the boulder and find Vasyl again. Although I was a mess inside, my cottage wasn't destroyed. Noisy was alive and well. My cows and chickens were healthy. If I could convince him that he was wrong, then perhaps I could convince myself that every-thing was fine.

Nina Ivanovna had told us to go straight home, but the boulder was just a short detour. As I was hesitating, deciding what to do, I realized I had another reason for stopping by the boulder. I remembered that I had forgotten my baby *matryoshka*. I needed to rescue her. Then afterwards, I could ride home and check on my father.

Climbing onto my bike, I hurried alongside the cars, other bicycles and people. When I reached the end of the block, I again faced the new Ferris wheel. Although I felt dark inside, the gleaming yellow circle shining against the blue sky still managed to lift my spirits.

I was certain of one thing: the day we celebrated the solidarity of all workers, May Day, was right around the corner. This was the most important holiday in all of the Soviet Republics; it wouldn't be canceled unless the world had ended. It was as plain and simple as that. Whatever had happened at the station, Pripyat would be back to normal by May Day. But would I be? When I tried to feel excited about riding with Sergei, I couldn't. Angelika's angry words had ruined my anticipation.

I raced as fast as I could towards the boulder. At the top of a small hill, I began panting. I struggled to identify the acid taste that had coated my tongue. Car Battery.[3] I had never tasted one before, but somehow this seemed right. What a strange flavor, I thought as I kept pedaling towards the woods.

When I reached the rushing stream, Vasyl was nowhere to be seen. I stepped closer to the boulder and saw ants feasting on the sausage and cheese that I had left last night. I dropped to my knees and examined the dirt. Although I noticed scuff marks, my baby *matryoshka* was gone.

I thrust my hand underneath the boulder, but all I felt was my muddy cup, an old fishing reel, a ball of twine…. My green blanket had disappeared, too. The green blanket was so worn that my frugal mother had no problem giving it to me for my outdoors picnics.

[3] *The Truth About Chernobyl* By Grigori Medvedev, page 150, 1991 Perseus Books Group, New York

It was dirty and worthless. But now its absence was proof that Vasyl was dishonest, and the proof made me happy.

"So you *are* just a common thief," I muttered. All of my imaginings that he was special now seemed fanciful. What I had learned from Granny Vera were childish tales. Papa was right. Science was the only truth.

I leaned my bicycle against the boulder and set off into the woods. After traveling a few hundred yards, I spotted a square of fabric. It lay underneath an oak tree whose low outstretched branches reached out towards me like gnarled hands. Although I must have walked by this tree many times, I had never noticed the tree's unusual branches before.

"Vasyl," I called out cautiously.

When no one answered, I bent down and crawled on my knees towards the trunk. A thin sheet, a blue towel and a piece of foam rubber lay on the ground. I ruffled through the damp material but found nothing interesting. I was about to leave when I noticed a candle stub at the base of the tree. It was almost burned to a nub. Used matches littered the ground.

I moved closer to view a carving. Someone had cut into the tree trunk a crudely drawn heart. Who had been coming to this secret space? Could it be Boris and Marta?

But people their age didn't hide underneath trees. This had to be Vasyl's hiding place. It was clear to me that something was going on in these woods I never knew about.

To catch Vasyl, I just needed to watch this tree. When I spotted him, I'd call out, "Liar." Nothing was wrong with my cottage. I'd tell him, "Give me my blanket and my doll back." But at the thought of the confrontation, my heart began pounding.

Better, I would tell Papa that a boy had stolen my belongings from me. I would send Papa to find Vasyl, who was a thief and a liar. I wasn't bound to keep my promise to him. Not at all!

When I returned, my father's car was still parked in front of our cottage. Mama was standing in our front yard talking to Boris' mother, Inna Boiko.

"Why aren't you at school?" Mama asked.

"I found his hiding place," I choked out. "There's a boy in the woods. He stole my blanket and my baby *matryoshka*."

"What are you talking about?" Mama plucked a tiny twig from my uniform. "You're all sweaty."

"I saw a boy in the woods. He was wearing my green blanket around his shoulders." I started to tell her about the baby *matryoshka* but in a panic, I realized that I couldn't talk about the doll without admitting my nighttime trip.

Mama and Inna Boiko looked at each other. "Have you heard about any thieves in our neighborhood?"

"No." The dark hairs above Inna Boiko's lip were quivering with disapproval.

"Where exactly is this hiding place?" Mama looked serious and angry.

I felt badly about getting Vasyl in trouble, but as I remembered the boy's cruel words, they hardened my heart. "In the woods. By the boulder."

Mama yanked my arm. "And what were you doing in the woods by the boulder? You are supposed to be in school!"

I had misread her anger. She was angry with me, not with Vasyl. "I'm sorry, Mama…" I started to object that Vasyl was the one who was guilty, but she interrupted.

"Return to school right now, and *never* look for boys in the woods again!" She shook me. "Do you hear me?"

Inna Boiko turned away as if to give Mama some privacy to discipline me.

"But, Mama. You don't understand," I protested. "Nina Ivanovna let us out early today, because of the fire."

Mama stared blankly at me. "Why?"

As weak as my explanation was, I felt superior as I offered it.

"Radiation. The air," I said.

"Nothing's wrong with the air," she said. "It's easy to get a good tan today.[4] Look," she pointed at her dark shoulders, mottled with freckles. "So you really don't have school?"

"No," I assured her.

Inna Boiko turned back to us now, and when she spoke up, I knew that she had been listening all along. "My Boris must be at the station by now." Her face was stricken with worry. "Did your teacher say anything else?" Mama asked.

I saw the confusion in her eyes, and I was afraid.

"Not really," I said. "But a man came to our classroom to talk to her. He had a star on his uniform." I was proud of myself for recalling this particular detail.

Inna Boiko caught Mama's eye. "Maybe the chemical protection unit. You know the force that Oleksandr Bilozir's first cousin trained for."

"Well," Mama said, "go change into your gardening clothes. We have some planting to do."

That's when I remembered my father. "How is Papa?"

"Still asleep. So be quiet."

As I walked towards the cottage, I heard my mother sigh and begin speaking to Inna Boiko, "Granny Vera filled Katya's head with so much nonsense. She plays with wood sprites and elves, and now a boy in the woods. At least, I hope the boy is make-believe. I don't know what we're going to do with that child. She can't tell the difference between the truth and her imagination."

"Better you than me," Inna Boiko answered. "I'd spank a girl for that."

My own mother had refused to listen to me. But as I walked inside the cottage, I was angriest with Inna Boiko. I wanted to tell her, I wouldn't be your daughter-in-law if you begged me.

After I had changed, I stopped by to see Noisy. He was chained underneath the oak tree. He jumped up and licked me all over. It didn't matter, since I already felt sticky with pine gum and sap.

[4] *The Truth About Chernobyl* By Grigori Medvedev, page 150, 1991 Perseus Books Group, New York

"Katya, come on," Mama called.

I walked over to the garden gate and lifted the latch. Mama was on her hands and knees, digging in some of the prettiest dirt I'd ever seen. It was deep brown, like chocolate. Not sticky or chunky with clay, it was so fine that it poured through my fingers. She handed me a glass jar of russet carrot seeds and pointed towards the far end of the garden. "I thought we'd plant our carrots over there."

Breathing in the earthy smell of grass, manure and animals, I picked up a trowel, crawled over to the spot she'd indicated and began digging. I had been told over and over that my ancestors had been farmers for generations, and I felt like I was born knowing how deep to plant a carrot seed in the dirt. "What's for lunch?" I asked.

"Shush." My mother pointed at the bush on the side of our cottage.

The first nightingale that I had heard that spring was trilling away.

Both my mother and I stopped digging and listened.

My mother's eyes held a faraway look as if she were trying to view the world from the nightingale's eyes.

After the bird was quiet, Mama said, "I think it's a sad song."

"Why, Mama?"

Ignoring my question, Mama asked, "What do you think the bird is singing about?"

"I think it's just happy to be right here in the Ukraine."

Mama laughed. "You are your father's daughter—so patriotic."

Both Mama and Papa were members of the Communist Party. But I always sensed that only Papa was proud to be a Communist. Once on a meeting day, Mama had urged Papa to go on without her. She claimed to be sick. Later, I saw her working in the garden. When I heard her humming happily as she weeded the radishes, I was certain she had lied.

"You don't really find the bird's song sad, do you?" I asked.

"Sometimes." Mama wiped the sweat off her forehead with the back of her hand. "I don't think our country is as perfect as you and your father do."

I had no idea what Mama meant. I knew for a fact that the nightingale loved our garden. But, for once, I was too absorbed in my task to ask questions. I dug a shallow hole in the earth and poured a few seeds in my cupped palm. I picked up one between my thumb and forefinger and stared at the small brown speck, not much bigger than a flea.

I dropped the seed into the hole and pushed the good earth over it. Was it magic or science that would cause this little seed to grow into a carrot? I let the earth flow through my fingers and decided *the dirt in Ukraine is magic dirt.* This black soil is so rich all things grow well. In just a few months, the green carrot tops would be the length of my fingers.

"Do you think Papa will wake up soon?" I asked.

Almost as soon as the words were out of my mouth, we saw him standing straight and tall in the doorway. Dressed in camouflage, his bulk filled the entire space.

"Where's my lunch?" he bellowed in his usual voice.

"Papa," I yelled. "You're well!"

"I'm better," he said. But when I flew out the garden to him and threw my arms around his neck, he staggered backwards.

Never one to show any weakness, Papa ruffled my hair and said, "Katya, you caught me off guard."

As I explained what I was doing home from school, his eyebrows knit closer and closer together. One hand curled into a fist. Mama joined us at the door.

"Natasha," he said to Mama. "Before I eat, I'm going to try to get in touch with the station. My boss may need me to come in early."

"Ivan, please tell Hryhory Larin that you are sick, and take a day off," Mama said. She was wiping her hands on her canvas work apron.

"Have you listened to the radio this morning?" Papa asked her.

"No," Mama shook her head. "I've been planting. We've gotten the cabbages, cucumbers, and tomatoes in. We need your help to finish the carrots, sorrel and peppers."

Normally at the mention of all these fresh vegetables, Papa would start talking about the feasts that we would have this summer: the *salo*—pig fat, salted and spiced—the new potatoes dripping in butter, the *borsch* made from homegrown beets and the piping hot apple pie topped with homemade sour cream. But now he turned to go inside.

"You need to help your mother in the garden, Katya," Papa reminded me as he entered the cottage.

Desperate to prove that I was a good girl, I called out to his broad back. "Yes, Papa."

Chapter Nine

Глава девятая

AFTER DINNER, I SAT AT MY NEW DESK. The pieces of the Russian doll were strewn in front of me. I tossed its blue box and, sadly, began reassembling the doll without its baby.

Right when I had begun to twist the schoolgirl doll back together, Noisy let out a series of unusually loud barks. Noisy had a special bark for my father's car, for strangers and for our family. Tonight, he was barking because he wanted my parents' attention.

I listened more closely and heard voices. Curious, I abandoned the *matryoshka*, unfinished, on my desk.

The main room of our cottage was empty. The magazines— *Rabotnitsa*, *Working Woman*, *Krestjanka* and *Farm-girl*—which my mother loved for their patterns were spread out at her place on the table. Papa's gun was on the table, and on the floor was the oily rag that he used for cleaning it.

Stepping onto the front landing, the door slapped closed behind me. Moths fluttered around the lone light. As I was wearing only my long T-shirt, the air felt cool. Wrapping my arms around myself for warmth, I identified the shadowy figure conversing with my parents, Uncle Victor Kaletnik.

On any other night, I wouldn't have dared to eavesdrop on my parents, but overhearing Uncle Victor's words, "One poor man is dead," I was filled with curiosity and dread. Many of my friends' parents worked at the station, and I probably knew the family of the man who died. Besides, the adults were talking so intently that they hadn't noticed me.

"I think we should both disappear, Ivan," Uncle Victor urged. "The authorities are not being honest with us. The danger is much greater than they say."

"But the reactor is intact," Papa interrupted.

"Ivan, you're not listening to me. Our bosses know that the situation is dangerous, but they're not telling us," Uncle Victor said.

"I have a duty to the station, to my country," Papa said.

"You talk about your duty, Ivan," Mama said. "But what about your duty to Katya and me?"

"Ivan," Papa's old friend interrupted. "I was at the station this afternoon. I saw a field of graphite in front of Reactor Number Four. If Number Four didn't blow up, why is the graphite, which we both know is stored in the reactor's core, all over the yard?"[5] he asked. "The reactor must have exploded. You can't deny the evidence of my own eyes."

"That's impossible," Papa argued. "Yakyhm Beregovoi would have made an announcement. You know that the Soviet reactors are the safest in the world."

"Ivan, listen to Victor. The station is dangerous," Mama urged.

Papa laughed. "A little radiation won't hurt me."

Mama threw up her hands. As she rushed past me into the house, her face looked as stricken as the day she learned that Granny Vera had died. She didn't even stop to ask me why I was on the porch.

"Natasha!" Papa called to her.

After the door slammed closed, Uncle Victor shook his head. "I guess I'll be going." He took a few steps towards the car.

We all knew that arguing with Papa was a waste of time.

"Victor, station guard is the best job that I could ever hope for," Papa called to his friend's back. "You know without this job I'd be a peasant. Tilling the land, barely selling enough potatoes to feed my family."

This was the first time in my life that I had ever heard Papa plead with someone.

Uncle Victor stopped walking and turned to face Papa. "Well, I'm not going back until I know it's safe."

"Many men have deserted. Hryhory Larin ordered me to return to work tonight," Papa said.

"Is your job worth risking your life?" Uncle Victor asked.

With those words, my worry burst out of me. "Why is the station unsafe?"

The men turned toward me, surprised.

"Mama needs you, Katya," Papa said.

Uncle Victor cleared his throat. "Your daughter deserves a serious answer, Ivan."

In the moonlight, I could see the scowl on Papa's face.

Uncle Victor stepped up onto the stoop, leaving Papa in the shadow of the oak tree. "The station generates electricity by harnessing the strong and dangerous power of radioactive materials." He paused as if seeking a simple explanation. "Those materials are like animals pulling a cart. When they are tied together, all goes well, but it becomes dangerous when the ropes and harness break. When the reactor exploded, the nuclear reaction became uncontrolled—like a small, slow detonation of an atomic bomb—and radioactive poisons saturated an area of many kilometers around the station." He lowered his voice, which sounded sad. "We can't undo the contamination. Mankind can only wait for thousands of years for the various radioactive molecules to lose their evil power."

"Victor, you could go to prison for talking nonsense like that," Papa said. His disembodied voice arising from the shadows of the oak tree was stern.

Uncle Victor Kaletnik in prison? Thousands of years? What did all this mean? Most frightening of all, the adults seemed confused, too. My chest was constricted with worry as I blurted out, "Is Angelika Galkina's father all right?"

"Khodenchuk is the name of the poor devil who died," Uncle Victor said. "But a lot of men have radiation sickness and are at the clinic."

I wanted to ask, "what's radiation sickness," but Papa broke in.

"That's enough, Victor," he snapped. "Go inside, Katya."

Although I was shivering from the cold, I lingered. "I'll play you in checkers soon," I said to Uncle Victor.

His head cocked in puzzlement as if unable to comprehend how to answer me.

When I returned to my room, the first thing that I saw was the flowery divan. I regretted that I had forgotten to ask Mama to get out the sheets and blanket for its bed. Now that it was so late, I didn't think she would be eager to help me.

"I'm going to work," I heard Papa shout from the front door.

"But Victor Kaletnik said…" Mama called from her bedroom.

"I don't trust his judgment," Papa said.

"Ivan!" Mama cried.

"I'll be careful. Listen to the radio, and I'll see you tomorrow."

A few minutes later, I heard the roar of a car engine. Papa was leaving for the station.

There were so many things that I wished for. I wished I had given Papa a hug. I wished that I could travel back in time to the night before—when everything was still perfect. I wished for my little baby *matryoshka* doll.

Chapter Ten

Глава десятая

ON SUNDAY MORNING, my mother and I faced the transistor radio. It was a small black box. Normally, we used it sparingly in order to conserve the battery, but we had been listening to it all morning. Despite the crackle of static, we were stunned at what we had just heard.

The announcer said, "We have a minor problem at the Chernobyl Nuclear Power Plant." We heard that we were not allowed to go outdoors or anywhere near a window. We were going to be evacuated, but only for two or three days. "Stay calm. Pack sparingly and wear light clothes."[6]

Heavy footsteps approached the front door. Thank goodness. Papa had returned from work. He would know what to do.

But then, a loud knock sounded.

"Panic is forbidden," the radio announcer said. His voice was solemn, like I imagined God's to be. A bit of static crackled on the radio, then we found ourselves listening to a Beethoven sonata. It was a joke around our village whenever the authorities wanted to change the subject, they played classical music.

Mama nodded at me, and I ran to open the door.

A man dressed in camouflage stood on our front stoop. Such a stern expression didn't belong on his young face, but then, self-

[6] *The Truth About Chernobyl* By Grigori Medvedev, page 186, 1991, Perseus Books Group, New York

importance was common in Communist Ukraine. "Gather your things. We are evacuating this area."

My mother appeared at my side. "My husband works at the station. We will wait for him."

"Your husband will meet you in town," the man promised.

How did he know this? I wondered.

"What do I need to take? Will our things be safe here while we are away?" my mother asked. She wrung her hands and looked helplessly around our cottage.

"Everything will be safe until you get back," the man said quickly.

"But who will take care of our animals?" my mother asked.

The man hesitated, then blurted, "Don't worry about them. Your lives are at stake."

"Our lives?" Mama asked. Her voice trembled, and she shot a worried glance at me.

The young man looked down at his shoes, but his voice rose in impatience. "Just turn off your gas and your electricity. I'll wait for you outside."

"What is going on here? How will my husband find us?" Mama protested. "Please explain this, this…"

"Leave him a note," interrupted the man. He spun on his heels.

I chased after him and tugged on his shirtsleeve. "Can I bring my dog?" I asked.

"No pets!" the man snapped.

As if on cue, Noisy slipped through the man's khaki- and green-colored pant legs, ran across the room and jumped onto Papa's chair. The dog knew that he wasn't supposed to be inside, but he curled up in the chair as if he slept on its soft cushions every night. In Papa's favorite spot, he looked like a king of the doggy world.

"Katya, take your dog out," Mama said. I could hear the relief in her voice. Dealing with Noisy was a situation she knew how to handle.

As the man strode away, he called over his shoulder, "Hurry! I have to visit many more houses."

"Katya, leave some food for Noisy," Mama said.

I grabbed stew bones from the bowl in the refrigerator and went outside. The man was smoking underneath our big oak. As if he were punishing the cigarette, he took one puff after another, smoking it furiously. I was heading to Noisy's bowls, when the man spotted me.

"What are you doing?" he asked.

"Feeding the dog," I said.

"I told you. Someone will feed your animals."

I didn't remember this promise.

The man pointed at our cottage. "Go pack. Now."

I put the bones down and glanced at the bowl for water. I was glad that it was almost full, because under the man's watchful gaze, I didn't dare fill it to the brim.

When I returned to the cottage, Granny Vera's cuckoo slipped out of its house and chirped eleven times, eleven o'clock in the morning. From my room, I could hear my mother shouting out the window at Inna Boiko next door. "A man is here at our door demanding that we evacuate. The station doesn't answer."

Despite my worries, I felt my excitement growing. I pulled out my battered suitcase and opened it on my bed. What do you take for an evacuation? I had no idea. I spied the motorcycle poster that Boris had given me for my birthday. I hadn't yet had a chance to hang it on my wall. On a whim, I put the cylinder inside my suitcase.

After I had packed a change of clothes, my brush, a few pencils and a notepad, I took another quick glance around the room and noticed the mirror carved with the little *domovyk*. I would have liked to take him with me, but the frame was too big. I remembered Granny Vera had told me when families wanted to take a *domovyk* with them on a move or a trip, they carried an empty box and invited the house elf to jump in.

I went to the trashcan and pulled out the box that had held my *matryoshka*. On its bright label, a blue *matryoshka*, not as pretty as mine, was cracked open revealing the smaller doll inside. I thought briefly about taking my own beautiful redheaded *matryoshka* until I remembered I had left her baby with that Vasyl. He was ruining everything. When I came back, I would have to deal with him.

I considered my other gifts, and what I should take, but I couldn't decide which would fit in my suitcase. Reminding myself that I would be away for only three days, I decided they could wait for me.

I stuck the empty blue box in my suitcase and said out loud, "Come with us, *domovyk*."

Nothing happened, but then, I was too nervous to wait more than a few seconds. I snapped the suitcase shut and went out to see if Mama had finished packing

She was picking up her ashtrays, potted plants and knickknacks and then setting them back down. I could see that she was more confused over what to take than I was and had made even less progress. Sweat circled the armpits of her casual white blouse.

A banging on the door startled us. "Let's go!" The man's voice was insistent.

I grabbed her hand. "Come on, Mama. We're coming back," I pleaded with her.

"Let me go, Katya. Right now!" she snapped.

Feeling hurt, I dropped her hand and sat down in a chair by the breakfast table.

Mama rushed into her bedroom. Through the open door, I could see my mother, who was normally so careful in her movements, throwing an armful of papers and her pajamas into a small suitcase. She put her piggy bank on top and clicked it closed.

When she came back in the room, I expected her to apologize. Instead, she didn't even seem to notice me. She hurried over to the drawer in the kitchen and scrawled a note on a piece of paper.

I decided to stop pouting and find out what she was writing to Papa.

But by the time I had reached the counter, she had the note in her hand. "Let's go, Katya," she said irritably. She stopped at the door to put her garden hat on her head and straighten her skirt.

Together, we walked outside into the bright sunshine. The man was waiting for us. He was smoking another cigarette and tapping his foot impatiently.

"We'll walk to Pripyat," Mama told the man as she carefully locked the front door. "It is only a half mile from here."

The man shrugged as he started for his car. "Suit yourself."

"But why, Mama?" I tugged at her dark skirt.

"We'll go look for the Kaletniks. Victor Kaletnik can tell me what we should do," she explained. "Katya, get me a rock."

Eager to be of use, I scouted around under the large oak tree until I found one. I rushed back to the stoop.

Before weighing the note down, I read it. In place of the usual flowing Cyrillic letters of Mama's handwriting, the note scrawled across the piece of torn paper: "Papa, we have gone to Pripyat to catch a bus. I trust that we will find you somehow. Love, Your family."

We had started out the gate when I noticed Noisy. On a whim, I ran back and released him from his chain. There was a chance he might dig under the fence and escape into the forest, but he never wandered far. I trusted I could find him when we returned. I hated the thought of Noisy tied up for three days.

I closed the gate. My suitcase banging at my side, I followed Mama down the dusty lane. Every few steps, I looked back at my cottage.

Noisy was jumping against the fence and barking as if his heart might break. I knew he didn't understand that we would be back. He was just a dog. He thought we were leaving him forever.

Chapter Eleven

Глава одиннадцатая

PRIPYAT'S SIDEWALKS WERE PACKED WITH PEOPLE, and passenger buses with either red, yellow or green stripes lined the streets. I overheard one man say that the line of 1,100 buses stretched for some twelve miles.

My mother gave a little gasp when she saw the panicked scene, but I had a strange feeling that I had witnessed all this before. Staring into Vasyl's fire, in the heat of the dream—or whatever the horrible things I had imagined were—I had envisioned crowds of frightened people and lines of metal buses driving off into the darkness.

Although a few people were chattering and laughing as if they were celebrating an early May Day, just as many people were crying. Soldiers stood on corners and leaned against buildings. Some were wearing ugly gas masks. They all held their guns as if they expected to use them. One *babushka*, dressed all in black, held up an icon and was mumbling, "Save us."

Despite the icon, I was sure that something evil was happening, and Vasyl had tricked me into being a part of it. "The boy who stole the blanket told me about this," I muttered.

"Katya!" Mama jerked my hand. "Stop making up stories. I don't have the patience for you today."

"Mama," I moaned, "I'm not making this up."

Her gaze stayed fixed on the scene in front of her as if she didn't even hear me.

A little boy wearing an embroidered shirt and a black jacket fussed next to me. He was squirming in his mother's arms. "Where are we going?"

Without a pause, his mother answered, "We're going to a circus."

Even I knew we weren't going to a circus.

"Which circus?" the little boy lisped.

"I don't know. Maybe one in another country," the mother said.

The little boy beamed up at her, and I couldn't help feeling sorry for him. But the mother's comment started me thinking.

Was it possible that the buses would take us out of the country? Papa had said the government would not let us leave the U.S.S.R. Ukraine shared its borders with Belorussia and Russia, both part of the Soviet Union, as well as Poland and Romania, which were not under Soviet control. I had always wanted to go to Belorussia, the country just north of Ukraine, where Mama had a cousin. Perhaps we could go stay with her?

I felt a twinge of excitement. My longest trip had been to the city of Chernobyl, about twelve miles north of Pripyat and Yanov.

Many of our neighbors and friends were gathered in clusters on the sidewalk, but not the Kaletniks. It was as hard to locate them in the anxious crowd as it would have been if it had actually been May Day. Searching for them, we hurried from group to group, not stopping to talk to the others.

Everyone was dressed differently. The gay hat that Mama wore for gardening sat atop her head, making her look slightly festive. Some women had worn embroidered or lacy party dresses and their expensive woolen shawls. Others had stayed in their everyday clothes. I spotted one old woman wearing her gray robe and slippers. As if the occasion were a formal one, I noticed that a number of kids had worn their school uniforms. I was glad that Mama had let me keep on my slacks.

And people carried fascinating objects. A boy had his guitar slung over his back. An old man held a goat in his arms. A cat jumped out of a basket carried by a girl. The girl started crying and running after the animal. The shouts of the policemen added to the chaos. "All residents need to board a bus immediately!"

One piece of the surrounding confusion was especially puzzling. I pointed at the large puddles of white liquid on the asphalt street. "What's that?"

"The government is trying to wash the roads," Mama said.

I wanted to correct her—to say the outdoors can't be cleaned like a house after a party—but right then I saw Galina Galkina, Angelika and her older brother, Oleg, huddled near the street light.

"Mama." I tugged on Mama's hand. "I see Comrade Galkina."

Mama and I hurried toward them.

"Angelika!" I shouted. The sight of her face—pale against her brown uniform shift—made me afraid. "Are you O.K.?" I cried as I reached for her hand.

Angelika jerked away. She kept her eyes on the sidewalk, but Oleg said quietly, "Our father is very sick." He was a tall, studious boy who wanted to be an engineer like his father.

"What's wrong with him?" I asked.

"He has radiation sickness," Oleg said.

Angelika lifted her eyes and nailed me with them. "You knew about this. What did that boy in the woods tell you?" she demanded.

From the coldness in her brown eyes, I could tell that she thought I was responsible for her father's illness. "Angelika," I protested. "No, I had no idea." I shook my head. Not me.

"Tell me what that boy told you," Angelika demanded.

I felt Oleg watching me, too, and I drew my eyebrows together in feigned confusion. "Boy. There was no boy." I lowered my voice so Oleg wouldn't hear. "You know I always pretend." As soon as I told this lie, I felt a terrible loneliness. As lonely as any boy living in the woods by himself.

"What are you silly girls babbling about?" Oleg asked crossly.

Angelika turned her back on me and began walking away. She

called over her shoulder, "Ask Katya to tell you. She's a liar…and a thief."

Hearing the words that I had used to brand Vasyl flung back at me felt strange, and I struggled to understand what she meant by her charges.

I knew why Angelika had called me a liar, but a thief? Why, she must be talking about Sergei. I realized that I had forgotten all about him.

Before I could react to Angelika's accusations, I heard Mama screaming behind us. When I turned around, I saw Comrade Galkina patting Mama's cheek.

I ran over to them. "Mama, what's wrong?"

Tears overflowed Mama's eyes. As if the garden on her hat had been lashed by a thunderstorm, the straw flowers hung at odd angles. "Last night, when your father went to work, he got too close to the reactor. Victor was right. It was damaged. Papa's sick again."

I grabbed her hand and started tugging on her. "We've got to go to him."

"Comrade Dubko is at the clinic. He will be fine," Galina Galkina said stiffly. "We need to board the bus now, Natasha. Be brave." In a gesture unusually tender for her, she touched my mother's cheek again. "Until we meet again."

Mama wiped her eyes and looked at her. "I hope your husband…" Her voice faltered.

Galina Galkina met her eyes. She assumed again the stern, humorless demeanor which characterized her. "My husband is dying for the Motherland." She turned away.

Angelika's father was dying. How could this be?

A policeman holding a megaphone walked up to us. "Please board the closest bus."

My mother gripped the policeman's arm. "My husband works at the station," she begged. "We have just learned that he is sick. We have to go to him."

"Impossible," the policeman said, throwing off her grasp.

I looked, but could find no pity in the officer's eyes. My suitcase was getting heavy, and the crowd around us had grown.

"We can't leave without making sure that he is all right," Mama insisted.

"Get on the bus!" the policeman ordered before turning away.

I grasped Mama's hand but her fingers were sweaty, and as a large man pushed past us, I lost my grip. Suddenly, I was alone among strangers, all carrying suitcases, purses, babies. As the group tightened, I was frightened to be staring into the face of a bright-green parrot. Behind the cage bars, he was cleaning his claws. His dark tongue curled around the talons.

"Mama!" I screamed.

"Mama," the parrot mimicked me, his voice full of distress.

I tried to breathe and gagged on a perfume that smelled like roses. As bodies crushed against me, I despaired, Mama will never find me.

The bodies shifted, and I lost sight of the parrot, turning my gaze instead on the ground, at shoes of all sizes and shapes. A pair of thick-black boots looked particularly ominous. In a wave of nausea, I realized those black boots were the fate of bad girls who snuck out in the middle of the night and brought boys food; of girls who stole their best friend's boyfriend. The boots would trample them until all that was left was their clothes. With one hand, I covered my eyes and waited, helpless as suitcases and bodies poked and prodded me. I had given up all hope of being rescued when I felt someone snatch my arm.

I looked up through the sea of bodies and spotted Mama. Although her face was streaked with tears, I've never seen her more beautiful than at that moment. At the cottage, the shock of the evacuation had been too much for her. But now, her determination to find me had lit up her features and made them glow.

Gripping my mother's hand once again, I was eager to let the crowd push us toward the nearest bus and away from those black boots.

Chapter Twelve

Глава двенадцатая

THE WINDOWS ON THE CROWDED BUS were all closed, and the air was hot and stuffy. Mama and I sat down in one of the few open seats at the back, next to a peasant. He wore a crumpled dark-green cap on his head, and tobacco had outlined his teeth in black. He held a sack full of cabbages in his ample lap.

A few minutes after we sat down, the man used his speckled hands to open the window, letting in both light and air. One by one, most of the other passengers followed the man's lead. The breeze that blew in smelled faintly of batteries again,[7] but the air was so much better than the stuffiness of the bus. When the bus lurched off, I remembered that I had no idea where we were headed. I wanted to ask Mama, but her hand was pressed to her forehead, and her eyes were closed. I could tell that she didn't know either.

We passed the hospital and the sign advertising its familiar slogan: "The Health of the People is the Wealth of the Country."

A woman in front of the bus was crying out the window, "Alexander!"

I leaned across the old man and stuck my head out to see a German shepherd chasing us. His dusty sides heaved from the exertion, and his pink tongue lolled out of his mouth. As I watched, the dog pulled even with the bus and began biting at its back tires.

[7] *The Truth About Chernobyl* By Grigori Medvedev, page 150, 1991 Perseus Books Group, New York

"Good-bye, old friend. I'll be back," the woman called to her dog.

Gazing out the window, I saw a road sign: "Kiev, 280 kilometers" or 174 miles. So Kiev was where we were headed. I had always wanted to visit our capital city. But the bus had traveled only a few hundred yards when the bus driver slammed on his brakes, and we all flew forward.

©Igor Kostin/Corbis

I spotted the cause of the delay. A peasant wearing baggy black pants and a white shirt was leading his herd of brown and white-spotted cows across the road. The smell of dust and fur blew in through the open window.

The bus driver yelled at the peasant, "Why are you on the road with those cows? Why don't you take them through the fields?"

The peasant called back, "It would be a shame to trample the rye and the grass." He gestured around him at the shimmering new green fields. I knew soon the rye and grass would be joined by oats, wheat, corn and barley. The crops would be so plentiful that there was no way that such a small herd could do significant damage.

Still, I understood why the peasant would choose to block our progress on the road to protect some grasses. All of us knew the land was important.

When the bus began moving again, I heard a clatter as glass jars banged against each other. A red-faced man in the seat in front of us yelled at his wife, "I can't believe you are so stupid. Everyone else brought valuables, and you brought pickle bottles."

"My mother needs them," the wife said, clutching two bulging burlap sacks more closely than she had before.

Without warning, Mama started crying. She didn't cry often, and until today I had never seen her cry in public. I reached out and patted her hand, but I had no idea what to say. Papa would know how to comfort her. I missed him so much that I felt like crying, too.

I would have broken down except I had a feeling that it wasn't Katya Dubko who was riding on the bus, listening to the pickle jars rattle. This was Sunday afternoon, the real Katya was finishing planting. Right now, she was probably up to her elbows in the rich earth of our garden.

This person bouncing along in the red bus was someone else. I had no idea what her relationship to me was. And I didn't want to find out.

No, she was someone the real Katya Dubko wouldn't want to know.

Much later, the bus jerked to a stop. I heard people around me muttering that we were in Kiev, and I opened my eyes. When I looked out the open window, I found that it was night. Six or seven policemen waited for us. One man held a megaphone. Another a clipboard. Several carried rifles. A few had on white medical coats over their blue uniforms. All of them wore grave expressions identical to those of their counterparts in Pripyat.

One of the first to exit, an elderly woman in a black shawl, began arguing with one of the policemen. "Where are we going?" she demanded.

"To a clinic," the policeman answered.

"We're tired and hungry," the woman protested.

Another policeman pointed at a short squat building across the parking lot. "It's a short walk, Comrade. The clinic is right there."

When Mama and I finally clambered off the bus, I looked around trying to get my first view of Kiev, but it was too dark. I hoped perhaps Mama and I could visit the Caves Monastery for which Kiev was famous. I had heard that tourists were able to see the mummified monks, but I was too exhausted to feel any excitement.

As we approached the ugly gray cement building, I wondered why we needed to go to a clinic. I didn't feel sick. But at this point, I had so many questions that I had lost the ability to ask even a single one. Without a word, I grabbed Mama's hand, and we followed the crowd.

A guard held the door open, and we passed into a waiting room packed with men, women and children of all ages. All the people looked healthy.

The bags, sacks and suitcases of the evacuees made it hard to navigate the floor. Mama and I were relieved when we found a spot on a bench next to an old lady. Although it was hot in the room, she was dressed in multiple layers of clothes, topped by her black winter coat. She had cherry-red cheeks and a matching nose, but the old woman didn't move or talk. In my depressed state, I began to wonder if she was dead. My suspicion seemed confirmed when a fly landed on her head, and she didn't knock it off. In our barn, I had seen the way flies landed on dead chickens and animals. From then on, I looked in the other direction.

I didn't have much to look at. The view out the lone window was dark. The couple who had argued over the pickle jars on the bus were quarreling about which of them should find a phone to call their relatives. Like Mama and I, most of the other people in the room were quiet and dispirited. "Mama, I'm hungry."

"Try to go back to sleep, Katya," she said.

I leaned against Mama's shoulder and did try to sleep. But I couldn't seem to get comfortable. Finally, I gave up and just leaned my head against the wall and closed my eyes.

After a while, I began to imagine I really did have a fever. I nuzzled closer to Mama. When I could stand my growling stomach no longer, I complained again, louder this time, "Mama, I'm hungry."

"It should be our turn soon," she quieted me.

To my surprise, the old lady next to me stirred. I looked over at her. She had opened her eyes and was pawing around in her bag. Finally, she pulled out a cooked potato. I looked away again. I couldn't bear to watch someone else eat. Mama nudged me.

The old lady with the cherry cheeks was offering the potato to me.

"Thank you." I reached out and accepted the wizened potato. Although it was stone-cold, it tasted better than even my chocolate birthday cake.

"Comrade Dubko," a nurse dressed all in white called from the doorway. She had on a surgical mask and a white cap on her head. I had never seen gloves so long before. They covered her elbows.

We threaded our way through the waiting area and passed into a smaller room containing only a few families. All the doctor and nurses wore white coats, pants, and caps, and the same long gloves. As the doctors examined their patients, their eyes glowed spookily above their white masks.

A nurse was shaving a little girl's head with a razor. Tears were flowing down the girl's dirty cheeks. Her long black locks had fallen to the ground in twisted curls.

No one had to tell me. My turn was next. Then Mama had her turn.

"Climb on up," the nurse said to me.

The chair was too high. Papa always told me that he loved my hair. It reminded him of Granny Vera. In protest, I stared deeply into Mama's eyes. She bit her lip, shook her head and helped me into the chair.

I took a deep breath.

"It will grow back, Katya," Mama's voice was saying.

I felt the cold razor travel up the back of my neck. The nurse turned to dip the razor in water. I reached back and touched a bald stripe. My bare skin felt naked and ugly.

PART II

KIEV, 1986

Chapter Thirteen

Глава тринадцатая

TWO WEEKS AFTER THE ACCIDENT, Mama and I knocked on the plain brown door of an apartment in Kiev. Each of us carried our small suitcase. Both our heads were covered in ugly stubble, and to add to my disappointment, my own hair seemed to be growing back brown.

"We're so lucky to get this apartment for our two families," Mama said. She must have sensed that I wasn't feeling very lucky because she kept talking away. "Of course, Aunt Olga Pushko's persistence helped a lot," she continued. "She is one determined woman." Mama knocked again, louder this time.

Not only is Kiev the capital of the Ukraine, it is also my country's largest city. Since arriving, we had wandered by St. Sophia Cathedral's thirteen golden domes and the Mariyinsky Palace's gorgeous blue and cream façade, and I had already verified with my own eyes what I had always heard. The city was beautiful. It stood on a series of steep wooded hills and was bounded on both sides by the Dnieper River which flowed south towards the Black Sea. Flowering chestnut trees lined the streets. The domes of St. Sophia's weren't alone; hundreds of other golden domes gleamed in the sunlight.

There was so much I wanted Papa to see.

Although I eagerly awaited his return, Mama had cautioned me

that it wouldn't be soon. Uncle Alexander Pushko and Papa were recovering at a sanatorium from mild cases of radiation sickness. Already, Papa had warned Mama that when he got well again, he was going to apply for a job, helping to clean up the station. A position at the station meant that he would have to live apart from us.

"Welcome." Aunt Olga threw open the door. She was surrounded by my four cousins, all with shaved heads.

Yuri, the youngest, grabbed my hand. "Come see, Katya. The water in the shower is so hot."

On our second day in the flat on St. Petersburg Street, Mama and I stepped into our creaky apartment elevator. Our arms loaded down with groceries, we were returning home from the market. The occupants of the elevator, a man smoking a carved pipe and a woman holding a mongrel puppy, stared at us. Even their dog's eyes bugged out with interest and curiosity.

I assumed that the couple was simply intrigued by our shorn hair until the woman suddenly demanded, "Get off this elevator!" The man used his body to block the elevator door from closing. Both of them waited, expecting us to leave.

"I'm sorry. What do you mean?" Mama asked. She had a country woman's natural grace and inability to grasp rudeness.

"We don't want to get sick. Get off,"[8] the woman ordered us.

The man took a drag on his pipe and blew smoke in my direction. I started coughing.

Mama took hold of my arm and began pulling me out of the elevator.

"We're not sick," I cried.

"Hush, Katya," Mama said. She steered me back onto the landing.

Before the doors slammed shut, I thought I heard the man tell the woman, "They say fish are being born without heads[9] and babies without blood."[10]

"What were they talking about?" I asked Mama.

Mama had turned pale. "People can be radioactive, Katya. A nurse at that clinic told me."[11]

"They don't know anything," I cried. Since we arrived in Kiev, we had listened to the radio. The government had repeated over and over. "Everything is safe. The danger has passed. Few have been harmed." Papa was recovering, and soon we would all go home. I could already feel my hair growing back. I wasn't sick.

"It's O.K.," Mama comforted me.

When I had a cold, Mama would make me throw away my dirty tissues. "You're infectious," she would say. Now I asked, "Can those people catch radiation sickness from us?"

Mama shrugged. "I don't know whether we are *still* radioactive or not." Now that she had no hair, her dark eyes looked huge, and I could see in their dark pools so much that she didn't know.

"And Papa. When is Papa coming to Kiev?" He always knew what to do.

Mama sighed as we stepped onto the next elevator. Thankfully, it was empty. "I've told you. Soon." I had asked her this question again and again, terrified her answer would change.

"May I go see him?" I asked.

"No. Papa will visit when he can. You know how stubborn your father is. Every day that he is safe, we should be thankful."

Chapter Fourteen

Глава четырнадцатая

THE FIRST FIVE MONTHS OF FINDING MY WAY around Kiev, attending a new school, feeling self-conscious, hoping for my hair to grow and waiting for news of our loved ones and friends ran together into a blur of pain, loss and discovery.

One night, my cousins and I arrived home, sweaty and out of breath, from a walk in the park. When I opened the door, I found Papa sitting at the dining table with Aunt Olga and Mama.

"Papa!"

I hurried to greet him. Staring into Papa's handsome face, I realized how much I had missed him. I burrowed into his arms, which smelled of sun and earth.

"Oh, how I've missed you, *donechka*! And I bring good news," Papa said.

"What?" I asked.

"The station has reopened, and Uncle Alexander and I have jobs as drivers." He beamed at me.

"But is it safe?" I asked.

"Of course," Papa waved his hand dismissively. "They're fixing it all up."

"How's Noisy?" I asked him.

For an answer, he squeezed me so hard that I felt like I might pop.

After a few moments of aimless fun during which Yuri challenged Papa to an arm wrestling match, Aunt Olga gathered her children saying, "I'll leave you three to talk. My kids are too young to hear."

Puzzled, I looked at Papa for an explanation. Although I was impatient to hear what he had to say, whatever it was, it couldn't be too bad. Now that Papa was back, the worst was over.

"Katya," Papa said slowly. He pulled out a chair. I sat down next to him.

When Mama had joined us and grabbed my hand, Papa leaned over the breakfast table towards me. He hadn't shaved for the last few days and stubble smeared his face. He touched his forehead and both sides of his chest, mimicking a gesture that Granny Vera had used on solemn occasions. "Katya," he said. "I am so pained to have to tell you this when we have just been reunited." He took a deep breath and said, "They are shooting our animals."[12]

"Who is?" I cried.

"The government hired hunters to shoot Yanov's cows, pigs and horses," Papa explained.

"What about the dogs?" I asked.

"Not dogs," Mama said. She squeezed my hand hard.

Papa didn't say anything. He just continued gazing blankly at me, and I knew the truth. In my mind, I pictured a terrier's small body lying in front of the cottage. I had no doubt that Noisy had been so lonely that he had run out to greet the hunters. He was always eager to see me or any visitor. He would jump up, all the while barking nonstop. If I ignored him, he would run through my legs so that I couldn't walk until I noticed him.

"That's not the worst," Papa said. "You must be very brave."

My poor Noisy. How could anything be worse?

Papa took another deep breath. "Most towns like Pripyat are just going to be closed. Because of the terrible contamination, the authorities are actually going to bury Yanov."[13]

"Bury Yanov?" I asked. "What does that mean?"

Mama let go of my hand and covered her face with her fingers.

[12] *The Truth About Chernobyl* By Grigori Medvedev, pages 188-89, 1991 Perseus Books Group, New York

"You remember how we buried Granny Vera?" Papa asked.

I nodded. Of course, Granny Vera lay in the cemetery in Pripyat under a big oak tree. We had tied her photo to an iron post next to her grave and decorated her headstone with tinsels and plastic flowers. Papa and I had liked to go to her graveside and read the long

©James B. Willard

rambling epitaph that my grandmother had composed herself.

"Soldiers are going to dig a huge grave and push the house inside it. Then, they are going to cover the hole with dirt," Papa explained.

"But why?" I asked.

"Because our home, our possessions, everything we own is radioactive," Papa said.

"Can't we at least retrieve our photographs?" Mama asked through the mask of her fingers.

Until this moment, it hadn't occurred to me that we would never go back. In my worst dreams, I thought it might be a year or two before I got to unfold my divan into a bed and have Angelika to sleep over; before I got to visit my woods, my boulder and my stream again. The total loss of my beloved home was too enormous to comprehend. My thoughts turned to my birthday presents. My divan was too large and bulky for Papa to carry. Although I was getting too old to play with dolls, my *matryoshka* and my Barbie would fit in Papa's pocket.

"How about my dolls?" I asked.

"I will bring back our papers, but saving anything else is too dangerous," Papa answered.

My dolls were dangerous? I didn't understand.

Papa shook his head. "I think I forgot to tell you, Natasha. Our whole area—Yanov, Chernobyl, Pripyat—has a new name."

"But Chernobyl has had the same name for thousands of years," Mama protested.

"They're calling it the Dead Zone," Papa said.

I stood up from the table. The new name told me so much. Granny Vera was dead, and I couldn't see or touch her. I started for the room that I shared with my young cousins.

"Katya," my mother called.

"I have to do my homework," I lied.

"Katya," she repeated.

"Let the poor girl go," Papa said.

I threw myself on my bed. Although I tried to wipe out all the thoughts that exploded in my mind, they came screaming back. I recalled every single fun time Noisy and I had ever had together. I thought about our visits to the woods. I relived the time that Noisy led me to the nest of baby squirrels. Noisy had liked to amuse himself by running back and forth on the stream bank barking at the minnows, while I picnicked with my forest creatures. Once Mama forgot to hook Noisy's collar to the chain, and he slept in bed with me. Now I wept for my little dog.

Suddenly, I felt the bed jolt. Yuri had jumped up next to me. He grabbed my pillow, exposing my tears, but he didn't seem to notice. "Come play hide-and-go-seek, Katya."

I didn't answer. He bounced up and down until Aunt Olga walked into the room.

"Stop it, Yuri," she scolded him.

"Mother, Katya's lazy. She won't get up."

I pulled the pillow over my head.

"Katya's asleep," Aunt Olga said.

I don't know if you could say that I slept. But I had many dreams of this new Dead Zone that used to be my home. I saw Vasyl's blue eyes, and the fire that he had started. The fire grew and grew until it reached the heavens. I imagined worms burrowing in the earth by our cottage, so radioactive they glowed. What were the hunters going to do with the insects? Kill every mosquito, every dragonfly? I imagined a new breed of dog created by a few that had escaped the hunter's guns. Like wolves, they were so fierce and wild the hunters couldn't shoot them. I imagined real wildflowers sprouting out of the cushions of my new divan.

Why had Vasyl picked me to share news of the accident? He must have sensed that I was different from everybody else. Something must be wrong with me. If only Vasyl hadn't chosen me to talk to. If only he hadn't made me somehow responsible for this horror.

"Katya, dinner," my mother called.

"No," I moaned, and jammed the pillow over my ears.

My mother came into the room and stood over me. "Look at me."

I rolled over. I felt her cool hand seek out my forehead to check my temperature.

"She doesn't have a fever," she reassured my father.

I flopped back over on my stomach and pulled the pillow on top of my head again.

"Let's leave her alone," Papa said.

The laughs, howls and arguments of my cousins drove me further inside myself until, gradually, the apartment grew quiet.

I didn't move until after I was sure that Yuri and the cousins were asleep. For a while, I had been listening to the murmur of adult voices coming from the living room. Now, I got on my knees and crawled to the cracked door. I lay down in front of it.

"If a woman milks her cow, the soldiers must stand nearby and make sure that when she's done, she pours the milk on the ground,"[14] Papa said.

"But that's terrible." I recognized Aunt Olga Pushko's voice.

"I've seen pools and pools of white milk on the grass," Papa said.

I heard some quiet sobs. I guessed they were my mother's.

"The farmers dig up their potatoes, but—can you imagine?—the soldiers force them to rebury them."[15] Papa sighed.

I closed my eyes.

"Night is the best time," Papa said. "We sit next to campfires. The Ukraine is still so beautiful."

I felt myself drifting off to sleep.

"I drove a group of soldiers to Yanov and saw Inna Boiko there."

"I thought civilians weren't allowed to return," Mama protested.

"Inna Boiko snuck in. She wanted to check on her garden. Even the death of her own son hasn't shaken her faith in the land."

I sat bolt upright.

Even the death of her own son…. Boris was dead.

Unable to listen any longer, I managed to crawl back to my closet where I had stored the suitcase I brought from Yanov.

I pulled out the suitcase and opened it. Because of the radioactivity, Mama had made me throw my clothes away, but I had kept the poster Boris had given me for my birthday. With the moon as my only light, carefully I unrolled the poster.

The poster showed a shiny red Yava, parked in front of an apartment complex.

I hadn't noticed before, but the motorcycle was riderless.

Chapter Fifteen

Глава пятнадцатая

ALTHOUGH WE HAD LIVED IN THE APARTMENT for several months, I hadn't gotten used to the unusual colors of Kiev's many buildings: Lime, aqua, and tangerine. The violet facade of the store on the corner still stunned me with its muted beauty.

I was by myself on my walk home from school but was surrounded by pedestrians and groups of students as well as clusters of schoolgirls like me, all wearing brown or navy dresses with black aprons and red ties around the necks.

In Kiev, I had quickly learned that the features—hooked noses, puffy bangs, knobby elbows—I had believed were unique to the people in my village were found everywhere. Once, I had seen a man with his face hidden by a newspaper he was holding.

The hands were familiar. Their thick fingers looked exactly like Boris'. I grew excited thinking that the adults were wrong. Boris was alive, reading a newspaper at a sidewalk café in Kiev. But as I joyfully approached, the man set the newspaper down on the table. The man's lined face—he was at least forty years old—made my heart sink.

Another time on a crowded street, I was walking behind a set of blonde pigtails that I recognized as Angelika's. But when the girl stepped onto a bus, I found that she was much younger than

Angelika and really looked nothing like her. Having been tricked so often in the past, I was no longer certain when I saw familiar features.

Now, the boy walking in front of me had white-blond hair the color of Vasyl's. He was the right size. I didn't understand what Vasyl would be doing in a big city like Kiev, but I didn't understand what I was doing here either. With the sun beaming down on us, he stopped to take a drink from a water bottle he carried in his pocket. I was able to draw so near that I could see the black roots of his dyed hair and the freckles on his brown weathered skin.

Why, he looks nothing like Vasyl, I realized in disappointment.

"Hey, you."

I understood someone was calling to me. Over my shoulder, I saw a group of older girls following me. I turned to face them. They looked to be five or six inches taller and twenty pounds heavier than I was, so they were probably in the seventh or eighth grade.

The biggest one stepped out from the group. This girl had a pillow of fat around her stomach and folds of thick skin on her neck, making it easy for me to imagine the overweight factory worker that she would become.

"You're from *there*," she said, a sneer slashing across her rough, red cheeks.

I didn't have to guess how she knew. My cropped hair was still much shorter than current fashions for young girls. If I happened to glance in a mirror or catch a glimpse of myself in a store window, I saw a stranger. I felt like one, too. When I'd gotten off the bus in Kiev, I'd become different, a Chernobyl person—someone whom everybody was curious about but no one wanted to befriend. And I was one of the lucky ones. At least I was alive. Boris was dead.

"Was it scary?" another girl asked. She had uneven dimples and blonde hair that turned up in perfect waves on her shoulders.

I shook my head.

"What did you see?" her friend who was eating a green apple asked. She was tall and skinny with a crooked nose that looked like it had been broken.

"I was asleep," I answered shortly, hoping the girls would go away. When the foursome continued staring at me as if I were a zoo animal, I added, "Just a plume in the sky."

"Did you smell the smoke?" the girl with the blonde hair asked.

Before I could answer, the heavyset girl turned her malicious gaze on me. "Can you have children?"[16]

"What do you mean?" I asked.

She pursed her lips. "Your insides are probably all messed up."

My stomach felt like I had swallowed a tub of ice. When I had asked Papa why his skin wasn't burned by the radiation, he said, "Radiation penetrates your skin and burns your insides. One victim got blisters on his heart." Papa's remark lent the girl's claim a frightening plausibility. I turned away and started hurrying towards my apartment complex.

"Hey," the one eating the apple said. "Don't go. We want to talk to you."

"I have to go," I stuttered.

The girls caught up and walked alongside me. I wondered whether I should start running.

"Look," the heavyset girl pointed at me. "Shiny's angry."

"Shiny's angry," the other girls started reciting in a singsong voice.

"Shiny head. Shiny nose. She comes from that place, Where nobody goes," the apple girl chanted. It sounded like any jump rope chant that Angelika and I would have sung in the school yard in Pripyat, but it was all wrong.

The girls all started laughing.

"If you don't leave me alone…" I searched for the most terrible threat that I could dream up and found myself thinking of Vasyl. I realized that although I didn't want it, he had given me power. The worst fire that the world had ever known was my fault. I didn't know exactly how to use that power, until I remembered why the girls had noticed me in the first place: I had ugly hair. I turned and faced them.

"I'll rub my head against you and make your hair fall out!" I shouted.

To my amazement, the girls screamed and took a few steps backwards. The girl with the green apple threw it at me, but it landed harmlessly and rolled in the gutter. When I didn't back down, they scurried away, laughing and shouting in fear and excitement.

For the next five or six blocks, I pretended I was no longer in Kiev. I was on my way home from school in Pripyat. Instead of concrete, the streets were dirt. And instead of the colorful buildings looming up beside me, tall trees lined the rough streets. I heard Noisy bark as I walked up to our cottage. When I entered my room, I saw my divan, covered in the bright colors of spring. I felt such relief as I sat down on it. I told myself: Those girls can't get inside my cottage. I'll be safe.

Chapter Sixteen

Глава шестнадцатая

AFTER A VERY COLD, LONG WINTER, summer arrived. It has been one whole year since we had moved to Kiev, and the trees had turned green again. When I entered our apartment after school, I found Mama talking to Papa on the phone. While I eagerly waited for my turn, I looked out the window at the bustling street below.

We were still far from finding a permanent home or leading a normal life. For one thing, Papa and Uncle Alexander remained absent, making only infrequent visits.

Yuri ran through the living room. He was going to be a big boy. Although we had recently purchased his gray vest at the mall, it was already tight across the chest.

On weekends, my mother and Aunt Olga took us shopping to try to cheer us up. My mother and aunt liked to brag about how their husbands' pay was unbelievably good. I looked down at my own new blue leather shoes. And I thought about the expensive winter clothes I had hanging in my closet and stuffed into my drawers. A blue wool coat. A dark scarf. Warm wooly gloves. Thick socks. We had all bought department store clothes in the latest fashions to replace the mostly homemade ones we had left behind in Yanov.

My hair had grown out, more brown than red. But now that it was shoulder-length hair again, I was convinced that my unhappiness showed in some other more subtle way, because I still didn't have any friends. Although these days I looked like the other students at my school, I felt so different inside. I sensed that my classmates all had happy childhoods and that none of their birthdays were tragic memories. Like a lily that died in winter but could bloom many seasons later, I was dormant, waiting and wondering if I would ever have a new life.

Yuri pretended to drive a truck. "Beep. Beep."

"Hush, Yuri," Aunt Olga scolded her son. "Uncle Ivan is on the line."

"Ask him when we can go home," Yuri demanded. My young cousin was the only one who still questioned the adults about when we could return. I noticed that Mama and Aunt Olga never answered him.

I was beginning to grow impatient when Mama handed me the phone.

"What have you been doing, Katya?" Papa said. Through the brightness in his voice, I could hear the exhaustion.

"I hate school," I began. In the village, I had belonged. Here, I was an outcast.

"You remember Oksana Evtushenko, who lived at the end of our street?" Papa interrupted my complaints.

"Yes," I answered. Our elderly neighbor always wore black dresses and black shoes.

"I saw her yesterday. She was kneeling in front of the cemetery. She was holding her crucifix, like your Granny Vera's. One of the captains told her that she had to leave."

"She's so old, Papa. Why can't she stay?" I said.

"Listen, Katya," Papa said. "I'm trying to make a point."

I desperately missed Papa and wouldn't see him for several weeks, so I was quiet.

"'I won't leave,' Oksana Evtushenko insisted. 'You've got to leave, *Babushka*. This is a war,' the soldier said."

It was a war, I thought. I longed to tell Papa about the older girls who for the past year had picked fights with me. Today, one of them had pushed me into the gutter, and I had gotten another bruise. I could feel the ache on my side, just under my rib cage. I wanted to tell my strong father that I, too, fought.

"Oksana Evtushenko said, 'You call this a war? There are white clouds in the sky. The apple trees are blooming. This isn't a war. I was in the Great Patriotic War. I remember the planes and the soldiers, the blood and the bullets.'"

Out the window, I stared down at St. Petersburg Street at the pedestrians rushing past with their packages and at the cars racing by.

"The soldier told Oksana Evtushenko, 'This is a war, and its name is Chernobyl.[17] And we will do what has to be done.' I want you to remember what the soldier said, Katya."

I wanted to make Papa proud of me. I would be strong. "Yes, Papa," I gripped the phone tightly, wanting him to know that I understood.

Chapter Seventeen

Глава семнадцатая

In such cramped quarters, my cousins and I fought often. But as an only child, I was mostly glad to be surrounded by their noise and love. Papa and Uncle Alexander appearances continued to be rare highlights.

Our second fall in Kiev, Papa was home for one of his monthly visits. He always showered me with trinkets—inexpensive rings and necklaces— and Mama new fabrics. Although we could afford to buy all the food that we could eat, sometimes the markets in Kiev were nearly empty. On this particular windy day, Papa and I were returning from shopping. We had hoped to purchase meat for dinner but had ended up with only a few jars of pickled beets and a loaf of *chorni khilib*—a black bread made of buckwheat and rye flour that tastes slightly of vinegar.

The leaves swirled around us in beautiful patterns of red and orange. Papa kept his hands thrust deep in his coat pockets and his head down. I could tell that his spoiled dinner plans had not put him in a good mood.

At the corner, we came upon another line. This one held so many people that it bent and twisted around the corner. To jolly him up, I joked, "Oh, Papa, maybe we were in the wrong line. Maybe that's the meat line."

He answered sharply, "That's not a market; that's a medical clinic."

I noticed a woman in the line wearing a colorful scarf. The purple and blue wool wrapped around her head for warmth contrasted with her sallow complexion.

I had the young person's usual fascination with someone who looked a little abnormal. I guess I gazed at the woman too long because, keeping her eyes fixed on me, she began shaking her head and clucking noisily. Embarrassed, I turned away.

"Those people have radiophobia," Papa said.

"What's radiophobia?" I asked.

"The *fear* of radiation sickness.[18] We have an epidemic in this area." I recognized the special scorn in Papa's voice that leaked out when he was referring to people who weren't as tough as he was. "Victor Kaletnik's organization is stirring people up, making everyone afraid. That man is a traitor to the Ukraine."

Although I was surprised Papa had called his oldest friend a traitor, I didn't dare ask about Uncle Victor. Instead, I asked, "You mean that woman isn't sick?"

"That's right." He frowned. "It's all in her head. She has just convinced herself that she is sick."

I nodded and deliberately kept myself from turning to look at the bad woman. Papa worked at the station. He knew what was really happening.

Chapter Eighteen

Глава восемнадцатая

ONE NIGHT AFTER THE BITTER UKRAINIAN COLD had passed, our second spring in Kiev, I was alone in the apartment. Enjoying this luxury, I had turned up the volume on the radio.

"Now for the latest news," the announcer said. "The Nuclear Ministry today announced the implementation of new safety protocols…'"

I quickly changed the channel. I didn't like to be reminded of the accident.

Hearing a knock on the door, surprised, I ran to open it. Unlike in Yanov, where our house was a meeting place for neighbors and friends, here in Kiev we rarely got visitors.

It was Uncle Victor. He was holding his hat in his hand. I had not seen him since the night after the accident, which was not so strange considering the disaster had scattered our close-knit community. Maria Kryko had told us that traveling from place to place, "We feel like trees out of the ground without roots." But something different was happening with the Kaletniks.

"Katya," Uncle Victor cried. Strands of gray intermingled with his black hair. "You look so beautiful."

Hugging him, the familiar feel of his soft waist reminded me of other better times. "How old are you now?" he asked.

"Thirteen," I told him.

"Is your mother here?" he asked.

I shook my head. Since Mama had been unable to find customers in Kiev, she had enrolled in night school to get her teacher's certificate. Aunt Olga had taken her kids to the laundry.

His friendly face fell. I remembered Uncle Victor's estrangement from my father, but Papa didn't live with us, and Mama set the rules now. I asked myself: what would my mother do? "Come in. Come in," I said, opening the door wide. "Mama will be home from her classes soon."

When Uncle Victor stepped inside, I saw the disorganized apartment through his eyes. Despite all our hard work, the room was always messy. Diapers, baby blankets, and puzzles littered the floor. A globe that my mother used for her studies sat on the table.

"Would you like some tea?" I asked in my most grown-up voice.

He shook his head. "I can't stay. We're in Kiev only for a short while. Julia and I are emigrating to Canada next week."

"Canada?" I cried. Since my father had called him a traitor to the Ukraine, I was not surprised that Uncle Victor was moving. But Canada was so far away.

Following me into the kitchen, he sat down at the table. I was embarrassed my guest had to push a plate of old toast out of the way.

"What does it mean to emigrate?" I asked.

Uncle Victor threw back his head and laughed. "Katya, you were always a bright child. I have a cousin in Canada, and he has helped us get visas. We are moving there to live."

"So we won't see you again?"

"We'll be back to visit," he said kindly. He glanced at the door. "I have much to do."

Despite my father's estrangement from Uncle Victor, I was sad that he was leaving. I would never forget the day that he had patiently explained to me the rules of checkers. Suddenly, I realized that his unexpected visit presented me with a unique opportunity. Victor Kaletnik had always talked to me like an equal. I could say, "Uncle

Victor, no one talks about the accident," I could ask. "Could you tell me what really happened? Why did the reactor explode?" I knew that he would answer my questions and tell me whose fault the disaster was.

"My work keeps me busy," Uncle Victor was saying. "I am trying to assess the damage to our health. Our government still denies everything." He smiled at me.

Ask him. Ask him. Did men really bury Yanov? Are we in danger? Are the levels of radiation still high? What are the consequences to all of us in the Ukraine? But to ask Victor Kaletnik these questions would suggest that I didn't trust my Papa's answers.

"We do have some good news," Uncle Victor said, but his voice sounded weary, not happy. "The government has constructed a concrete structure to keep the contamination from leaking out of the damaged reactor. It's called the Sarcophagus."[19]

I managed one question, "What does that mean?"

His mouth tightened, and he looked grim. "A sarcophagus is an Egyptian tomb. We were never able to find the body of the poor engineer who died inside the reactor. Ukraine's Sarcophagus is being called the most expensive tomb in the world." He spread his hands out on the table. "The Sarcophagus is built to last thirty years, but of course, the contamination from the plutonium will be here for at least 250,000." His eyes held much suffering as he said, "But by building this shelter and sending a few engineers to prison, the government can pretend that they've fixed the problem."

He gazed at me as if expecting—and in fact, welcoming—some harder questions.

After a long pause, Uncle Victor smiled at me. "The Soviets are constructing a new city, Slavutich, to house the workers at the station. It'll be right next to the Dead Zone."

At the mention of the new village being built for families like ours, I felt my heart leap to my throat.

"Your father is still working for the station?" he asked.

"Yes," I said.

"I bet he will qualify for an apartment there. I hear that the government plans to make the living spaces unbelievably luxurious."

Although Uncle Victor sounded as though he thought he was conveying good news, I felt only dread. "How close is the new city to this thing, the Sarcophagus?"

"Forty miles."

"I don't want to move near the station again," I told him.

The smile dropped off his face. "I'm sorry. I didn't mean to upset you."

I didn't tell him that I had been upset every single day of my life since we moved away from our cottage.

Uncle Victor looked at his watch. "I've got to go. Tell your mother I stopped by."

"I will."

He stood, and we hugged. "Katya, take care of yourself."

I'm not an engineer, I thought. I don't run the Chernobyl Station. How in the world can I take care of myself?

Chapter Nineteen

Глава девятнадцатая

A FEW MONTHS LATER, as Victor Kaletnik had warned me, Papa told us that we were moving again. It was the summer before the eighth grade. Although I had begun to doubt the wisdom of Papa's job at the station, I confess I never turned down a single one of the many gifts paid for by his good wages.

"Put it on, Katya," Papa said, as he handed me a delicate silver chain.

"It's beautiful," I cried and slipped it around my neck.

This night, Aunt Olga and her family had gone to stay with relatives. Mama had spent the day preparing a great meal. As a consequence, Papa was dipping his bread into his *yushka*, a nutritious soup of whole wheat bread, chicken, veal, ham, egg yolks and celery. He was in a wonderful mood, smiling and talking.

I fingered the silver chain on my neck and wished that I didn't have to hear what he was saying.

"The apartment will be ready in two or three months." He took another sip of soup. "It's brand-new with two bedrooms and central heat. The most modern in all of the Ukraine. Cable is piped in free of charge." Papa directed his dark eyes on me. "Katya, you're quiet. I thought you hated living in Kiev."

Somehow, I had endured two featureless years at Kiev Secondary

School # 37. Although I had managed to learn a few things, I had a hard time concentrating. Since I no longer took pride in being a good student, my grades had slipped. My attitude might have been improved by a few good friends, but I had none. I couldn't understand if it was my own unfriendliness that made me stand apart and feel different, or the suspicion that other students had toward me, the Chernobyl refugee. Still, as little as I liked my situation, ever since my conversation with Uncle Victor, I'd known that Kiev wasn't the worst place to live.

"At least Kiev is two hours away from the station," I told him. "I don't want to move closer."

"The station's pay is ten times higher than anywhere else in all of the Ukraine." Papa's fist hit the table. "How can you fail to understand the opportunity?"

"The pay is great because of the horrible risks," Mama said quietly.

Looking at her downcast eyes, I sensed that Mama, too, had her reservations. But she never opposed Papa.

Somehow, I found the strength to break through our habit of silence. I had never told them that I had overheard their long-ago conversation. This night, I had grown tired of never speaking about the things that were most important to me as well as hiding my fears. "Boris died at the station," I said.

Papa and Mama exchanged quick glances. "We know," Papa said sadly.

"Why didn't you tell me?" I asked.

Mama sighed. "Maybe we were wrong. We were trying to protect you. There's been too much sadness…" Her voice trailed off.

"Boris was a hero," Papa said firmly.

"But why?" I asked. For so long, I had been groping with the question—why did Boris have to die so young? My head throbbed with memories of Boris and the fishing trips he used to take me on. How patient he had been when he baited my hook. How many fish would he have caught by now if he were still alive? Hundreds of

128

sparkling trout.

My parents sat there looking uncomfortable. When my father continued, his voice was reasonable.

"Katya," Papa said. "Many of the families who we know are moving to Slavutich. The other day, I saw Comrade Galkina. Your good friend, Angelika Galkina, is moving, too. You want to see Angelika, don't you?"

I shook my head miserably.

"I talked to Sergei Rudko's father and Lyudmila Pikalova's. Your old class will be united again. Aren't you excited?" Papa asked.

Do I look excited? I wanted to say. But I knew I had already pushed my luck.

"I will be happy to live together as a family again," Mama said simply.

"I want to move away to a far-off country," I said. "Like Victor Kaletnik."

"Victor Kaletnik?" Papa raised his eyebrows.

I picked up the globe that Mama had been using to plan a geography lesson and spun it.

"Don't mention that man's name," Papa snapped. "I've heard that his group is trying to close the station. The station is our livelihood."

With my eyes closed, I dragged my finger along the cardboard surface. The globe stopped spinning. When I peeked, I saw that my finger had stopped on a patch of blue, smack in the middle of the Pacific Ocean. I thrust the globe at my father.

"Here, Papa. Here's where I want to live."

PART III

SLAVUTICH, 1990

Chapter Twenty

Глава двадцатая

THE NAME *SLAVUTICH* MEANS GLORY in Russian, and the nation's best builders were tapped to construct this model city. Crews from eight Soviet Republics worked overtime to complete high-rise office buildings and concrete-block apartment houses in the styles of their homelands. When the town was finished in 1987, almost 25,000 people moved there. Virtually every adult resident worked at the station.

It was February, a few months before my fifteenth birthday. We had been living in Slavutich for almost two years.

Although Slavutich was surrounded by woods and streams, I had never visited them. When I asked Papa to take me hunting or fishing, he always made up an excuse. He muttered he had seen too many dead animals. As a consequence, my memories of my childhood woods had grown dim. Now that I was almost fifteen, my early belief in magic embarrassed me. I had decided that Vasyl had been some kind of horrible nightmare. He was the result of birthday excitement and too much sugar.

In fact, my transition from villager to townsperson was nearly complete. When I approached my home, I no longer expected to smell manure and grass as I had when I was younger. I didn't listen for a dog to bark out a welcome. I didn't long to feel the cooling shade of an old oak tree.

Just like everything else in our new city, Slavutich Apartments was made out of quickly poured concrete. Our home was a standard two-bedroom unit. The parking lot was devoid of trees and stunk of auto exhaust. We had no garden. "No Pets Allowed," the sign in front read.

My bedroom was not a granny or a teen room, just a nondescript, modern space. I had a brand-new desk, an oak bureau and a new bed fitted with soft sheets, all paid for by my father's wages at the station. Although I could have covered my walls in posters, I had hung only one, the poster of the Yava that Boris had given me.

Like my bedroom, the shiny walls of our living room were blank, too. My parents hadn't snapped any photographs to replace the ones that had been buried. Perhaps to them as well, our new lives in Slavutich felt too unreal to be documented.

Papa was still big and strong, although he had a touch of gray in his hair. Crow's feet fanned out from his eyes. While he had kept his job as driver for the station, Mama had begun a new career as a teacher's aide. Her tan had faded, and her latest glasses were almost as thick as Aunt Olga's. Of my two parents, I would have to say that Mama had aged the most.

Angelika Galkina, Sergei Rudko, and Lyudmila Pikalova and I were finishing our freshman year at Slavutich High School #1. Angelika was now the best student in our entire grade, and I certainly didn't care enough to challenge her for the position. Sergei was almost six feet tall and a soccer star, and every girl in the entire school liked him. In Kiev, I had spent two years hiding from my fellow classmates. Now, even though I had grown tall, almost 5'10", and had thick, shiny brown hair and unusual eyes that Mama said were the color of new leaves, no one at school seemed to even see me. I passed through my classes and the halls, unnoticed and unengaged.

My only friend was Lyudmila Pikalova. While our shared history kept Angelika and me apart, Lyudmila and I enjoyed listening to each other reminisce about Yanov. Lyudmila humored me by hunting through magazines with me for a shade of blue, the same color as the shutters on my cottage. We liked to argue about whether we had been studying math or science when the policeman appeared in our doorway that morning shortly after the explosion. I remembered a newly drawn picture of the solar system on the blackboard; she claimed we were dividing fractions. We enjoyed sharing stories about our old pets. Lyudmila had had a mutt named Leo who ate mushrooms.

Lyudmila liked giving me fashion tips, such as "Wear short skirts. White nail polish looks best." I never followed her advice. "Why should I care about my appearance?" I asked her. "So you can get a boyfriend, Katya," Lyudmila would say.

I never responded seriously to her quips, but I thought to myself, why would I want a boyfriend? Some days, I felt like boys had destroyed my world.

This particular noon, as always, I sat by myself in the large indoor cafeteria, surrounded by tables of laughing and talking kids. Many of them were eating food purchased from the school's kitchen, sausage and sauerkraut or corned beef and slaw, but like me, most were enjoying home-made sandwiches. We were all dressed in the uniform of Slavutich High. The girls had on brown or navy dresses with black aprons. The boys wore their dark suits.

Lyudmila plopped down next to me. Because I had known Lyudmila as a kid, I understood that her sex appeal was manufactured. Back in Nina Ivanovna's class, she didn't swing her hips when she walked. She didn't purse her lips at the end of her sentences. Her voice wasn't low and husky. In fact, as a young girl, she rarely said anything at all. Now, she acted the part of a French movie star.

Lyudmila glanced at me to make sure that I was watching her. She slipped a photo out of her pocket and set it down on the table in front of me. I felt as if she were issuing a challenge.

"What's this?" I said.

"A freak of nature," Lyudmila said with the air of an expert.

I picked up the photo. At first, I thought it was a giant spider, but on closer examination, I found that it was an animal. A colt, but with eight legs.[20] No longer hungry, I abandoned my cheese sandwich.

"Where did you get that?" I asked.

"The radiation is causing birth defects," Lyudmila said quietly.

I remembered the girl in Kiev who had asked me whether I could ever have children. Involuntarily, my hands touched my stomach.

"But the Dead Zone is clean now," I protested. Although the authorities admitted that the area would be uninhabitable for thousands of years, they had buried the most contaminated villages and forests, removed topsoil, and resurfaced roads so that people like my father could work there safely.

Lyudmila laughed. "Katya, you're so gullible. Lots of animals and people are sick."

I rushed to defend my father's position. "But Papa said…"

"Your father works for the station," Lyudmila interrupted. "Of course he's going to say that everything's perfect."

Although I had been raised to trust my father absolutely, I couldn't clamp down and control my thoughts with the self-discipline he encouraged. Hadn't both Angelika Galkina's father and Boris Boiko died of radiation sickness? Even my own father had been sick after the accident. It was four years ago, but I still remembered the people standing in line at the clinic in Kiev. In my mind's eye, I could still see the woman at the clinic who had visually scolded me for staring at her. My father had mocked her. He had claimed that she only thought she was sick.

I'd taken a gymnastics class at school in Kiev, and I would always remember my first back bend. With my head upside down, my hair streamed to the floor. Suddenly, the blood rushed to my head, and the gym, the bleachers, and the students all looked different.

Sitting at the lunchroom table with Lyudmila, I felt my mind perform a trick that it had never attempted before. In a mental back bend, I reached my own conclusion.

Perhaps the woman with the sallow face standing in line wasn't imagining she was sick; perhaps she truly *was* sick from the radiation.

"What's wrong?" Lyudmila asked.

"Oh, nothing," I said. If Papa had been mistaken about that woman, what about all the other things he had told me?

I felt dizzy as if I had stood up too suddenly from a back bend.

"Come with me to my aunt's," Lyudmila said. "I got this photo from her. She has lots of information." I had heard about Lyudmila's aunt before. She had moved to Slavutich from Kiev a few months ago, and Lyudmila proudly described her as crazy, in a good way.

"When?" I asked.

Lyudmila's fuchsia lipstick spread into a grin. "After school today."

Margarita Pikalova, Lyudmila's aunt, kept an apartment on top of Café Sunflower where Lyudmila and her mother worked. That afternoon after school, Lyudmila and I began climbing up a windowless stairwell that wound its way upwards. On the third floor, the stairs stopped and picked up again in a corner. Although this last flight of stairs was narrower and darker, we had no problem finding the way because the steps shimmered. Trying to identify this unusual glow, I remembered the snails that I used to watch as I sat by my boulder. The stairs sparkled as if a large snail had preceded us and deposited its shiny slime.

The stairs dead-ended into one door. It was small and gray.

Lyudmila knocked. "Margarita Pikalova."

A woman flung open the door. "Hello. Hello."

When I ducked inside under the low door frame, I realized immediately that I didn't know anyone else who looked like Lyudmila's aunt. She was a big, fleshy woman, a common type in Slavutich, but she was dressed as if she were a young beauty. Most of the older women I knew wore their hair short or in a bun. Margarita Pikalova's stringy hair fell loose past her shoulders. Unlike Mama's dark sensible skirts, hers were purple and flowing. A string of crystals hung around her wrinkled neck.

"Welcome to my crystal palace," Margarita Pikalova said. Her arms expanded as if to embrace the whole world. "Who's your

friend, Lyudmila?"

"This is Katya Dubko."

After our exchange of greetings, my gaze turned to her living room. Crystals of all sizes and shapes hung on every available wall, and separated and spread the daylight flowing in from the windows throughout the otherwise ordinary apartment. Even the ceiling was unexpected. Although the green and the pink bands had smeared, an artist had painted an impressive rainbow over the breakfast table.

The way the light filled the room reminded me of my stream. The sunlight and rocks had broken down the clear water into bits of colors similar to those gleaming around me. I stood for a moment enjoying my memories of my forest stream. It had been a long time since I remembered the way the water looked when it had tumbled over the rocks on a sunny day. Too long.

Margarita seemed to notice and approve of my gaze. "I'm so proud," she said, gesturing at the crystals, "to be healing our damaged land."

Margarita described her business, *Crystal Creations.* "I sell three lengths of necklaces with five different auras. The auras promote healing, happiness, wealth, spirituality, and love. Upon receipt of the crystals from a supplier in the U.S., I bless each in a mysterious process and designate its aura." These ceremonies took place at night after Lyudmila and I had gone home. Following the blessings, the rocks took on light hues: health was green; happiness, violet; wealth, blue; spirituality, yellow; and love, red. The gradations in shade were so slight as to be almost imperceptible.

"Auntie," Lyudmila's tone was wheedling. "Katya wants a job."

Again, Lyudmila was arranging my life without consulting me, but I immediately liked her idea. It was time for me to get a job. I hated asking Papa for money. He never complied without grumbling.

Margarita gestured toward the packages of crystals piled on her breakfast room table. "Katya, you can be my assistant in this noble venture."

I wasn't sure about her theories or what she was offering. But I wanted to learn more about the birth defects, see more pictures like the one of the colt. "O.K.," I agreed.

Margarita slipped a crystal tied on a green ribbon around my neck. It bumped against the silver chain that Papa had given me.

"What's this for?"

"To guard against radiation. It's your first week's pay in advance," Margarita said. She clapped her hands. "Now, girls, don't just stand there. We need to get busy."

"Katya, you can help me," Lyudmila called from the kitchen counter. It was piled high with order forms, envelopes, plastic baggies, ribbons and crystals of all shapes, sizes and colors.

"Katya, the first thing you must understand is this: my little apartment in Slavutich is doing more to keep us safe than the entire Soviet military industrial complex," Margarita began.

I sat down eagerly next to Lyudmila. I so wanted to believe.

Two months later, I was still stringing crystal necklaces at Margarita's. That was long enough for me to earn several prize crystals as wages and to discover that my employer knew very little about the effects of radiation. One afternoon, I had finished work and was walking down the stairs of Margarita's apartment when I saw a boy's blond head, glowing in the dark like a light. At that moment, I felt none of the shyness that had kept me quiet for so many years, and I called out: "Vasyl!"

He turned then and showed me his profile. In the dark stairwell, I shouldn't have been able to see his eye color, but I could. His eye was bluer than blue; as blue as the sky on the day of the explosion. And it was round and glittered like a marble.

"Wait!" I shouted. But Vasyl passed through the door. This time, he was dressed in brown pants and an ordinary soft-brown shirt. When I stuck my head out, I saw that he had been swallowed up by the crowd.

Trying to reach him, I pushed through the throng of people with grocery bags returning from the market. I spotted him ahead of me. "Vasyl, wait. Wait," I called. He was dodging into the market.

It was a small market with booths of brightly colored vegetables and fruits and a single bread vendor. A rickety fence separated the booths from the adjacent parking lot.

Vasyl had stepped behind a vegetable vendor's stall. A woman with a careworn face and a dark shawl covering her head was selling a customer a string of beets. She didn't seem to notice Vasyl as he brushed past her, heading towards the fence behind.

I was running blindly towards him, not looking where I was going. I had just seen Vasyl lift up a fence plank and slip through it when I bumped into a man bending down over a tub of luscious-

looking blueberries. I started trying to excuse myself and get around him when he lifted his head. It was Victor Kaletnik.

Not only did I tower above him now, but he wore glasses. I was so surprised to see him I just watched him, not saying anything.

Oblivious to the fact that I had just bumped into him, he directed his attention at the vendor. "I saw a local farmer unload these blueberries," he said quietly. "They're not safe."

"What else is there to eat?" the vendor asked, before shrugging his big shoulders and turning away.

"Don't buy the blueberries!" Uncle Victor shouted to all the surprised shoppers.

I cast one more glance in Vasyl's direction. But the plank was in place; the fence looked solid again, and Vasyl was gone. Why had he come back now? I needed to know, but Uncle Victor was leaving. I made a split-second decision and began following the man I knew was real.

A man wearing pants with dirt on the knees stopped Uncle Victor. "I'll buy the blueberries. For my boss." He gave a hearty laugh.

As Uncle Victor hurried towards the street, he was muttering to himself. "What ignorance! They think the contamination is funny. They don't realize…"

I tugged on his arm. "Uncle Victor," I said. "What are you doing here?"

He turned his penetrating black eyes on me. I caught sight of a rainbow in the lines of his bifocals.

"Katya!" He scooped me into his arms and hugged me. "How old are you now?"

"Almost fifteen," I answered. "What are you doing?"

"I am still working for an international health organization. We're investigating the disaster," Uncle Victor said. "My wife stayed in Canada, but I'll be here for almost a year."

"Why haven't you stopped by my house?" I asked.

His gaze dropped to the sidewalk. "I did. Your father and I don't agree on things anymore."

The pause was becoming uncomfortable. "What was wrong with those blueberries?"

"I just returned from the Dead Zone. I happened to see a farmer sitting in the back of a truck with some crates marked with black X's. When I spotted the same crates at the market, I became convinced that the blueberries were grown in the Zone; perhaps in an illicit greenhouse there." He gazed fondly at me. "That's my Katya. When you were young, you were always asking questions."

"I have lots of questions," I admitted.

Uncle Victor nodded. "I can imagine." He paused for a moment as if considering something.

"My apartment is around the corner. I have some information that is not available here in the Ukraine. You may be interested."

Without waiting to see if I was following, Uncle Victor hurried off, taking big strides, and I had to race to keep up. His khaki trench coat blew in the breeze. I noticed that its hem was torn and flapped above his unpolished boots.

When we got to the front door of his modest apartment, he said, "You can stay here. I'll be right back." He let himself into the apartment.

I waited impatiently, worrying about whether I had made the right choice. Should I have tried to track Vasyl instead of Uncle Victor?

A few minutes later, he returned, holding what looked like a stack of papers. He pressed them into my arms. "Please bring these journals back. A friend of mine translated them. I work at the station two weeks on and two weeks off, but if you catch me, I'll buy you a soda and try to answer your questions." Uncle Victor took a watch out of his pocket and looked at the time. "Now I have to go." His hand rested on my shoulder.

"Thank you," I said.

When I returned home, our apartment was empty. I passed through our large front room which served as a living room, small kitchen and breakfast area. The appliances, the carpet, the furniture, and the television were all new. Papa told me every day, "Katya, you should feel grateful." We did have so much more than we ever had in Yanov, and yet…

I closed my bedroom door and flopped down on the green blanket covering my bed. It was the third green one that my mother had knitted for me. In another life, Vasyl had stolen the first from under the boulder, and as far as I knew, the second still covered my bed in my cottage buried under thousands of pounds of earth.

The first journal article was entitled *Alas, Chernobyl*. As I began it, I experienced the curious sensation that I should have read this material a long time ago. After all, every word pertained to me—to my lost home. I wasn't a good student anymore. If a homework assignment had contained all these scientific terms, I would have lost interest after the first paragraph. But tonight, I finished the first chapter in no time and eagerly studied a radiation map, illustrating the fallout from the explosion.

The map used shades of color to show increasing levels of radioactivity, progressing from green to yellow to orange and onto darker shades of red. The worst patches from the explosion were deep brown and looked like lopsided pants legs. One leg was long and thin. It was about a mile wide and reached six miles to the west of the station before gradually fading to lighter colors for a full sixty miles. The other leg was a short, wider lobe that extended northwest over the Pripyat River. Between them, Pripyat was colored a lighter shade, but still the red that indicated serious contamination. Tiny villages like Yanov didn't appear on the map.[21]

My mother stuck her head in and said, "Time for dinner."

"Is Papa here?" I asked.

"He's leaving for the station tomorrow, so guess where he is?" Mama said.

Papa was at the gym. "I'm not hungry," I told her.

"Are you sure?" she asked.

"Yes," I said.

Mama, who never wanted a fight, shut my door.

I read much of the night. Of course, I already knew the outlines of the story of the evacuation, but the journal article filled in the details.

On April 27, the nearly 46,000 residents were evacuated from Pripyat. On May 2, the authorities decided to expand the evacuation orders and remove all residents within a thirty-kilometer (eighteen mile) radius around the station. This area became known as the Dead Zone. Over 135,000 people ended up being evacuated. Authorities flattened and buried seventy villages.[22]

By myself, I had figured out that the sinister black plume in the sky was radioactive. But now I learned that fifty tons of uranium fuel had vaporized in the explosion and were blasted into the atmosphere. Seventy tons of uranium and 900 tons of highly radioactive graphite exploded onto the ground around the reactor. The eight hundred tons of graphite that remained in the reactor core caught fire and created a radioactive inferno. It burned for ten days and discharged a continuous stream of radionuclides. These radionuclides eventually traveled to every country in the Northern hemisphere, polluting lakes in Japan, hill farms in northern Wales, and reindeer herds in Norway.

Before that night, I had been suspicious of the station. Now, living just forty miles away, I was certain that I had a right to be afraid. It was clear that Papa and the government had both lied to me. They told me that the reactor was safe. The Chernobyl accident was not just the worst accident in the history of the nuclear power industry; it was the greatest man-made disaster in all of history. And *Alas, Chernobyl* said that it could happen again.

I was about to close the journal when I spotted the word 'firefighters.' My eyes burning from exhaustion, I skimmed the section until I came to a sentence that both puzzled and troubled me. I reread the line: "Of course, since water doesn't extinguish a nuclear fire, the efforts of the firefighters were in vain."

So Boris had died for nothing! I couldn't believe it.

I rubbed my eyes and reread the sentence a third time, but its import stayed the same. Shocked and saddened, I threw the book on the floor. It made a satisfying loud thud. I turned off my bedside light and closed my eyes, but sleep wouldn't come.

Lying in the dark, I gripped the peanut-shaped crystal hanging around my neck.

Help us, heal us, I begged Granny Vera's God, that kindly father figure who cared about us all. Perhaps he wasn't just a superstition. But when I remembered the black plume that had appeared in the sky that day, the little rock felt puny in my fingers. My prayer seemed pointless against that devil's tail.

This night, when a fitful sleep finally rescued me from the horrors of the truth, I dreamed of Boris. He was wearing his firefighting uniform: Black pants. Black coat. Helmet. I knew it was Boris, although I never saw the fireman's face. He was sitting on top of my boulder facing the stream. "I'll go to him," I thought happily, but when I tried to reach him, I found the air was sticky like glue. As hard as I pushed, it was impossible. I couldn't work my way over to him.

Chapter Twenty-One

Глава двадцать первая

THREE OR FOUR HOURS LATER, I awakened to sounds of boots pounding on the floor above me. A water pipe groaned. A neighbor coughed. A cat in the alley yelped. Exhausted, I opened one eye.

I was about to pull my blanket over my head when my mother entered my room.

"Katya, time to get up," Mama said.

I glanced at my watch. "Give me fifteen more minutes," I begged. It was a Sunday, my only day to sleep late.

Mama tugged on my green blanket. "Papa starts his shift at the station, and he wants to have breakfast with you."

I groaned.

"Come on, daughter!" my mother demanded in an exasperated voice. "Your room is a mess. You need to clean it up this morning."

After her footsteps trailed off, I rolled out of bed. The journal article was splayed open on the floor where I had thrown it last night. As I stepped over it, I sensed that it had already changed my life, although I wasn't sure how yet.

I pulled on a plain yellow T-shirt —I hated logos of any kind— and blue jeans and boots. Although Lyudmila claimed that I dressed like a boy, I simply liked to be comfortable. Staring into the brand-new mirror, I tucked both my silver necklace and my crystal inside my T-shirt. I could no longer deny that my hair had turned almost completely brown. After all, although I knew a few redheaded kids, I didn't know a single redheaded adult. I was starting to face a painful fact. Some of my favorite things belonged exclusively to childhood.

When I entered our main room, my parents were sitting at the breakfast table eating porridge. They both wore sweatpants. On recent mornings, my mother had been returning sweaty and peevish from my father's attempts to teach her how to jog.

My mother looked up when I walked in, but my father kept eating. "Good morning," my mother said.

"Morning." I yawned.

"Ivan." My mother prodded him when he didn't seem to notice me.

My father frowned and looked up. "Hello, Katya."

I scooped some lumpy porridge into my bowl and sat down at the table. It was covered with a white tablecloth, embroidered with blue and green peacock eyes. The tablecloth was identical to ours in Yanov. Although I used to like the tablecloth when we lived in Yanov, I found my parents' attempts to duplicate our old life irritating.

To keep from looking at either of my parents, I fixed my gaze on the jar of foreign coins that sat on the counter. Papa collected them. He claimed that the rich foreigners at a nearby hotel were too lazy to pick up their dropped change. This jar was a prop in his standard lecture—"Katya, you need to save for the future."

Slowly, Papa put his hand in his pocket and withdrew one of Margarita Pikalova's prize crystals that she had given me in exchange for a week's work. "What's this?" he demanded. "I found it under my bed."

My mother sighed. "Please, Ivan. Let's don't argue. You leave for the station in just a few minutes."

I had heard the disdain in my father's voice, and my own response stiffened. I automatically prepared to defend Margarita, even as I realized that after my night of intensive reading, my last shred of belief in her fanciful theories was gone. "You know what it is. I've explained about crystals."

"What is this rock doing underneath my bed?" Papa demanded.

I touched the peanut-shaped crystal that I wore around my neck to make sure that it was hidden by my T-shirt. "I'm just trying to keep you safe," I said to Papa.

Papa got that stubborn look on his face that I had grown to hate. To keep myself from saying something that I would regret, I spooned another bite of porridge into my mouth.

"Crystals can't keep anybody safe," Papa said.

We had had this argument before. Besides, reading *Alas, Chernobyl* had raised new concerns. "Neither can the Soviet government."

My mother clapped her hands over her ears.

"What's this nonsense?" Papa's voice rose. "The government constructed the Sarcophagus."

"The Sarcophagus was built to last thirty years," I said. "The pollution will be here for hundreds of thousands."

Papa glared at me. "The reactors are perfectly safe."

As I answered him, I sensed two great forces battling. I had only a murky understanding of the fight between Communism and freedom, but I found myself beginning to choose sides. "What makes you so sure?" I said slowly and precisely.

My father's spoon clattered against his bowl. "Katya, what is wrong with you? Your crystals are ridiculous." His voice was clotted with scorn. "But your disobedience is worse!"

My mother's dark eyes darted between us. "Let's don't argue. Ivan, you were going to tell her about the birthday surprise."

My fifteenth birthday was the following week. Since neither of my parents had mentioned it, I was starting to think that they had forgotten.

"Please," my mother begged him.

Papa's face was expressionless. I felt badly that he couldn't trust my reaction even to his attempt at kindness.

"I bought a Moped," my father said cautiously. "We can share it."

"A Moped?"

A slight smile crossed his thick lips. "You used to want a motorcycle when you were a little girl."

"Don't look so disappointed, Katya," Mama fussed.

"It's just that I hadn't thought about a motorcycle in years," I said, explaining my stunned surprise.

"Well?" Mama said. Her smile was hopeful.

I pushed away my half-eaten bowl of porridge and tore out the door. It was early, and I risked waking up our neighbors. Still, I ran so fast that I practically fell down the two flights of stairs.

A Moped was parked on the street in front of our apartment. The exhaust pipe was bent, but its body was a beautiful bright red. The sight of the black helmet hanging off the handlebars made me remember last night's dream about Boris. As I slipped on the helmet and threw my leg over the seat, I found myself missing my former neighbor more than I had in a long time.

My father walked up to me.

"Where's the key?" I asked.

He stuck his hand in his pocket and held out a gleaming silver key. As far as I was concerned, at that moment, it was the key to the whole world. I grabbed it. "Thank you, Papa."

His face broke into one of his broad grins that didn't used to be so rare. "Come back and tell me what you think." He glanced at his watch. "I'm leaving in fifteen minutes."

The clatter of the Moped drowned out my answer. The days were still short, and the sun hadn't come up yet. Only a couple of pedestrians walked on the streets.

Although it wasn't as fast as a motorcycle, this Moped was almost my very own. I listened carefully to the sound of the motor so that I could memorize it. I checked the engine temperature with my hand. It was cool. The body of this machine was bent, but the motor ran smoothly. For years, I had studied the details of the different machines: the engines, the spokes, the exhaust and the pipes. Yet since we had moved to Slavutich, I had lost touch with my fascination for motorcycles and speed.

Driving down Slavutich's main thoroughfare, *Heroes of Chernobyl*, I passed its famous monument to its victims. Larger-than-life photos of the men who died as a result of the explosion were framed in two concrete mounts. Spanning the mounts like a rainbow, an artist had painted a mural featuring a liquidator, representing those people who were recruited or forced to assist in the cleanup after the explosion. He had long hair and was dressed in a gray suit. His hands were stretched out wide. Above him in English and Ukrainian was the inscription: We will build a new world. *Pobuduemo novy svit.*

I was probably going only fifteen miles per hour. Still, as the wind rushed through my hair, I remembered the night of my birthday so long ago, when Boris had taken me for a motorcycle ride.

I felt a lump in my throat. I swallowed, but it wouldn't go away.

My dear Papa was waiting for me in front of the apartment. At the sight of him, I started to smile, until I noticed the camouflage khaki pants and long-sleeved shirt that he always wore to work. He changed into his uniform at the station. Thinking of the articles that I had read last night, my feeling of warmth evaporated.

"Thank you, Father," I said to him with exaggerated formality as I handed him the key.

The happiness slid off his big features, and I turned away.

Chapter Twenty-Two

Глава двадцать вторая

UNDERNEATH THE DATE, MAY 1, 1990, Tatjana Petrovna had written a series of equations. She was a good teacher with a deep voice that sounded as though it belonged on radio. Although she had many small failings—for instance, her upper arms looked like bread dough, and she rapped the blackboard incessantly with a pointer—it wasn't her fault that I rarely listened in her math class.

I found much that I'd rather think about. Who would I have become if the accident hadn't happened? In the future that I should have had…in the future that I deserved…I would be popular in school. Sergei and I would go to dances together. Sometimes, I allowed myself to imagine our first kiss. We'd be standing in a forest glade like Boris and Marta.

Our classroom contained about thirty students. Angelika sat near the front with Sergei. Since I was on the back row, when I day-dreamed, my gaze rested on the backs of their blond heads. Lyudmila Pikalova's desk was next to mine.

Tatjana Petrovna rapped on the blackboard. "Attention, before we start reviewing our math problems for the day, I have some good news. The nuclear power industry has arranged for us to take a very special trip. Our class will go see the Chernobyl Power Station and Pripyat. Photographers will take some photographs. For the good of our country, we need to show that the station is now safe enough for students to visit. I think the trip will be very interesting."

After our teacher made her announcement, Lyudmila's eyes, heavily rimmed with blue eyeliner, turned to me. "Oh, Katya," she whispered. "Let's go."

I felt conflicted. I wanted to go, but no one seemed to realize that the station was dangerous. So I just shrugged.

"Other schools take field trips to beaches. We go to nuclear waste dumps," Mikhail Bazelchuk quipped in the seat in front of me.

Rumor had it that Mikhail's father conducted questionable business dealings. In any case, there was no disputing that Mikhail seemed to enjoy more material possessions than others in our class. Not even the smell of Lyudmila's flowery perfume could overcome the stench of the expensive cigarettes that Mikhail smoked in the alley behind the school.

I raised my hand. "Are students required to go?"

Our teacher looked surprised. "Why, no. It's not required."

"Why don't you want to go?" Lyudmila asked me.

"I've got good sense, that's why," I said.

"Tatjana Petrovna, may I visit my old apartment?" Angelika asked. I remembered how proud Angelika had been of her apartment and felt a stab of love for her.

"Can we go see the Ferris wheel?" Mikhail Bazelchuk asked.

"I don't know the answers to these questions. Your guide will decide what you can see and what you can't," Tatjana Petrovna said. She began passing around a sign-up sheet for the field trip. When she finished, she cleared her throat and said, "Students, I am appointing a class monitor to make sure that you behave. Our top student and a girl who is very responsible: Angelika Galkina. "

I had stopped competing with Angelika long ago. She received every honor. She was clearly the most outstanding girl in our grade. Lately I had noticed that she and Sergei had started eating lunch together. They would probably marry and have perfect blond babies. While I would be forced to live with my parents for the rest of my life.

If they would have me.

"Now turn to page….," Tatjana Petrovna began, and I tuned out.

During a break between classes, I was walking down the hallway when I spotted Sergei standing at Angelika's locker. She had her back to me, and Sergei and I caught each other's gaze. I don't know why, but I sensed he was thinking about Yanov and our childhood together.

I often wondered if Sergei remembered the note that he had written me: *Let's go out together.* I had never mentioned it to him. In fact, we had barely spoken since the accident. But at that moment, I walked up to him as if nothing had ever happened.

"Hey, Sergei," I said.

"Hi, Katya," Sergei said. "Algebra test is going to be tough, huh?"

Angelika, who was still kneeling at her locker gathering her books, twisted her neck to peer up at me. Her brown eyes held a clear message. They said: Keep away.

"Yeah," I replied and quickly started walking. I was pleased to see Sergei look surprised, as if he expected—and wanted me—to keep talking.

Chapter Twenty-Three

Глава двадцать третья

A FEW TIMES AT CRYSTAL CREATIONS, I had challenged Margarita. "This crystal is just a rock," I would say. But she would take the crystal over to a bright light and motion for me. Upon closer examination, I always had to admit that I did see something. Somehow, Margarita managed to sell between ten and forty necklaces a week. Her best customers were tribes of gypsies. Upon receipt of an order, Lyudmila and I strung the crystals on a velvet or silk ribbon.

When she needed to match a crystal to a request—say a man wanted a cure for bankruptcy—Margarita pressed her fingertips to her forehead in concentration.

One day after school, Lyudmila and I read a request from a man named Yves. On the form he had scratched the words, "major love problems."

Margarita looked over our shoulders. "I think this one will be perfect." She reached onto the table and selected a medium-sized crystal. It was strawberry-shaped. She spun it between her thick fingers, examining it.

"But, Auntie!" Lyudmila cried. "You already chose that one for the pig farmer's son who has asthma. That's a green crystal for health. Not a red one for love."

Margarita took the crystal over to the light and examined it. "You're right," she said after a moment. "Lyudmila, you have a good eye."

Lyudmila beamed. "Better than Katya's."

Margarita turned to me. Her gaze was bold. She had on a bright dress of emerald green that made her waist look vast and her long hair more eccentric. "Katya has other gifts."

I think this was the moment that I began to trust her in a new way. "Margarita," I said, "I can't come to work for you tomorrow."

"Why? Is something wrong?" she asked.

"No," I said. "I have an appointment."

Margarita looked to Lyudmila as if for an explanation. Lyudmila said, "She wouldn't tell me either. I hope it's a new boyfriend."

"You know I don't like anybody." For fear that Lyudmila would hound me unmercifully, I had never admitted my interest in Sergei. In fact, I hardly admitted it to myself.

"Who is it, Katya?" Lyudmila begged. "Tell me."

But I only shook my head.

The next day after school, I parked the Moped in front of Uncle Victor Kaletnik's concrete-block apartment building. It had been a few weeks since I first spied him at the market. Later, when I had returned the journals, he had mentioned that he needed an assistant. Despite my duties at Margarita, I believed that I could find the time to work for Uncle Victor. Today was the day that he had agreed to meet with me to discuss the job. My father wouldn't be happy, but if Uncle Victor paid me good wages, I thought I might be able to convince him.

I raced up the stairs to his apartment. After walking down a dark hallway, I found number 401 and knocked. Uncle Victor opened the door. He was wearing brown bedroom slippers, casual slacks and a T-shirt with *THE BIG APPLE* overlaid on a Manhattan skyline. "Come in. Come in. Have a seat." His smile was broad, and I realized he was happy to see me. It occurred to me that maybe I wasn't the only one who got lonely.

I followed him into a bare room dominated by the largest and most cluttered table I had ever seen. Floor lamps cast spotlights on different sections. Books, gigantic pinecones, photographs and letters crowded almost every surface.

Uncle Victor settled on a brown wool sofa. I removed a stack of books and sat across from him. "I'm afraid without Julia here, I have not bothered to keep house."

I found myself asking, "Don't you miss your family?"

"I do, but, Katya, I love my work, which brings me to your request. Although I could use the help, I've been worrying." Uncle Victor turned his direct gaze on me. "I can't have you become my assistant without your father's permission." He shook his head. "I doubt he'll approve."

"He'll let me. He is always telling me that I need to save for the future," I said.

"Didn't you tell me that you already had a job?" Uncle Victor asked.

"Not a problem," I reassured him vaguely. Just as I had avoided telling Lyudmila and Margarita that my appointment involved science, now I was too embarrassed to describe *Crystal Creations* to Uncle Victor.

The phone rang. "Excuse me," he said.

While I waited for him to finish talking, I found myself thinking about how precariously I straddled all my worlds. I wasn't scientific like Uncle Victor, I didn't believe in the government as loyally as my father, and I wasn't faithful like Granny Vera and Margarita. All I had were my questions, and none of the answers the adults in my life offered were enough for me.

Sitting in Uncle Victor's uncomfortable chair, I couldn't stop marveling over the fact that it was Vasyl who led me here. He certainly didn't fit into any world I knew.

When Uncle Victor sat down again on the couch, we engaged in a few minutes of small talk about my life at school and his new home in Canada before he said, "I have a confession for you, Katya."

I nodded, waiting.

"The organization that I work for—Canadian International Health Alliance (CIHA)—hasn't taken a public stand, but personally, I'm committed to closing the station."

I had guessed his position. I had seen it in his thoughtful demeanor when he answered my questions. In the way his eyes darted away from mine whenever my father's name came up.

"Of course, your father disagrees," Victor Kaletnik said.

As I spoke, I had to shut out an image of my father's face. I knew if he ever learned of my treachery, his lower lip would jut out and his hands would clench into fists. I managed to stammer, "I'm on your side."

Uncle Victor stared thoughtfully at me. "If we're successful, your father could lose his job." His keen eyes pierced me as he continued, "I don't know if a person your age can understand things like this, but your father and the other workers at the station enjoy an incredible standard of living. Ten times the national average."

I considered these options. I had come to believe that the station should be closed, but I knew that my father would be devastated if that happened. It was clear that our standard of living would suffer. How could I choose among my father, our way of life and our safety? They all seemed so mixed up together.

Uncle Victor grinned and leaned closer. "Despite all this, you really want to come to work for me?"

"Yes," I said. Taking a job with him didn't mean the station would close, I told myself. But I would learn more. That seemed to be all that mattered. Although my newfound knowledge had been making me feel afraid, it had also awakened me, made me feel more alive.

"Well, let's see what your father says," Uncle Victor said. "My schedule is the same as your father's. I go to the Dead Zone for two weeks, then return and write up my findings."

I nodded.

"I'll give you a key. While I'm gone, you're welcome to read my books." He stood up and pointed at the messy table. "In fact, let me introduce you to my filing cabinet." He winked at me. "It's really very organized." We stopped in front of the first section. "This end contains photos of the mutations that people claim have been caused by radiation."

I looked down at the stacks of photographs and saw a piglet without eyes, a pig with one eye the size of its head, a calf with a lip like an elephant's trunk, and a goat with hind legs three times longer than those in front.

Uncle Victor picked up one photograph and showed it to me. At first, I couldn't make out what it was. But then I noticed that although the animal's head looked like a dragon's, its body was that of an ordinary chicken.[23] "This is my next assignment."

The red and greenish-blue protuberances hanging from the chicken's face made me feel sick. I had seen Margarita's picture of the colt, and I had heard about the mutations, but to be standing in front of stacks and stacks of photographs containing so many of these distortions made me feel as if my nightmares were coming to life. "What do you do with these?" I asked.

"My job is to investigate whether the photos are frauds or not. If they're real, my organization sends a medical doctor or a veterinarian to visit the family." Uncle Victor stepped sideways and gestured towards some outsized pinecones and leaves. "I collected these specimens from the Zone myself. When certain trees are infected with high doses of radiation, their leaves and pinecones grow huge."

I gazed at a pine cone as long as my size eight shoe.

Uncle Victor faced the middle of the table. "You may want to avoid this section." He picked up a worn stack of photographs and letters. "This part of my filing cabinet deals with the human tragedy—photographs of children born since the Chernobyl accident. Some have heads twice as big as normal. A few have no hands or feet."

"You're right. I don't want to see them." But even as I spoke, I was edging closer to get just a tiny glimpse.

"Actually, it's difficult to prove that any particular birth defect is caused by the radiation, but CIHA is documenting a higher thyroid cancer rate in the area than the national average. Are you tested every year for thyroid cancer?" he asked softly.

His tone was kind, but as I nodded, I felt queasy. I was only fifteen years old. What an awful question. "Yes," I told him.

After a few more steps sideways, we faced the only square foot of the table that was free of paper. "If your father agrees, you can use this area as your work space," Uncle Victor said.

I didn't want to appear stupid, but I still wasn't clear what my duties would be. "What would you like me to do again?"

Uncle Victor smiled. "You may find this hard to believe, but with my wife in Canada, I need someone to look after me."

He looked so silly standing in front of the messy table in his house shoes that I laughed out loud.

"While I'm at the station, it would be great if you could stop by and check to see that I remembered to take out the garbage." His nose wriggled in mock disgust. "Too often, my apartment stinks when I return." He gazed around the room as if looking for more chores. "Also, you could check my voice machine."

I shook my head, puzzled. A machine for voices? "Excuse me. I don't know what that is."

Uncle Victor started walking to the kitchen. "Come here."

I followed him to a black box resting on the kitchen counter. "People can call my phone number and leave messages." He punched a button, and the machine began talking. "Uncle Victor, your laundry is ready." He picked up a pencil. "Now, where's a notepad?"

The kitchen counter was bare. I glanced at the long table, but all I saw was a mess.

As he turned off the machine, he smiled. "Your first job is to find a notepad. Then," he said, "I'd appreciate it if you'd jot down my messages." He glanced at me as if to see if I was finding all this agreeable. "I'll give you more assignments as we go along." He paused. "If your father agrees, that is. I pay fifty *grivnas* a month. Is that O.K.?"

"Yes." The money wasn't really important to me, only to my

father.

"In a few days, I leave for a shift at the station. I hope your father will have granted his permission by the time I return," he said.

I could tell that he was about to dismiss me. "Uncle Victor, do you have any more articles like the ones you showed me?"

He eyed me appraisingly. "I do," he said.

"Could I read them?" I asked.

"I wish everyone in the whole world would read about the accident," he said. He turned to his 'filing cabinet' and began hunting through the stacks of paper.

When he wasn't looking, I picked up a dirty sock from the table and dropped it on the floor. Uncle Victor made even me look neat.

When I got to the apartment that night, my father and mother were standing together next to the electric stove in the kitchen. Our freshly painted beige kitchen had brown linoleum floors that sparkled and broad windows that let in a lot of light. A factory-made cuckoo clock purchased in Kiev hung on the wall next to the sink. Papa liked to point out that the cuckoo and our family had changed places. "We live in a luxurious, modern apartment, and our cuckoo lives in a simple peasant's hut with a thatched straw roof. It's as it should be," Papa would say.

My father's T-shirt was drenched with sweat. As was his custom after a trip to the gym, he was slugging down glass after glass of water. He always worked out like a maniac before and after his return from his two-week stint at the station. Neither Mama nor I were ever very curious about the details of his work life. It was as if we pretended that he didn't spend two weeks of every month at the station, and his real life happened only when he was at home.

Mama stirred a big pot of something that smelled like beef. She had tied an apron over her teacher's outfit. Since Papa was well-paid, he insisted on eating meat at every meal. Most people considered themselves lucky to have it once a day. "How was your day, Katya?" she asked.

"Good," I mumbled. "What's for dinner?"

"I'm trying a new recipe for *varenniki*," Mama said. These large stuffed dumplings, the national dish of Ukraine, were one of Papa's many favorite meals. "I hope it's good."

Papa laughed. "What's not to like about beef, fried potatoes and onion?"

I had finished a cheese sandwich hours ago but felt as if I hadn't eaten all day. "When's it going to be ready?"

"Fifteen minutes," Mama said.

Papa walked over to the kitchen counter. "Come see," he said. "A friend from the station gave it to me." He unfurled a poster of a cartoon-like man who grinned up at us. By his camouflage uniform, gas mask and goggles, I knew the man was a liquidator.

As if I couldn't read, my father recited the poster caption out loud: "We understand what the homeland requires of us and we will do it. Therein lies the heroism of our Soviet man."[24]

"Yes, my dear," my mother said. "You are a hero." She patted my father on his broad back.

©Igor Kostin/Corbis

Papa beamed. I could see the outlines of his muscles straining his dark blue T-shirt.

From the little I had gathered about my father's job, I did know that for someone earning his living in the Zone, Papa was lucky. Unlike some, he wasn't required to handle any highly contaminated materials. Instead, his job consisted of just driving dignitaries around the Dead Zone. Still his frequent exposure to the contamination meant the government considered him a liquidator. I didn't like thinking about this classification. Uncle Victor's journals claimed that many of the liquidators had already died from illnesses caused by radiation. But as if something I read in a book couldn't have anything to do with me or my family, I brushed away this fact. "May I have the poster?" I asked him.

"Why?" he asked. He sounded suspicious.

"I don't know," I said. I wasn't lying. I had no idea why I wanted it.

Papa considered my request. "It will do you good," he finally decided.

Alert to a truce between Papa and me, Mama called happily, "Wash up. I think this is going to be the best *varenniki* ever."

I went into my room and found a shoe with a hard heel in the pile in my closet. I collected a few tacks from my desk. As I pounded them into the wall, I began thinking about the article that I had just finished reading at Uncle Victor's.

At 1:23:58 a.m., the explosions began. The initial blast tore off the reactor's roof and cast aside the biological shield as if these tons of steel and concrete weighed nothing at all. The blast broke apart the graphite and fuel with the force of about thirty to forty tons of TNT, throwing the most deadly debris outside the reactor.

The floor of the building housing Reactor Number Four started shaking. The engineers heard loud banging noises. The upper biological shield covering the reactor came to life, rocking and twisting. It was almost as if a four-story building made of concrete and steel started dancing a jig.[25]

About a minute later, at 1:25 a.m., as the yellow and white flames leapt up to 600 feet in the air, the alarm sounded at the fire station. Boris's unit responded.

Fiery sparks showered the sky and an unearthly glow poured up into the night—a shaft of radiation from the reactor core.[25] Vasyl's fire. How hard I had tried not to believe him when he said our world would change. How much it had.

I stepped back from the wall and reexamined the tough-looking liquidator. I decided that I liked the new poster; it reminded me of the stupidity of the top officials at the station. For three whole days, the government had tried to keep the accident a secret from the world. For several weeks, the managers still officially clung to the delusion that the disaster was only a 'trifling incident, with no lasting damage.'

Because of their trifling incident, my friend, Boris, had died. My old cottage was buried under mounds and mounds of earth. Not only could I never return home, I had to live next to the largest nuclear waste dump in the world. And the worst might not be over. Uncle Victor had told me, "It's not likely. But the damaged reactor could explode again at any time without warning."

I pounded the final tack in the wall so hard that the glass panes in the window shook.

If I were the Soviet Premier, I decided, I'd find every single Chernobyl official guilty. If I could, I'd lock them up in a dirty, drafty jail underneath the station and see how they liked living in such a contaminated place.

Papa appeared at the door. "Mama said that you had a biology test today. How was it?" he asked.

"Fine." This was probably not true. I hadn't studied and could have flunked.

My father stared at my wall. "The poster looks good there."

Papa sounded so self-satisfied that I just wanted to hurt him. "I hate the station."

He hurried over and drew so near that I could see the stubble on his face. "What did you say?"

---

[25] *The Truth About Chernobyl* By Grigori Medvedev, pages 73-77, 1991 Perseus Books Group, New York

"It could kill us all!" I cried.

"Ungrateful girl!" Papa yelled.

I clamped my hands over my ears and threw myself on my bed.

"That's where we get this beautiful apartment, our three hearty meals a day. That's how I pay for the clothes on your back, your Moped, and the jewelry you love."

I rolled over and looked at him. "I could make money, Papa. Uncle Victor has offered me a job."

"What?" he said, as if he hadn't heard me. "No!"

"It would be good experience working for a scientist. He's willing to pay me. You don't like Margarita Pikalova. You're always saying that I should get a new job."

"Not with that traitor," Papa muttered.

"Dumplings are ready," Mama called.

"Please," I begged.

"No daughter of mine…" Papa began, but words failed him. Following a few moments of heavy breathing, he stormed out of the room.

Mama stuck her head in my door. "Dinner."

"Not hungry!" I yelled.

I waited for my father to return and order me to eat, but he left me and my growling stomach alone. The smell of the *varenniki* reminded me of the happy times in our cottage that seemed so long ago. Why couldn't my father understand?

Chapter Twenty-Four

Глава двадцать четвертая

NOW THAT I HAD A MOPED, I could visit the woods on my own, and on a free weekend, I drove to the forest closest to Slavutich. I stopped the Moped next to a deserted path that I had been told led to a stream. Not wanting to risk a damaged tire, I pushed the machine over the bumpy path until I spied a clump of bushes. After I made sure that the bike was completely hidden, I pocketed the key and started hiking.

The gravel path meandered through a forest of thickly clustered poplar, aspen, pine and oak trees. Their dense branches blocked the sun and created the half-light of a forest shade that I remembered so warmly. From far away, I heard the rush and splatter of the stream. Sunlight cut through the branches and colored the air green. Hurrying down the path, I felt as if I were returning home.

But first impressions can be deceiving. When I reached the stream, I saw that the water was sluggish. Cattle patties dirtied the banks in rough brown ovals. I searched the banks, but the only stones were the size of pebbles. There was no boulder anywhere.

I found a clean place to sit and yanked off my tennis shoes. The soil was sandy, not the soft, squishy mud that I was used to. I parted some reeds and stuck my feet in. At least, the water was icy. I would have given up and left if the stream had betrayed my fond memories

by being warm. A minnow nibbled on my toes. I looked more closely and spotted a fish hiding among the mauve, pink, and gray rocks of the streambed. If only I had brought my old cane pole.

I picked up a rock to skip. Feeling it flat and hard in my hand, I tossed it aimlessly. It skimmed across the water and disappeared into the deep woods on the other side.

I hadn't been inside a forest since the day after the accident when I had gone to search for Vasyl. For so long I had thought of Vasyl's appearance as a nightmare, but after I saw him on Margarita's stairs and he led me to Uncle Victor's, I wasn't so sure.

When I was a child and wanted my forest creatures to appear, I had concentrated on the light. Now, I stared at a bright patch of sunlight that fell on a branch and created a dark shadow on the surface of the flowing stream.

If only Vasyl would appear now. I had so many questions I wanted to ask him. Why had he chosen to tell me, of all children, about the accident? Was he a person or a spirit? Was he good or bad? He said that I would come back. It seemed impossible, but then I reminded myself that everything else that he had said had turned out to be true.

Not believing that he was going to appear, still I waited for him.

Some trash floated by—a plastic bag, a soft-drink can. A turtle kerplunked off a rock. A dragonfly nearly lighted on my hand. With no strange boy or water sprites to keep me company, after about an hour, I yawned. Could I be growing bored in the woods?

Eventually, I felt a hard cramping in my toes from the icy water. When I yanked them out, I stuck on my tennis shoes. But my cold feet didn't bother me nearly as much as the feeling of dissatisfaction that buzzed around my head as irritating as mayflies.

I remembered when I used to sit next to *my* boulder by *my* stream. The forest, the wind and my creatures had all whispered to me, sharing their secrets. The whole world was clean and safe. My magic rock could cure any problem and make any dream come true. I could do anything and be anybody.

Now, the forest had become ordinary—just some water, trees and dirt. At least, that's how it felt.

I stood up and brushed myself off.

Hiking the path again, the light shifted as I passed into the depths of the forest where the thick branches overhead blocked the sun. I was about twenty paces from my Moped when I experienced a familiar sensation. The air sparkled as if it were a pane of glass. I responded instinctively, readying myself to see things differently.

I looked around, but everything was the same. I saw only the path winding through the woods and, in the distance, the bush where I had hidden my Moped. Beyond that, the highway stretched out wide and gray. But something inside me felt different. I was still waiting when I heard Boris' voice. *Hello, Katya!* He sounded as if he were standing in a room next to me, a room in the trees.

I looked around. Only the branches swayed in the breeze. No one was there.

I knew that the voice was in my head. Yet, it sounded real. Where was he?

Katya....

I felt as if I were five years old, and we were playing hide-and-go-seek again.

"Boris!" I cried out loud. A car honked on the nearby highway.

I was alone. Still, the same warmth filled my chest as I had experienced when I rode behind Boris on the Yava. As I walked back down the forest path towards my Moped, I kept studying the shadows of the deep woods, but I knew I wouldn't see him there.

Boris still had secrets to reveal to me. How could I find out what he was hiding?

Chapter Twenty-Five

AFTER SCHOOL ON MONDAY, I found Uncle Victor's door open. He was sitting at the long table reading a journal. I had brought a school notebook with me. I wanted to jot down some notes about the disaster—to understand more. If I couldn't completely understand, at least I wanted to get the facts right. "Hello," I called.

Uncle Victor looked up. "Katya, come in." When I had settled on the chair next to his, he asked, "So have you talked to your father?"

"I haven't had a chance," I lied.

At this evidence of my father's continued disapproval, Uncle Victor's face fell. They had known each other since boyhood. He quickly tried to cover his disappointment by taking off his glasses and cleaning them with a cloth. "I'm not comfortable without his permission."

"Give me a little more time," I said. "He'll agree. He's always talking about how I ought to earn more money."

Uncle Victor put his glasses back on and met my gaze. "O.K."

"Can I do anything for you?" I asked. "I mean, as a volunteer? You don't have to pay me."

Perhaps Uncle Victor was touched by my eagerness because he said, "What can I do for you?"

I didn't hesitate: "Uncle Victor, there's so much I want to learn."

Putting down his journal, he asked me, "What are you most interested in?"

I hadn't known what I was going to say beforehand. "I want to know about the firefighters."

Victor Kaletnik nodded. "Boris Boiko. He was your neighbor, wasn't he?"

"Yes," I said softly.

Uncle Victor sighed. "In Hiroshima, the bomb went off at 2,300 feet. Boris and the other firefighters were closer to a nuclear reactor than anyone in human history."[26]

"But Uncle Victor," I broke in, and the question felt urgent. "I read that water doesn't put out a nuclear fire, so what was Boris doing?"

"You're right," he said. "At temperatures of over 2,500 degrees centigrade, water itself breaks up into its explosive chemical components of hydrogen and oxygen. The firefighters were actually fueling, not extinguishing the nuclear fire."

"So why were the firefighters on the roof?" I cried. "Why did they put themselves in so much danger?"

Uncle Victor's tone was soothing. "In addition to the fire which raged in the reactor core, dangerous non-nuclear fires had sprung up all over the tar roof. The firefighters succeeded in extinguishing these ordinary fires. If they had failed, the remaining reactors might have ignited."[27]

Could this be Boris' secret? Had he truly died a hero? "I was afraid that Boris had died for no reason," I said, my relief thickening my voice.

"Not at all," Uncle Victor said matter-of-factly. "The firefighters' quick work prevented a disaster too horrible to think about."

He had no idea how happy he had made me.

Uncle Victor looked up at the clock on the kitchen wall. "Now I've really got to finish my journal article," he said. "I'm leaving on a

---

[26] *The Truth About Chernobyl* By Grigori Medvedev, page 89, 1991 Perseus Books Group, New York
[27] *The Truth About Chernobyl* By Grigori Medvedev, page 124, 1991 Perseus Books Group, New York

short trip to Canada tomorrow."

"Please, Uncle Victor, let me do something for you while you're gone," I begged.

When he didn't answer, I asked, "Can I check on your apartment?"

"You can come read my books." He pulled a key out of his pocket. "And you can help me by jotting down my messages for me." He gestured towards the kitchen. "Otherwise, the voice machine gets full." He shook his finger at me. "But nothing else unless your father approves."

Chapter Twenty-Six

Глава двадцать шестая

AT LUNCH THE NEXT DAY, I was sitting alone at a picnic table reading *Chernobyl, A Disaster for the Generations*. I always brought a book to keep me company. After years of being unfriendly, no one but Lyudmila was likely to disturb me.

When I saw her heading towards me, I quickly stuck the book into my backpack. At this point, I wasn't ready to tell Lyudmila about my job at Uncle Victor's. I was no longer working at *Crystal Creations*. I had lied to Lyudmila and Margarita and blamed the decision on my parents. My bad grades offered an easy excuse. I'm not sure exactly why I was so hesitant to tell Lyudmila the truth. But she was successful at the crystal business in a way that she wasn't at school.

Sergei Rudko and Stepan Yasko sat down at the next table. They looked over at us. Sergei was the captain of the soccer team; Stepan was the high scorer. As groups of kids walked by, they all greeted Sergei and Stepan. "Do you think we'll win the game Friday? Great goal, Stepan!" With their neatly combed hair and bulging muscles, the boys exuded confidence and fun. They were both eating oversized sausage sandwiches.

Lyudmila batted her eyes at the boys in a ridiculous way.

"Come have lunch with us, Lyudmila," Stepan called.

"I can't," she said, then added. "Maybe later."

Lyudmila was the most popular girl in our class with the boys. The other girls disliked her for flirting so openly.

While Lyudmila and Stepan were bantering, Sergei and I looked at each other. When he smiled at me, I felt myself blushing. "How was algebra?" I called out.

"I think I passed it," Sergei said. Then Stepan spoke to him, and Sergei turned away.

"So," Lyudmila asked as she plopped down, "why don't you go talk to Sergei?"

"Why should I?"

"Because you like each other," she said.

"I do not," I protested.

"I just saw it in your faces when you looked at each other."

Lyudmila should forget about her silly crystals and take up face readings, I thought.

"So now I've cracked the secret of your mysterious appointments." Lyudmila laughed knowingly. "You're meeting Sergei." She shook her pointed fingernail at me. "Angelika will be so angry when she finds out."

"I am *not* meeting Sergei," I protested.

Lyudmila smiled, and her tone became confidential. "I'm sure that Margarita Pikalova will let you borrow an extra-powerful love crystal, even if you're not working for her anymore."

I shrugged.

"Don't you ever want to go out with a boy?" Without asking, Lyudmila picked up a pear from my lunch. She carefully bit into it so as not to disturb her dark lipstick.

"You tell me every detail of your dates, Lyudmila," I said. "Why do I ever need to go on one?"

Lyudmila stood up and tossed the pear core into the trash. "You're so stubborn, Katya." As she walked away, swinging her hips, Stepan watched her.

I took out my book but instead of reading, I just sat there eating my cucumber and mayonnaise sandwich. I was about to take her advice and walk over to sit with Sergei when someone touched my shoulder.

I looked up, and Angelika stood there. The last few years had not improved her looks. Although her blonde hair, smooth skin and luminous eyes were still beautiful, in comparison with her china-doll nose, her mouth had grown outsized. Her crooked teeth, which I used to consider cute, now appeared crude.

"Are you going on the field trip?" Angelika asked. Her hands were on her hips. Her narrowed eyes gleamed with disapproval.

I was tempted to ask her why she was talking to me, but I thought I knew. The planned field trip had made me remember our childhood together, too.

I shook my head.

When Angelika's gaze fell on the table, I glanced down at my book, *Chernobyl, A Disaster for the Generations.* Her father had been one of the engineers running the safety experiment on Reactor Number Four. That made Comrade Galkin partly responsible for the accident. Quickly, I covered the title with my hand.

Angelika grimaced. "Why are you reading that propaganda?"

"It's not propaganda," I said.

Angelika's face had turned red. "Have you forgotten that my father was one of the engineers?" Her tone was bitter, and I understood its meaning. She had never forgiven me; my father had lived, and hers had died.

I answered her, gently, "I haven't forgotten, Angelika."

"My father gave his life for the station," Angelika said.

Since the engineers' mistakes had cost many lives, I couldn't come up with an answer that wasn't unkind.

"That's why I'm going to be a nuclear scientist, Katya. To help the station, but you..."

"Hey, Angelika," Sergei interrupted.

Angelika pursed her lips. Instead of finishing the sentence, she turned. Without so much as a backward glance, she walked away to join the boys.

I knew what she had been about to say, "Katya, you're a horrible person, a thief and a liar."

Even after the last four years, Angelika's distrust was still painful.

After school, I parked the Moped in front of Uncle Victor's concrete-block apartment building. He had left for Canada a few days ago. The landing smelled of cabbage and bacon. At the thought of his neighbors' dinner pot simmering on a nearby stove, my stomach growled.

Since the elevator was small and slow, I started up the narrow stairs to the fourth floor. As I fitted the key into the lock of his apartment, I felt proud to be entrusted with this responsibility.

I walked into the dark room, flipped on the light and examined the bare kitchen. I didn't smell any rotten trash. The bottom of the coffeepot wasn't black and smoking. The burners on his stove weren't red-hot. In his bedroom, even though the bed was unmade and the pillows and blankets had tumbled off onto the floor, the alarm clock wasn't buzzing. All seemed to be in good shape.

A wrinkled apple sat on the kitchen counter. I ate it hungrily before heading over to the stack of articles that Uncle Victor had given me to read.

I opened the journal to a collection of eyewitness accounts of the accident. I copied word-for-word descriptions like, 'I saw the fire from my apartment. It was white with red spikes. It looked radiant. Like a fire sent by heaven.'

After what felt like a short time, I shifted in my seat and noticed that my foot had gone to sleep. I stood up to try to wake it up. When I glanced at my watch, I couldn't believe what I saw. I had spent two hours in this chair.

Looking out the window, I noticed that it was growing dark. My parents would be angry with me for being late for dinner. I closed the journal and was preparing to leave, when I happened to glance at the voice machine.

I should check Uncle Victor's messages for him. He had said that the machine got full. Without further thought, I headed over to the kitchen counter. Readying myself, I tore a page out of my notebook and pushed, 'Play.'

"This is Leonid Tkachenko at the Ministry of Health. We received your report on the illegal strawberries. We are processing it." I jotted down *illegal strawberries* and the man's name.

Click.

"Victor Kaletnik. This is Olga Petrova. I have your laundry." I wrote *pick up laundry*.

As a Chernobyl kid, I knew that frightening things happened suddenly. But I also believed my life had already been altered as drastically as was possible.

"Bad news. Five liquidators have tested positive for cancer. Vitaly Bondar, Yuri Verovsky, Dmytro Paltayev." I was scribbling as fast as I could trying to keep up.

"I think you know one," a man's voice said.

I dropped the pencil.

"Ivan Dubko. Forgive me for breaking the news to you this way."

I realized what Granny Vera always said was the truth. "When you begin to accept your losses, expect another one." I wasn't able to hear the fifth man's name. As I pushed 'Off', my mind flashed to the day when I first saw the plume of black smoke in the sky. Back then I didn't know that the plume had anything to do with me. I remembered my cottage with the blue shutters. Boris. My forest with its ancient trees. Noisy and his blue-black terrier nose. The cross-eyed rooster named Pirate, who woke me most mornings.

The plume had taken my home, my friend, my forest and my animals. Now it was taking my Papa. My stomach rose in my throat.

I staggered into the bathroom and lost the apple in Uncle Victor's toilet. I gagged repeatedly until only harsh stinking liquid flowed out of my mouth. Leaning over the toilet, I wiped my mouth with the back of my hand.

My strong Papa!

Chapter Twenty-Seven

Глава двадцать седьмая

WHEN I GOT HOME, IT WAS MY FATHER, not my mother, who was sitting at the kitchen table covered with the white embroidered cloth.

Papa's thick fingers drummed the table, which usually meant that he had excess energy and needed to go to the gym. But tonight, I wondered whether his nervousness was related to his diagnosis.

His big hands closed around the jar of foreign coins. "If you were going to stay out late, why didn't you call us? We've been waiting for you," he scolded me.

"I'm sorry," I said.

"Mama went to buy some groceries. We thought we'd have a special family dinner tonight. She was going to try to find a chicken…" When his voice faltered, I was suddenly certain.

"Papa." I saw the fear in his eyes and felt a stab of pity. "I know," I blurted out.

"So you saw Mama?" The coins jangled as he passed the jar from one hand to another. When I didn't answer, he continued talking, "The doctor called this morning." His deep sigh made me recall his despair when he suffered even a minor cold. "As a liquidator, I'll be entitled to the best care."

"Papa…" There was so much to say, and I didn't know how to

say it.

"I'm glad that the government is going to cover the cost of my treatment," Papa mumbled as if to himself. "There's only one problem with that." He banged the jar of coins down so hard that the glass sounded as if it might break. "I'm the one who's going to die."

"You're not going to die, Papa," I cried out.

His dark eyes stared blankly at me as if he had gone blind and could no longer see the world that he had always been so sure of.

"What kind of cancer is it?" I asked.

"Thyroid," he said. "It's a good kind of cancer. At least that what's Dr. Sokolov said."

"I'll do some research. I bet Dr. Sokolov's right."

"There's no good kind of cancer," Papa said. His head fell into his large hands.

Despite the pitiful sight that Papa made or perhaps because of it, suddenly I was angry at him again—at his mistaken idea of patriotism. For hadn't Papa put himself into danger? Of course, on the day of the accident none of us had known that living near the station was so dangerous, but later, when he sought the job of driver, the risks should have been more obvious. But just as Papa believed his beloved country was the greatest in the world, he continued to insist that his government would protect him. I had no wish to hurt him now when he was so down, but I had to ask, "At least, do you understand now that the station is unsafe?"

"Katya," my father said. He looked stooped and more frail than I had ever seen him. "Part of health is mental toughness. I know I received a massive dose of radiation. I have tried to act as if I didn't. But I know…I do know that working at the station is not completely safe." He sighed. "I even know that it could happen again."

I couldn't help myself. "So why do you work there?" I felt my voice rising. "Why must we live in a city next door?"

My father started speaking more slowly than I had ever heard him. Every word felt like a fingernail tearing off, exposing the quick. "I am not a well-educated man. Ever since the accident, I have always known that I may not live a full life span."

I guessed that he had never spoken these words out loud before, even to my mother. It would have been admitting weakness.

"I am proud of my bargain." Papa held his head up and met my eyes. "I have done what I had to do to protect my family."

When my father's tears fell, I was amazed that they weren't giant's tears. Actually, they were no larger than mine. I had never seen Papa cry before.

"Katya," Papa said. His voice was heartbreakingly raw. "Chernobyl has taken so much from me. I don't want it to take my daughter, too." He sucked in a jagged breath. "I'm not talking about the cancer. I mean that I don't want you to hate me."

Suddenly, I felt the strong connection with him that I had had as a child. I felt like I did in the old days when we had hunted and fished, shoulder to shoulder in the woods. I never wanted to leave his side again. I threw my arms around his thick neck.

"I don't hate you, Papa," I cried into his shoulder. "It's just that… In the last few months, I've started to want to become a scientist." I struggled to find the words to explain. "I want to learn all about the accident. I want to prevent another one from happening."

Papa hugged me even tighter. "You are strong, Katya. You are smart. You have great academic ability. Your questions…" As his voice trailed off, he met my gaze.

In his gray eyes, I thought I saw his own growing doubts.

"Even as I've been afraid of your curiosity, I've admired it," Papa managed.

I realized that my Papa had been watching me. Perhaps, on my halting and difficult journey to piece together the truth, he had even been pulling for me.

"You'll get through this. You'll have a great future," Papa tried to reassure me.

"Papa, we'll have a future. All three of us."

Papa shook his head. "Nothing has been right for such a long time."

As I often had done as a child, I clung to my father and inhaled his distinctive smell of earth and sun, the smell of the Ukraine itself. With my face pressed to his thick neck, I felt closer to my home, and I realized how desperately I missed it.

Mama came through the door. Papa and I were still hugging each other.

"No chicken," Mama said. "But I bought three beautiful cutlets…" As she held her grocery bag in the air, she smiled at us. "I'll have dinner ready in about an hour."

I couldn't stand watching both my parents break down on the same day. "Mama, is it O.K. if I go by the library? I have a science report due."

Mama's face drooped. The bag dropped to her side.

"I'll be right back." I assured her. "I'll be on time, really." I stood up and made for my backpack by the door.

"Please don't forget and be late," Mama called, but she wasn't scolding me.

I returned and kissed Papa on the head. I noticed that a clearing of skin had appeared in the forest of his thick dark hair. Like most men his age, he was balding.

Chapter Twenty-Eight

Глава двадцать восьмая

STUDENTS CROWDED AROUND THE TABLES in the library. Everyone was working on the science projects due next week. Lyudmila Pikalova waved gaily at me. "Halllooo, Katya." She wore tight-fitting jeans and a T-shirt. As always, a pack of boys surrounded her.

I acted as if I hadn't heard her greeting and headed straight for the bookshelves. I grabbed a medical encyclopedia and flipped the pages until I found the word 'thyroid.' The illustration showed an organ in the front of the neck. The caption said: the thyroid, a ductless gland, regulates growth.

Next, I skimmed the text until I found that awful word 'cancer.' Still standing, I searched for the subtitle, "Thyroid Cancer Treatment." Trying to walk and read at the same time, I bumped into a sharp object, a table edge. Unable to take my eyes off of the book, I slouched into the closest chair.

If caught early, the encyclopedia claimed, *thyroid cancer is among the most treatable of cancers. Surgery or radiation therapy or a combination will cure many cases.*

After I had read for half an hour, I decided that my father's doctor was right. Unless Papa had an advanced case, thyroid cancer was a good type of cancer to have.

I closed my eyes and tried to imagine the scar my father would have following surgery. It would look like a shiny half-moon on his thick neck. But I reminded myself that I was picturing the best case. So much of our lives had been the worst case—Papa would probably have advanced cancer, too.

After searching through several newspaper articles, I found the official position on whether Papa's cancer was caused by exposure to radiation. Dr. Mykola D. Tronko, director of Ukraine's Thyroid Cancer Institute, said, "To tell you the truth, even…years after the accident, we have more questions than answers." So many more questions, I thought.

I lifted my head to consider what I had just read and was surprised to find Sergei standing in front of me. His slacks fit neatly over his slim hips, and his blue T-shirt was tucked in loosely. His blond hair was brushed back from his face.

"Have you changed your mind?" Sergei asked.

"About what?"

"About going back?" Sergei said.

"Going back?"

"To the Zone." He combed his fingers through his hair. "The field trip next week?"

"The field trip?" I said vaguely. I had forgotten all about this.

"Angelika is the student leader for the trip. She's asked me to help her with the count." Sergei's mouth broke into a smile. "Why don't you come?"

Do you want me to come? I wondered.

Sergei gazed slyly at me out of half-closed lids. "What ever happened between you two?"

"Between who?" I asked.

"You and Angelika," Sergei said.

I shrugged. "I don't know."

"Angelika told me once that you really let her down, but she didn't say how."

"I've barely said ten words to her in four years," I admitted.

Sergei shrugged. "So are you coming? What should Angelika tell

Nina Ivanovna?"

He blushed, catching his own mistake. Nina Ivanovna had been our teacher in Pripyat.

"Tell her I'll go," I said impulsively.

Chapter Twenty-Nine

Глава двадцатьдевятая

A FEW DAYS LATER, WHEN I ARRIVED HOME late from school, the apartment felt empty. I dropped my books on the breakfast table.

Seeing the large pot on the stove, I remembered that Mama had to take an exam tonight. *Chicken soup for dinner. Be sure to look in on your father.*

The day before Papa had gotten the call from Dr. Sokolov, he had been his usual athletic self. But ever since he had learned of his diagnosis, my father had spent a lot of time in his bedroom, leaving only occasionally for errands and walks. Several friends had stopped by to visit.

When Uncle Victor returned from Canada, I wondered if he would be among the visitors. I was curious and apprehensive about how my father would react to his old friend.

I headed down the hallway to my parent's bedroom and knocked on the door.

"Come in," Papa called in a husky voice.

My father was sitting up in bed leaning against a pillow. The stink of sweaty gym clothes was gone, replaced by the menthol scent of cough drops and the dry papery smell of tissues. Although I'd always been bothered by that locker room smell, now that it was too late, I realized I would miss it.

Not a single beam of light crept in through the closed curtains. "May I turn on the lamp?" I asked.

My father gave a halfhearted croak, "Sure."

I moved his unused jogging clothes, his XX Large T-shirt and black shorts, from the big chair next to the bed, and sat down.

"Hello, Katya." He was wearing his favorite pair of mustard-colored pajamas. The yellow pajamas made his complexion look unhealthy, like clay. "Did you have a good day at school?" he asked.

I thought of how I spent my days at school, fighting to pay attention to my teachers and rushing to get out of the building as fast as I could. "Yes," I said. "How about you? Have you been sleeping?"

"Some," Papa said. "The hospital called. I'm going to Kiev for an operation next week."

"Can I go?" I asked. How could it be that only a few days ago, I hated to be in the same room with him? Now I didn't want to let him out of my sight.

"Aunt Olga is coming to stay with you."

I wanted to see little Yuri and my other cousins, but I also felt grown-up enough to stay in our apartment alone. "I don't need a babysitter."

Papa sighed. "You're still young. Besides, it's all arranged."

Since I didn't want to start another argument, I forced myself to say, "I'll do what you want."

Papa nodded. "That's my obedient daughter."

This particular compliment grated. "What have you been doing?" I asked to avoid reacting.

"When you walked in, I was thinking about Granny Vera," he said.

"What about her?" I asked.

"It's so good to talk to you again," Papa said. He reached over and patted my arm. "I've missed you."

"Me, too, Papa." Even though we had lived together in the same apartment, I knew what he meant.

Papa sighed. "Sometimes, I wish that I had paid more attention to your grandmother. Once I got to a certain age, I refused to listen to her stories anymore. Back then, I was young and fervent. I thought that the old ways were holding us back from becoming a modern nation."

I knew that Papa adored Granny Vera, but I also remembered that Granny Vera had kept secrets from him. "Don't tell your Papa," she would warn me.

"Do you remember how she ended her stories?" Papa asked.

I nodded, and we both recited together, "And so it shall be until the end of the world."

Papa stared at the blank wall. "Sometimes I wonder what she would think of all that has happened." He sighed. "It goes against everything that I've been taught to believe, but I wonder if I'll see her again."

I leaned close to him. He didn't smell like a thunderstorm, but remembering Boris and the statistics that I had read in the journals, I worried. "Papa, you're not going to die."

I guess my voice was jarring because Papa closed his eyes.

When he stretched, his arms draped over both sides of the bed. His feet dangled off the end. "I'm sorry, Katya. I think I want to sleep." He pulled the blue blanket up. As he yawned, he looked as defenseless as the baby squirrels Noisy had once discovered. "Goodnight, *donechka*."

He hadn't called me "little girl" in so long. Although my thoughts spun uncontrollably, I leaned over quietly and kissed him on the forehead. I couldn't imagine a world without this man.

A few minutes later, I knocked on the door of Margarita's apartment.

"Come in," Margarita called.

Except for the light above the table, the room was dark. She sat at the table which was crowded with little bowls. Absorbed in her task, she didn't look towards the door. I squinted to make sure of what I saw. It looked as if she was dipping a medium-sized crystal in red dye, like an Easter egg.

Approaching the table, I called, "Hello, Margarita."

Unembarrassed, Margarita removed the dripping crystal and laid it on a napkin. A pile of wet crystals in front of her formed a mound. "Why so late, Katya? Lyudmila's already gone."

I sat down in the chair across from her. Overhead, the smeared rainbow glowed in the electric light. "I came by to tell you some bad news."

When Margarita sighed, her enormous chest heaved.

"My father's sick," I said.

"I know. Lyudmila told me," Margarita said.

On her way out of the library the other night, Lyudmila had stopped by my desk, and I had shared the doctor's terrible report with her.

"I'm so sorry," Margarita continued. "It's as you feared."

This wasn't the reaction that I had expected. "I didn't know that Papa was going to be sick," I protested. "He's such a strong man. Why I thought he was going to live to be one hundred and..."

Margarita smiled gently as she interrupted, "But, Katya...Of course, this was why you have been so angry with him."

"What do you mean?" I asked.

"Your father must have picked up a massive dose at the time of the explosion. By spending two weeks in the Zone each month, he's been risking his life." Margarita's tone was matter-of-fact. "For what?" She shrugged her broad shoulders. "For money?"

For no reason, I thought about the jar of foreign coins that Papa always pointed to when he lectured me about saving for the future.

Margarita's fingers quickly dropped another crystal into the red dye. "Why? Money's not more important than a man's life."

How could I have been so stupid? Papa wasn't an overzealous patriot. He worked at the station to pay for the Moped and jewelry he thought I liked so much.

Margarita dropped the wet crystal on the white napkin where it dripped pink tears.

I had come seeking comfort because I had felt so raw and scared about my father's illness. Now I realized I had come for something else, too. My question burst out. "Do you believe in your crystals?"

Margarita thoughtfully stroked the large crystal that hung around her neck. "I believe in not giving up. If my crystals provide hope, they're worth every *kopeika*."

I wasn't sure I agreed with her. We were silent for a moment as her fingers nimbly finished the stack of red crystals. She pulled a bowl of yellow dye towards her. "Have I ever showed you how I use this leftover water for fortune-telling?" she asked.

"No." I shook my head, uninterested in the tricks she played on people.

Margarita started twirling her finger around in the water.

Rainbows created by the crystals' refraction of light danced around the white tablecloth. I reached out to catch one, but my fingers closed on air. "Margarita?"

"Yes," she said. My tone must have alerted her to the importance of what I was going to say, because she pushed the bowl aside.

"Something happened when I was younger. I've never understood it." Since I had failed to convince Angelika so long ago, I had never tried to describe my meeting with Vasyl to anyone else. "Just a month ago, I saw a boy in your apartment stairwell. He has really blond hair and round blue eyes. Have you seen a boy like this?"

"No," Margarita said. But I could tell by the directness of her gaze that I had captured her attention.

I told her every detail of my first meeting with Vasyl. "It wasn't a regular fire." I searched for the words that would persuade her. "As the boy was talking, I smelled the smoke. I felt the heat from the flames." I kept my eyes on her high-cheekboned face, trying to gauge her reaction, but her expression was inscrutable.

"What do you think?" I asked her when I had finished.

When Margarita smiled, her eyes lit up with excitement, and she looked much younger. "It sounds like you saw your *domovyk*."

"My *domovyk*?" I asked, remembering the little figure in the corner of the mirror. I hadn't thought of him since we left Yanov. Besides, Granny Vera said that *domovyk*s were house elves. "I saw this boy by the stream, never in my house."

"If he doesn't feel welcome in his house, a *domovyk* can travel anywhere. He warns his people of danger or misfortune. His visits can be like nightmares," Margarita shrugged, "or just interesting."

"Have you ever seen yours?" I asked.

"Many times," Margarita said. "Mine has the figure of a small boy with pointy ears and round eyes. He is very hairy."

Thinking of Vasyl's blond hair, I asked, "What color hair?"

"Jet black," Margarita said.

"When was the last time you saw him?" Katya said.

"Before the accident. I looked out the window of my apartment. My *domovyk* sat on the curb." Margarita got a faraway look in her eyes. "He was crying red tears."

"Red?" I asked.

"Bright red," she said. "I knew that something terrible was about to happen." She sighed. "But I never dreamed that it would be a nuclear accident."

I was grateful Margarita believed me, and doubting her story made me feel guilty. Besides, I had experienced too many unreal things myself to dismiss the red tears.

It was almost 7 p.m., and my hunger had grown unbearable. I looked over at her kitchen counter. Her usually overflowing fruit bowl was empty except for a blue *matryoshka*. The pattern on the doll was of a young girl in the middle of a snowstorm. I remembered that on the night of the evacuation, I had asked my *domovyk* to jump into my *matryoshka*'s box and come with me, and for the first time in a long time, I thought of the tiny *matryoshka* baby lost in the woods.

"Thanks for listening. I've got to go now," I said.

Margarita smiled at me. When I stepped into her arms, she folded me into her ample breasts. I breathed in cinnamon and cloves.

Chapter Thirty

Глава тридцатая

ON THE SCHOOL BUS FOR THE FIELD TRIP, I held the dosimeter that I had borrowed from my father. It was a small gray box with a screen. Although the radiation levels had come down throughout the Zone, I had heard extremely high levels still existed in places. I had brought along the dosimeter to look out for these 'hot spots.' When the radiation rose, the dosimeter would start beeping.

Right now the screen said twenty microroentgen, a little lower than the typical reading in Slavutich of twenty-five or twenty-six, and about double that of a city in America, where a dosimeter normally registered about ten to twelve microroentgen per hour. Some places in Europe maintained higher readings because the streets were made out of stone.

I could never look at the instrument's screen without thinking about Boris and his last night. He had climbed up on the roof of the station and gazed down at the nuclear reactor. It must have been blazing like a fallen sun. I had read that the temperature was so hot that the tar covering the rooftop had melted.

The radiation on the roof reached 20,000 roentgen an hour. One thousand microroentgen equals one milliroentgen, and 1,000 milliroentgen equals one roentgen. One roentgen is 100,000 times the average radiation of a typical city. So Boris was exposed to radiation one billion times my current reading. Near the core, levels reached 30,000 roentgen per hour. In such cases, a man would absorb a fatal dose in forty-eight seconds.[28] I recoiled just thinking about it and tried to bring my thoughts back to the present.

I had a seat at the back near the window. Excused from wearing uniforms, we were all dressed in slacks and T-shirts. Lyudmila was next to me. Three or four seats ahead of us, Sergei and Angelika sat side by side. Why had Sergei asked me on the field trip if he was going to ignore me? I wondered. Since that night in the library, I had replayed his words again and again. "Will you come?" It was the one cheerful note in these anxious days before my parents left for my father's surgery.

To my surprise, I had to persuade my mother to agree to let me join the field trip. My father's illness had broken the uneasy trust she had tried to maintain in the station's safety.

Over the weekend, Papa had repeated to her the information that he overheard the station guides tell foreign scientists. Stuff like: Although background radiation up to a dozen of times the usual levels is still the norm in the Dead Zone, it's comparable to the amount given off by the naturally radioactive sands of the Brazilian coast.[29]

Despite his support and my pleas, Mama had refused to agree to let me go. Finally, I pointed out to her that since Papa was allowed to spend twenty-six weeks a year in the Dead Zone, I should be safe for four hours. Reluctantly, she gave in.

Now, I was silently repeating these arguments to myself.

The highway to Pripyat was still well-paved, although the closer we got, the more potholes we seemed to hit. It was a peaceful drive, and we didn't see a single other car. I was glad to be returning in the spring, but as I looked out on the green fields, I wished it was a little later in the year. It was still too early for the wildflowers.

The bus passed hundreds of transmission lines attached to rows of wooden poles. These lines carried electricity from the station to the rest of the Ukraine. Seeing that web stretch on, I realized that the station generated so much power, that the government would never

[28] *The Truth About Chernobyl* By Grigori Medvedev, page 83, 1991 Perseus Books Group, New York

allow it to close.

Many of the kids were laughing, talking and singing, but I noticed that—except for Lyudmila—those of us from the Dead Zone were quieter.

Already the bus had cleared double rows of barbed wire fencing and yellow radiation signs that announced the first checkpoint. Only a few more miles and we would reach the second checkpoint and Pripyat.

Lyudmila was flirting with Mikhail Bazelchuk in the seat in front of her. She wore her blue T-shirt as tight as our teachers would allow.

"I'm a Gemini," Lyudmila told Mikhail. "That means I'm very friendly."

"Who are Gemini supposed to marry?" Mikhail asked. He was not handsome. His lips were too thin; his eyes too hard; and his hair too frizzy.

As Lyudmila whispered her answer, I was grossed out when I thought I saw her pink tongue touch his ear. I wanted to warn her to leave this particular boy alone, but since she cared as little for my views on boys as I did for hers, I turned my back to them both and stared out the window.

A roadside sign caught my attention. "Open fires, mushroom and berry picking, hunting and fishing are forbidden."[30] How I used to love every one of these forbidden activities, I thought.

Lyudmila nudged my shoulder. "I've figured out how we can settle our argument, Katya."

"What argument?" Mikhail asked.

I wondered too.

"We were studying math when the policeman came to the door of Nina Ivanovna's class. But stubborn Katya insists that it was science," Lyudmila said.

Lyudmila was wrong. I remembered a crude drawing of the solar system on the blackboard.

"How are you going to settle that?" Mikhail asked. "Your teacher isn't going to be in the classroom."

"The blackboard!" Lyudmila said triumphantly. "The lesson will be on the blackboard."

It was eerie to realize that Lyudmila could be right. I had heard that the Dead Zone had been looted, but no one would steal a blackboard. It might be exactly as our teacher left it four years ago. I felt a sharp pang of desire to return to the schoolroom. I wanted to see if my books were still in my desk. The books of the real Katya.

Angelika turned around. "I agree with Lyudmila," she said. "We were studying math."

Sergei frowned at her. "No, Angelika, it was science," he said.

I grinned openly at him. When he smiled back, I felt a surge of hope.

Comrade Mokhoyida, our guide, put an end to our debate by standing up in the front of the bus. Her ill-fitting gray suit clung to her plump thighs. A helmet of brown hair framed her pale face. With a huge smile, she announced, "Thank you for your courage in coming today."

I looked around at the kids on the bus and was pretty sure that I was the only one who was afraid.

"Chernobyl is the site of the largest nuclear accident in the world," Comrade Mokhoyida announced.

"People are proud of the strangest things," Mikhail muttered. He picked up his comic book and began reading about Conan the Barbarian.

"The Zone is heavily guarded to keep the nuclear materials safe," Comrade Mokhoyida continued. "To protect their health, the scientists and support staff who work here are limited to two-week shifts." She continued talking about stuff I already knew until the bus hit a rough patch of concrete, and she had to steady herself against the dashboard. "I'll resume when the road gets better," she apologized, before sitting down.

I thought about the day of the evacuation. My mother and I had ridden a red-striped bus out of Pripyat. I remembered being grateful to the old peasant who had opened the window next to us so that we could have fresh air. Now I knew how dangerous that air had really been. "Did you leave Pripyat on a bus, Lyudmila?" I asked.

Lyudmila nodded. She twirled her long hair around her finger.

"Were the windows in the bus open?" I asked.

Lyudmila looked at me curiously. "I don't remember."

Mikhail whipped around and narrowed his small eyes at me. "I don't like talking about that day."

"I didn't know you lived in Pripyat," Lyudmila said.

"We had just moved there," Mikhail said.

As Lyudmila leaned over the seat in front of us to tell him, "What bad luck!" she thrust her bottom in my face. Although I playfully slapped her, that didn't stop her from whispering into Mikhail's ear.

We passed more abandoned barns and silos and rotting cottages overgrown with weeds. One large poplar sprouted out of a farmer's roof. I remembered this drive from when I was a kid. In April, these same fields used to be planted in neat rows of corn and hay. Now, only tall green grass blanketed the ground.

No matter what I saw or how hard I worked to distract myself, I couldn't get my mind off the bad news. When Mama and Papa returned from the doctors, she had told me that Papa didn't have an early case of thyroid cancer. "The surgeon says it's an 'advanced case,'" she had admitted.

Ahead, a candy-striped bar blocked the road, and the bus braked to a stop. This was the last checkpoint guarding the Dead Zone. A guard dressed in camouflage gear exited a nearby guardhouse. Holding a clipboard, he took big strides toward the bus.

The bus driver opened the door, and Mokhoyida exited the few steps onto the ground. She approached the guard.

While the guard slowly examined all of our documents, I found myself studying the guardhouse. It was a small wooden building with a chimney and a gray roof. A high rectangular window provided the only view of the checkpoint from inside the hut, and I wondered how the guards knew when a visitor had arrived. They must rely on the sound of the cars, I had decided when the guard finally waved us on.

After Mokhoyida climbed back on board, our cumbersome bus rumbled over the cattle guard, leaving the checkpoint in the dust.

A few seats ahead of us, Stepan pulled out a radio, and Lyudmila began singing along. It was one of our favorite English songs, "*This is not a technological breakdown. This is the road to hell.*"

I closed my eyes. Lyudmila's voice, which had been loud in my ear, stopped.

"Is the bus making you sick to your stomach?" Lyudmila asked. "You're even more quiet than usual."

"I don't feel well," I said, to cover up my real problem. I didn't want to share my father's latest bad news. If I kept the doctor's report secret, I hoped I could keep it from coming true.

"Almost there," Comrade Mokhoyida called out.

The bus grew silent. In the seat in front of us, Mikhail started coughing in that hacking way that smokers do.

"We're going to just drive by the station. At Pripyat, we'll get out of the bus. It's very exciting. A photographer for the Ministry of Health is coming to take your photo. People all over the Soviet Union will see your picture."

For a fleeting instant, I felt the urge to escape. I didn't want to let the nuclear industry use my photograph to prove that the station was safe. But I felt that helpless feeling again: there's nothing I can do.

"Our last stop will be the car graveyard, where the authorities buried the contaminated cars," Comrade Mokhoyida said.

Mikhail sniffed. "I've been to the Zone many times with my father."

"Doing what?" Lyudmila asked.

"My dad has an auto parts business," Mikhail said. His voice was proud.

"*Kruto*," Lyudmila said, using our word for cool.

"He's probably a bootlegger," I hissed to Lyudmila. Everyone had heard rumors about criminals who stole highly radioactive televisions, car parts, and appliances from the Zone and sold them on the black market to unsuspecting buyers.

Lyudmila turned to me and whispered, "You always think the worst of everyone, Katya."

Mikhail heard her. "And you always think the best, Lyudmila. You're a sweet girl." He glared at me. "And Katya, you should go back into your cave."

"You're right, Mikhail. Katya is uptight." Lyudmila faced me. Her gaze scolded me. I could tell that she was thinking, *Katya, no boy is ever going to like you.* She turned away and threw her arm around Mikhail's shoulder.

Mokhoyida stood up again and faced us. "We've arrived at V.I. Lenin Nuclear Power Station, Chernobyl."

I turned away from the kids and looked out the window.

In my imagination, the station had become a dark fortress, an evil emerald city with a terrifying fireball on the throne commanding people to do its bidding and then consuming them. Now with the bus parked one hundred yards away, the ordinariness of this complex of five- and six-story buildings surprised me. It resembled any other boring factory.

Water towers and some construction cranes rose up alongside the buildings. The whole compound was gray, except for random panels. A few were metallic, and others were painted yellow or light blue. The metallic surfaces were rusted and glinted in the sun. The painted ones added a playfulness to the scene which seemed out of place. The entire compound was enclosed by a concrete fence topped with barbed wire. Men dressed in camouflage guarded the gates.

"The station," I overheard Angelika tell Sergei. "I haven't been here since I was a little girl."

I found Angelika's reverent tone irritating and was tempted to challenge her, but what would I say? Although I hated Reactor Four and the men who were responsible for the explosion, many brave liquidators had given their lives to clean up the nuclear debris. It took 90,000 of them to assemble the Sarcophagus.[31] This place was a crime scene all right, but I realized it was a shrine, too.

A man dressed in black pointed a camera at the bus and snapped a photograph. Mokhoyida waved at him.

I examined my dosimeter. It was thirty-two microroentgens an hour. Pretty normal.

"That building next to the tall tower is the Sarcophagus," Comrade Mokhoyida said. "It shares a divider wall with the third reactor unit, which is still operating."

Until that moment I hadn't looked for the Sarcophagus, but now that the guide identified it, I gasped at the sight. It was a rectangular structure, constructed out of concrete blocks. On some floors, the blocks appeared uneven, and sloppy spaces gaped between them. Yet the pathetic nuclear shield was all that stood between the world and another horrible disaster.

"The radiation was too high for humans to approach," Comrade Mokhoyida said. "So not a single rivet or weld holds the Sarcophagus together."

I had read about the Sarcophagus' construction. The government had assembled the twelve-story structure using remote-controlled cranes and giant military helicopters. Too radioactive to be removed, these large machines now lay buried somewhere in the Dead Zone— alongside 12,000 other cement trucks and bulldozers employed to clean up the accident.

"To collect the graphite from the roofs, the government purchased robots from Japan, but the machines were useless," Comrade Mokhoyida said.

The robots couldn't function on the rough ground. Instead, for this most dangerous job, the government hired men. They were called "biological robots." Few of them understood the risks that they were running.

"Some 3,400 army reservists with picks and shovels were hired to clear the roofs. The men were given strict time limits, sometimes as little as twenty seconds, to reduce their exposure and keep them safe," Comrde Mokhoyida said.

Keep them safe? I wondered if our guide knew that many of these biological robots had already died? Uncle Victor told me that the doctors were forbidden to tell the men their illnesses were caused by the radiation.[31] Even my own father's doctors had lied to him. Dr. Sokolov had claimed that his thyroid cancer was probably unrelated to his exposure to the radiation. "Why does anyone get cancer?" he had shrugged. "Who knows?"

"Today, only twenty-five percent of the Sarcophagus can be entered by humans," Comrade Mokhoyida said. "The remainder still contains four times the lethal dose with readings of up to 3,300 roentgens an hour."

I looked over at Lyudmila. She was calmly chewing gum. But I had read that if a person stayed for just two minutes inside the forbidden areas, she would be overcome by radiation sickness. After ten minutes, she would die.[32]

"The Sarcophagus is believed to contain up to 200 tons of melted nuclear fuel in addition to thirty-seven tons of radioactive dust. You are looking at a building which safely houses more radioactive waste than any other facility in the whole world," Comrade Mokhoyida bragged.

The guide's propaganda was too much to bear. "That building is not safe!" I protested loudly enough for the whole bus to hear. I knew that the Soviets built the Sarcophagus to last only thirty years, but the plutonium alone would be radioactive for another 250,000.[33]

Lyudmila punched me in the arm for making a scene, and Angelika glared at me in annoyance. I was about to add more, when Sergei craned his neck to stare. I remembered Lyudmila's look, *no boy is ever going to like you.* And I shrank back in my seat. I wanted him to notice me, not think I was a freak.

"You better be quiet, Katya, or I'll report you to Tatjana Petrovna!" Angelika yelled.

Comrade Mokhoyida smiled calmly at me. "Don't worry. We are already planning another stronger structure, to contain the contaminants for a longer period of time. We will build this structure over the Sarcophagus."

"That's right," Angelika broke in. "The authorities have the situation under control."

I was tempted to ask, *Then, why are they already planning to build another 'stronger structure?' And why haven't they built it yet?* But for the moment, I managed to contain my anger.

"What's wrong with you?" Lyudmila hissed.

As I pointed out the window at the Sarcophagus, I could feel the heat rising in my cheeks. "That's what's wrong." I told her. Although I knew Lyudmila wasn't interested in the facts, I couldn't stop myself. "Another explosion could occur any hour, any minute, or any second." I was furious at her—at all of them—for not knowing enough to be afraid. "If the reactor explodes again, the consequences could be even worse than last time."[34]

Lyudmila cocked her head and peered closely at me. She was wearing at least three coats of mascara. Her eyelashes were so stiff that they looked like small swords. "You never show any emotion," she said. "And now, *you're so angry.*"

When I met her gaze, her blue eyes were full of curiosity. She looked as if she had never really seen me before.

I turned away from her towards my watery reflection in the window. During our many arguments, my parents had said the same thing to me. "*You're so angry.*"

"No, I'm not," I always answered. Yet as I stared out the window at the clumsily built Sarcophagus, I felt as red-hot as the reactor core on the night of the explosion. A few minutes passed, while I breathed deeply, trying to regain control of myself.

"Hey," Mikhail pointed at the Sarcophagus. "A bird just flew in there."

I looked in the direction that he was pointing.

Since the Sarcophagus was over 100 yards away, it took me a moment to spot the crow. Its black head poked out of a crack in the nuclear shield. The crack appeared to be about the length of my arm. Flapping its midnight-blue wings, the bird began flying towards us.

"That crow probably built a nest inside the damaged reactor," Mikhail said. "It will have radioactive babies, and then the whole family will fly away to… Norway." He shrugged expressively. "All over the world."

Chapter Thirty-One

Глава тридцать первая

AS THE BUS CROSSED THE BRIDGE, I caught my first glimpse of Pripyat. The town's tree-lined streets were crumbling. Decapitated streetlights dangled on electrical cords. Grass poked out of cracks in the sidewalks. I saw only one sign of life. A long-abandoned piece of gray laundry flapped in an open window.

Our bus pulled up in front of the square, concrete plaza and jerked to a halt. "This town of 45,000 people was so young that the city fathers never gave this plaza a name," Comrade Mokhoyida said.

It looked like an ordinary plaza dotted with benches and surrounded by trees. But where were the cars, the people and the pets? I remembered all the May Day parades that I had watched from the vantage point of this plaza. How I had hurried across this square on my way home from school. I missed the vendors selling punch from the roadside stands, the mothers pushing strollers, and the blooming gardens.

Pripyat was a ghost town. I knew that cities weren't alive and so couldn't die, but looking at the spooky emptiness of the plaza, I still felt sad.

I checked my dosimeter: Thirty-six microentgens an hour.

"Is that high?" Lyudmila asked.

I shook my head. "It's only a little higher than Slavutich."

"You're so good in science, Katya. I'm so bad," she said in a little girl's voice.

Mikhail turned around in his seat. "I can help you in science, Lyudmila."

She and Mikhail began whispering again. I did my best to ignore them.

"First, we'll go to the apartment house across the street," Comrade Mokhoyida said.

I looked over at it. It would have been a typical ten-story apartment project except that the windows were all shattered or missing. The doors were either gone or hanging on their hinges. The paint peeled from the window sills, and the stucco was dirty and cobwebbed.

©James B. Willard

"How many of you went to school here?" Comrade Mokhoyida asked.

About ten of us, including Lyudmila, Mikhail, Sergei, Angelika and me, raised our hands.

"So you've come home." In this one short remark, Mokhoyida brushed past all the heartache of our broken lives, and without showing any sympathy, she began issuing instructions concerning our tour.

Still keyed up, I looked out the window. Thick yellow rays of the sun only partly illuminated an alley, igniting the dust into luminescence.

Then, I spotted him. With my face pressed against the glass, I caught a glimpse of a small figure. As he hurried away from the apartment building into the alley, one moment he was standing in the sunlight and the next he was in shadow. I saw only his back but he was dressed in dark pants and an embroidered shirt. As always his blond hair was too blond. I knew what his eyes would look like if he turned. I felt the need to follow him.

"Katya. Katya," Lyudmila shook my arm. "What are you staring at? You look like you've seen a ghost."

"I'm fine, Lyudmila," I said. The doors to the bus were still closed, and now the alley was empty again. Trapped inside, I had lost Vasyl again.

"Listen carefully, kids," Comrade Mokhoyida raised her voice. "We need to stay together. You are only permitted inside apartments 102, 104 and 109. In about thirty minutes, we'll all gather in the lobby."

She turned her back on us and exited the bus.

Since the first bus had already unloaded, I could hear voices wafting from the lobby of the apartment complex. I passed a line of mailboxes, open and empty like rusty mouths.

I spotted Angelika and Sergei ahead of me as I followed Mokhoyida into apartment 102. Inside the apartment, everything was covered with a layer of dust as thick and wooly as a blanket. The mold and mildew tickled my nostrils.

Comrade Mokhoyida looked around the room. "The looters have been everywhere."

The apartment was empty, without furniture or lamps. Holes

gaped where the appliances should have been. Cracked paint peeled off the walls. Glass, magazines, papers and small objects littered the floor. I spotted a Coke bottle, a gas mask, some shoes, a pair of broken eyeglasses and a dead potted plant. Outside the room's open window, a lush green forest blocked the light.

The ravages made me grateful that our cottage had been buried. Although I knew the liquidators had crushed its walls, I hoped nothing had been stolen. For some reason, I wanted to believe that my home had been buried with my teen room still intact.

"The apartment has two bedrooms and one bathroom," Comrade Mokhoyida continued.

Lyudmila and I began examining the trash on the floor.

Mikhail walked up to us. "She sounds just like a regular real estate broker," he joked. "Buy an apartment in hell. Very reasonable."

A group of kids trailed after Mokhoyida into the bedroom. I noticed that Angelika and Sergei were among them. They were walking side by side, and Angelika's hand brushed against his.

"When's your next soccer game?" I overheard Angelika say to Sergei.

"Friday night," he said.

Angelika grinned. "I'll be there."

I thought I saw a shadow cross Sergei's face. "Yeah, sure," he said. As Angelika and he waited for the throng of students to enter the room, I could have sworn that he was looking at me. It must be my imagination, I told myself, and then I realized that it wasn't. Sergei Rudko was definitely gazing directly at me.

To hide my blush, I quickly turned my attention to the floor. I spotted a yellowed copy of *Izvestia*. I leaned closer and read the date, January 29, 1985. Just like a time capsule, everything in this apartment was old.

"Ooohhhh," Lyudmila cooed. "I found a souvenir I want to keep." She held up a little tennis shoe. With its laces hanging down, the dirty shoe looked as if it were weeping.

"Lyudmila, that's radioactive," I warned her.

"Oooh," Lyudmila squealed and dropped the shoe on the floor.

Without any warning, Mikhail appeared from nowhere. He swaggered up to Lyudmila. "I have something I want, too."

"Oh, yeah." She grinned at him.

Mikhail grabbed her face in his hands. "A radioactive kiss." He roughly pressed his mouth to hers and began pushing her towards the wall.

"Quit!" Lyudmila ducked underneath his arms. She stopped running a few feet from him. She smoothed her hair and brushed off her clothes as if to rid herself of his touch.

"You know you're hot for me," Mikhail said as he lunged for her again.

Lyudmila was almost able to escape, but Mikhail slapped her bottom.

She called to him, "I was just flirting."

I turned to Mikhail. "Leave her alone," I hissed.

"I'll meet you in the lobby, Katya," Lyudmila called.

"O.K.," I said.

Mikhail, who had a smirk on his face, was leaning against the wall. "She's been coming onto me all morning."

"Lyudmila plays around. But it's just an act," I explained to Mikhail.

"Oh, so she's really an unfriendly outcast like you," Mikhail said.

"That's just an act, too," I said.

Mikhail snorted. "You both fooled me." He bit his lips to keep himself from coughing, but a hacking cough burst out anyway.

"You should quit smoking," I told him.

"I have," he called over his shoulder as he walked away. He knew I could see the pack of cigarettes bulging from his back pocket.

Mokhoyida reentered the room, surrounded by a group of students. She examined her dosimeter. "Thirty-five microroentgens. This reading is lower than you would get on a round-trip flight from New York City to Paris."

"Why are radiation levels high on airplanes?" Angelika asked. She had that eager, good-student expression on her face.

"The higher the altitude, the thinner the atmosphere and the greater the exposure to cosmic rays,"[35] Mokhoyida said. "How many of you have ever been on an airplane?" she asked.

No one in her group raised a hand.

Mokhoyida's face broke into a broad grin. She seemed to be endlessly cheerful. "Well, I promise you that you don't notice the higher radiation at all."

Although Mikhail had claimed that our guide sounded like a real estate broker, I found her upbeat tone almost deranged.

To get away from her grating voice, I walked out of the apartment into the lobby. It was as wrecked as the apartment. Handprints spotted the walls. The sheetrock was peeling. Algae and mold blackened the foundation.

How long had it taken to build this apartment complex? One year? How much time would pass before nature had completely reclaimed it? Twenty or thirty years?

A giant spider had made its home in the corner of the room. For a few minutes, I stopped and gazed at the cobweb so huge and intricate that it looked like it had taken months to build. No one was likely to disturb it. Lucky spider.

Unlucky people…. Poor Papa!

Although this morning I had heard Papa tell Mama that he was going to run some errands, he was probably already back home, lying on the bed in his dark room, all alone.

Lyudmila and Sergei passed through a door to the lobby. She must have recovered from her encounter with Mikhail because giggling and batting her eyes, she was already flirting again. With Sergei! I watched them nervously.

Sergei's blond hair was the only bright thing in the dark room. I was surprised that Angelika was nowhere to be seen. She was probably still buttering up the guide.

"Lyudmila," I called.

"What?" she turned, but didn't make a move toward me.

"I have to talk to you," I insisted.

Lyudmila whispered something to Sergei. I took a step toward the entrance, and she followed me.

"Don't be angry," Lyudmila looked into my eyes and pleaded. "I don't like Sergei. I'm trying to help you."

"I'm not worried about you flirting with Sergei," I said, relieved.

Lyudmila moved closer to me and began whispering into my ear. "Sergei thinks Angelika likes him more than he likes her, and he doesn't know what to do about it." Her voice rose with excitement. "He didn't say it, Katya, but I think he likes *you*."

At some other time, this piece of news would have been all-absorbing, but now…I took a deep breath and confessed what had been bothering me all morning, "My father is really sick. His thyroid cancer is more advanced than we thought."

Lyudmila stared solemnly at me. Her eyelids, at half-mast, revealed stripes of different-colored shadow. "Poor Katya," she said, as she grabbed my hand.

I didn't respond because, behind her, I spotted Sergei heading over to us.

Sergei grinned at us. "What are you two whispering about?"

Lyudmila winked at me. "I'll talk to you in a minute, Katya." Before I could object, she squeezed my hand and hurried off.

"So what's going on?" Sergei repeated.

The sun streamed in through the open door. Staring at the little dust particles hanging in the light, I thought of Vasyl, running down the alley. Why, he might have been heading to Yanov. To my cottage with the blue shutters.

With the image of my cottage, a plan popped into my mind, as vivid as Vasyl's fire had been. The only thing that might pose a problem was the electric fence.

"Sergei," I said. "I have this crazy idea."

Sergei's face brightened. "I love crazy ideas," he said.

"I'm going back to my cottage. Do you want to come?" I asked.

"Yanov is buried, isn't it?" Sergei asked.

"Yeah, but we could try to find it." I said, trying to keep my tone casual, not desperate like I felt.

"Sneak off?" He shrugged. "Just like that? Why?"

On the day of the accident, I had seen him riding his bike towards the plume. He was adventurous, I was sure of it. "Why not?" I asked. The real answer was too complicated to understand, even for me.

Sergei looked around as if to see if anyone was watching us.

"We can be back before the bus leaves." I barely recognized my own voice, it was so soft and cajoling. You sound like Lyudmila, I thought.

From the next room, I could hear Angelika talking to someone. "I'm looking for Sergei. Have you seen him?"

Sergei nodded towards the door. "What are we waiting for?"

The two school buses were parked on the street. The bus driver closest to us rested his head on the wheel. The other bus appeared empty. No one was on the sidewalks. No cars were driving down the street.

I pointed at the spot where I had seen Vasyl, and we ducked into the alley. When we emerged onto a parallel street, we turned right. Despite the fact that Pripyat seemed completely deserted, instinctively we both walked close to the buildings, traveling in their shadows.

After the first block, I recognized this street. As it was on my route home from school, I had walked down this same street every day for many years.

"What's this street's name? Do you remember?" I whispered to Sergei. He shook his head.

My forgetfulness added to my impression that I was dreaming. Unlike my last day in Pripyat, this street was so quiet. I had never been to a city this still before. It was even quieter than the woods, and it was clear that soon all the concrete would be overtaken by nature. Once trees and bushes had only timidly lined the street, but now they had boldly advanced. A bird nested in a broken streetlight. Tall grass grew in the cracks in the sidewalk. Would the new woods eat up the buildings of Pripyat and swallow them totally? Or would odd features like doorknobs in the branches and windows in the tree trunks hint of the city that the forest had devoured?

Sergei pointed at a passing street sign: Lenin Street.

Of course, this was Lenin Street. "How could I have forgotten?" I wondered, but as I asked the question, I already knew that answer. The Lenin Street of my childhood had been bustling with pedestrians, cars, and bicycles.

In the distance, I could see a familiar building. Even with its missing front door and windows, I recognized Angelika's home. It used to be the most modern complex in the city with the hottest water and the newest appliances. Now it looked like a haven for squatters. "Angelika's old apartment," I told Sergei.

"Hum," Sergei said. He looked thoughtful. I wondered if he was imagining Angelika's anger when she learned that Sergei and I had snuck away together. I know I didn't begin to breathe easier until we had passed by the unhappy gaze of the building's broken windows.

From a distance, we could see the small guardhouse at the outskirts of town. The smoke pouring out of the chimney was the only sign of life. The guards must be inside. Too soon, we reached the fence that I had dreaded.

"Isn't the fence electric?" Sergei said.

"Yes. But maybe it's not activated," I said.

We both contemplated the sharp barbs on the fence for a few moments. Then Sergei glanced back in the direction from which we had come. "I have an idea. Why don't we go see the Ferris wheel?" he said.

Although the circumstances were stranger than any I could have imagined, I felt like Sergei was inviting me on a date; the date he had asked me for all those years ago. In my mind, I could hear Lyudmila's voice encouraging me: Go!

"Do you remember we were going to ride the Ferris wheel on May Day?" I asked him. I had been quiet for so long, but now I felt comfortable talking to him.

"Sure," Sergei said. "I was excited."

"Me, too," I said and blushed. "Would you mind, Sergei? Could we go to Yanov first?" I realized now that while I had thought my interest in the guardhouse earlier had been just idle curiosity, the information I had gathered could help me now. "I think we can get past the guardhouse. No one walks in the Dead Zone. The guards will be looking for cars."

"You want to sneak past the checkpoint?" Sergei asked, incredulously.

"Yes," I said. "And I need you to come with me." Not wanting to give him an opportunity to object, I hurried forward undercover of the trees. Commando-style, I slinked up to the back of the building. After a few moments, I heard Sergei's footsteps. I was glad that he was following me, but I think I would have continued even without him.

When we reached the shack, we pressed our bodies to the building and listened to the sound of our own breathing. Except for the low murmur of a radio, the guardhouse was as quiet as the abandoned city that it guarded.

"Is anyone at the window?" Sergei mouthed.

"We'd have to backtrack to find out," I said.

"You're right," Sergei said.

Surely it was some other Katya Dubko—neither the obedient girl from Yanov nor the silent one from Slavutich High School—who said. "Let's gamble. If we sneak directly under the window, even if a guard were standing at his post, he might miss us."

Sergei stroked his chin. "That window *is* high."

"Come on," I urged him. "If we hurry, we can go see the Ferris wheel, too."

Just then, we heard the sound of a car, and we were forced to scoot to the back of the building. Careful to stay out of sight, we listened to tires screeching to a halt, to boots trudging to greet the car and to a few mumbled words. Then, we heard the whoosh of the bar, the thud of the boots retreating and the sound of a door. The car drove past.

"Let's wait a minute," I said. "Give the guard time to get settled."

"I agree," Sergei said. After a pause, he added, "I've always wanted to go back to the amusement park."

"Do you think about the past much, Sergei?" I asked.

"My brothers and I used to hunt and fish. Almost every weekend," Sergei said. His voice was dreamy.

"I miss that, too," I said. "Did you ever see our cottage in Yanov?"

"No," Sergei said.

"It was surrounded by woods. My grandmother and grandfather lived there," I said. "My grandmother used to tell me stories in front of our stove."

"Mine, too," Sergei said. "I was always terrified of Baba Yaga and her house on chicken legs." He paused, remembering. "But I loved to hear my granny talk about her *domovyk*."

"Yours had one, too?" I asked, excited.

"Yes," Sergei said. "She called him 'a peculiar, little fellow.' She said he ate only bread."

Sergei's comment reminded me of Granny Vera's story about her *domovyk* stealing a loaf of bread. "What else did your grandmother say?"

"How long do you think before the bus leaves?" Sergei asked, and his question brought me back to the present.

"At least forty-five minutes." I reminded him, "Remember *that photographer*." I couldn't keep the scorn out of my voice. But if Sergei shared my scorn for the nuclear industry, he didn't show it.

"We should go," he said.

"Yes," I agreed.

"I'll lead," Sergei said. Before I could answer, Sergei bent down and ran toward the candy-striped bar. When he reached it, he squatted underneath. Every second, I expected to hear a man's voice ring out, but he slipped by the guardhouse without incident. Careful not to kick any gravel or to scuff my shoes, I followed.

In just a few moments, I joined him under the cover of the nearby woods. We hid behind a pine tree and looked back at the checkpoint.

Sergei grinned. "So much for the airtight security system."

I laughed as I plunged into the woods. "Let's go." My forest was much denser, greener and taller than I remembered.

"There's no path," Sergei said.

"It's just overgrown," I said. "I know the way."

Welcome home, Katya, the trees seemed to say. *Welcome home.*

Unlike the town, the forest was as wide-awake as I had ever seen it and more beautiful than I remembered. It seemed that birds and squirrels inhabited every tree, that all the bushes were budding and that green grass blanketed every inch of the ground. Sparrows, magpies and blackbirds sang in the trees. The wind blew fluffy seeds past me. It was the spring that I hadn't experienced. The spring that the accident had stopped.

"My father and I liked to hunt boar," Sergei said. "We had just killed a big sow. Its body was at the taxidermist in Kiev on the day of the accident. It's the only thing my parents let me keep."

"All I have is a motorcycle poster," I confessed. "I didn't even get to keep my other birthday presents. My new Barbie—that Angelika gave me, actually," I paused, thinking about my teen room and the things I had left behind. "And a beautiful *matryoshka*."

"A motorcycle poster?" Sergei asked.

"Did you know the Boikos, my neighbors? Their son, Boris, was a fireman."

"No," he said.

"Boris gave it to me," I said.

"Your boyfriend?" he teased.

"No, he was engaged," I said simply.

When I was younger, I had needed a bicycle to make the trip from Pripyat to Yanov. Particularly in the winter, the trip had been exhausting. But now, we had already reached my lane.

At first, I couldn't believe it. The Ancients, those old homes, had survived the Great Patriotic War and others. But now, they had disappeared. As if the ground had grown boils, mounds of dirt bulged where these wooden cottages had once graced the earth.

"Is this Yanov?" Sergei asked.

The all-consuming ache that I felt started in my stomach but quickly spread out into my limbs, filling my head. I wondered if cancer hurt like this. My cottage was truly gone. And the Ancients were buried, too. Until I saw this field of dirt, I had never truly believed my father. When I didn't answer, Sergei said, "I'm sorry, Katya."

I began running to shut out the pain. "Help me find my house, Sergei," I called. I counted mounds until I arrived at what I guessed was the location of our dear cottage. I couldn't be sure because our oak tree was buried, also.

I pointed at a heap of dirt, all that was left of the home my grandfather had built to keep our family safe so long ago. "I think this is it."

Sergei and I both hunted around in the grass which had grown past our ankles. Eventually, I stepped on something. I bent down and scraped the dirt off a slat of wood. It was blue, but more faded than I had remembered it. "A piece of our shutters."

I wanted to kneel there and dig until I reached our cottage. I wanted to rescue it from its tomb of earth and let it feel the sun again.

"Hey, what's this?" Sergei said. He raised a chain—Noisy's chain, still spiked to a chunk of earth.

I ran to him and grabbed it out of his hand.

"What is it?" Sergei asked.

Noisy had been such a good dog. "It's my dog's." I stood there squeezing the end of that mud-encrusted chain. "I should have found some way to sneak him out."

At least I had let Noisy loose before we left. Perhaps he had found his way out into the forest.

"My sister brought our cat, Aneta," Sergei said quietly. "But the police took her at the clinic in Kiev." He shrugged. "They killed her anyway."

I dropped the chain, and its clank sounded so final as it hit the ground

The lumpy field looked like nothing more than an abandoned construction site—never loved by anybody. My home had vanished as completely as if it had never existed. It was as if my childhood had never existed either. The achy sadness crept up my throat. What if the boulder was gone, too? That's when I realized something that I should have known all along. It was the boulder that I had come for, the boulder that I wanted to see. The boulder would make everything feel right again.

"Could we go just one more place? Then we'll go to the Ferris wheel. I promise."

I knew that Sergei was ready to return, that he didn't understand what we were doing in that desolate field, but I also hoped he understood how I felt losing Noisy and everything else.

Sergei nodded and started walking alongside me. "But we should hurry."

I tore down the path toward the stream. It was completely over-grown, but just as before, I knew exactly which way to head. I walked another few yards and a deer jumped across the path. I watched its white tail bob around in the forest until it disappeared.

So beautiful….

The branches slapped my legs. My head, arms and legs began itching as if I were being attacked by a swarm of invisible mosqui-toes. I didn't want Sergei to get impatient, so I hiked as fast as I could. The clomp of Sergei's boots sounded behind me. Once we ran into vegetation so dense that I had to find a way around.

"Are you sure you know where you're going?" Sergei called out.

The trees blocked my view of him. "Yes!" I yelled just as we entered a familiar clearing.

When I turned the bend, I noticed the stream first. I knew that the water was radioactive now, but it rushed past, as innocent and as carefree as always.

Next to it, shimmering in the morning light, I spotted the boulder. With all the changes and destruction, somehow, my boulder had managed to remain exactly the same. I felt like it had waited for me. Was Vasyl here, too? Is this where he had led me?

I ran and knelt down by its side. "Sergei, come here." I motioned to him. "When I was a kid, this was my magic boulder."

"We came all this way to see a rock?" He obviously couldn't understand.

I stared into his dark eyes. "You know what I mean."

"Yeah," Sergei said. He didn't meet my gaze. "I touch that boar's tusk before every important soccer game." He looked around. "Well, now that we've seen it, can we go?"

"Just give me a minute," I said. As I plopped down next to the boulder, I heard a kerplunk, kerplunk.

"Did you see that, Katya? The rock made it all the way across the stream," Sergei called.

Glad that Sergei had found a game to keep him busy, I crouched low and reached my hand into the hollow underneath the boulder. My fingers bumped into the softness of my green blanket. Eagerly, I pulled it out and unwrapped it. Never a neat child, it had been my habit to simply stuff it into the cavity. But today the blanket formed a small neatly folded bundle. I knew that my hands had never created these tight folds. The last time I had seen this same blanket, it had been draped around the boy's shoulders.

He had returned the blanket. And that wasn't all! I felt a small bulge at the folded edge.

As I unwrapped it, a feeling of warmth flooded my body. My *matryoshka's* baby rolled into my hand, her blue eyes gazing trustingly up at me.

Vasyl. Vasyl must have hidden these things here. There was no other explanation. That strange boy did exist.

I had called Vasyl a thief, but he had put everything back. And I had called him a liar, but what had he really said?

I had dwelt mainly on the terrible part of Vasyl's words, *Our world will be destroyed.* He was right. But now I realized he meant more than just my cottage.

And I remembered what else he told me. "You'll come back," Vasyl said. "You need to."

And here I was.

My heart started pounding with the magic of those days. I thrust the blanket aside and slipped the little *matryoshka* into my pocket before quickly continuing my search for other treasures.

Sergei laughed and called from the stream, "You look like you're hugging that rock."

Stretching my hand back into the farthest recesses of the cave, my fingers closed around something soft. I pulled out a rumpled, dirty motorcycle magazine. It was turned to page 55. I stared at an advertisement for a Yava before holding it up.

"See, Sergei. I put this magazine underneath here because I wanted a motorcycle. My dad bought us a Moped a few months ago."

Sergei laughed. "So the boulder granted your wish."

I stretched my arm and crouched even lower until my fingers scraped against the back wall. On its way out, my hand grazed some objects. Eagerly, I pulled out my old fishing line along with a few muddy eating utensils.

Looking through the remains of the props for my fairy feasts, I discovered Sergei's note stuffed into a coffee cup. I had hidden it there, of course. But not until my fingers closed around the torn and dirty piece of paper had I realized I wanted to find it. I reread the childish script. "Katya, let's go out together." Then I looked over at Sergei. He was still skipping rocks across the stream.

Standing in the sunshine, Sergei's hair was golden blond. His shoulders were so broad. He caught me gazing at him. "What else did you find?"

I fingered the note, wondering if I should tell him. "Nothing," I said as I slipped the note into my pocket.

These things from my past were radioactive, but they were good, too. Somehow I felt I needed them to know how to go forward.

One last time, I swept my hand through the boulder's hiding place. My secret space was now empty.

Sergei threw a rock at the boulder, and it pinged off its side. "Too bad. If that old rock were really magic, I'd have a wish."

"What's that?" I asked.

"I'd want to move back home," Sergei said.

Chapter Thirty-Two

Глава тридцать вторая

ON OUR RETURN, WE SPOTTED A GUARD standing at the window. I don't know if Granny Vera was watching over us or if the guard had had too much *horilka* at lunch, but his eyes were half-closed.

Both of us were able to slip underneath the candy-striped bar without waking him from his doze.

I looked at my watch. We'd been gone almost forty minutes. Instinctively, we both picked up our pace. By the time we reached Lenin Street, we were out of breath and panting.

"Sergei, I don't think we have time to ride the Ferris wheel."

"You're probably right," he said.

"I'm sorry," I apologized. How could I ever explain the blanket to him?

Finding that old, dirty green blanket and the little doll changed everything.

I was now convinced that Vasyl was my *domovyk*. For some reason that I didn't understand, my house elf had chosen to appear to me in the woods instead of my cottage.

In the last five years, more unimaginable things had happened to me than anyone who wasn't from Chernobyl could even dream. When I was a child, I had believed my Granny's outlandish tales of beings from the spirit world, and I had pretended to believe in spirits and magic long after I realized that her stories were folklore. Then, the more I learned about the Chernobyl explosion from Uncle Victor, the more I had grown to realize that the truth can be fantastic.

Now, in a sudden shift, I understood the other side: the fantastic can be the truth as well.

As we hurried along, I did these mental gymnastics trying to make sense of everything, yet understanding that I never would know all the answers. Then I saw it: the yellow Ferris wheel against the blue sky.

It was hard to believe that something so fun and joyful had never once turned.

Maybe Sergei's note emboldened me, or maybe it was the little baby safe in my pocket, but I reached for Sergei's hand. When I was much younger, Boris had led me on walks in the woods. Sergei's hand wasn't callused, like Boris's, but soft and young.

He threaded his fingers between mine. Both of us were looking at the Ferris wheel. Without a word, we started toward it.

When we reached the amusement park, I surveyed the merry-go-round, bumper cars and Ferris wheel. "Why would anyone guard an amusement park?" I muttered my thought out loud.

"I don't see anyone," Sergei agreed.

We ran past the small merry-go-round and bumper car ride toward the Ferris wheel. One booth rested on the ground. Another swung about five feet above it. An emergency repair ladder led all the way to the top. Eagerly, Sergei scrambled into the booth nearest the ground. I climbed in after him. We kicked our feet, but the booth barely swung. "This is no fun," Sergei said. "We're too low to the ground."

Without waiting for a response from me, Sergei climbed onto the top of the booth. I steadied it while he strained every muscle to pull himself onto the next higher one. Despite my best efforts, the seat swung wildly.

"It's just too far—even for me," Sergei said.

The sadness in his voice made me ache for the ride that we had never taken together. All the laughs I had missed. The divan I had never slept on. The Barbie I had never played with.

I looked up at the crisscrossed metal tower. That's when I noticed the ladder. It appeared so rusted as to be dangerous, but I realized I had to take some risks if I ever wanted anything wonderful to happen to me. I would not leave here with another disappointment. "Look, Sergei." I pointed at the ladder.

"Yes!" he said. He jumped off the rocking booth.

With no more thought, I began climbing ahead of him. The rust scraped my hands, but I didn't care. I wanted to laugh at the wonder of Katya Dubko scaling the Ferris wheel with Sergei Rudko.

Halfway up, I paused. My legs trembled as I balanced precariously on the rung and surveyed the scene before me. All I could see were the tops of trees, but the forest looked as clean as the day of creation.

"Don't stop," Sergei urged me.

I looked down. Sergei's golden hair was below me. My hands had grown sweaty. Just a few more rungs, I told myself. Then you'll see everything that you would have seen if you and Sergei had ridden the Ferris wheel on May Day.

"We're so close," Sergei said.

I turned my gaze upward and pretended that I was climbing to heaven. A few white clouds dozed above me. As I took those final steps, I was as calm as the blue sky.

At last, I stood on the top. If I hadn't been so focused on Sergei, I might have been able to imagine my whole future mapped out in the patchwork of forest and meadow laid out before me.

"Hold on tight. I'm coming up next to you," Sergei said.

His body jostled mine. Soon, we were standing side by side, pressed close together.

Why had I never noticed that his brown eyes held tiny flecks of the truest blue? The wind was blowing through his blond hair. I'm sure that my smile was an invitation. When his lips grazed mine, I felt an electric shock so severe that it reminded me of an explosion.

I even heard clanging in my ears.

Then, Sergei pulled away. He gazed down at the base where a man was banging on the structure with a stick.

"What in the heck are you kids doing?" a man's voice called out.

I looked down. Despite the wind, my body felt warm.

The man was the color of concrete. His clothes, his face and his beret were all gray. His beet-red nose was the only thing that stood out. I guessed that he was a security guard.

I tried to think of any excuse that would explain our actions, but my mind was blank. My hands were sweaty and, suddenly, my legs had begun quivering.

"We're Chernobyl kids. We came back to ride the Ferris wheel," Sergei yelled.

"You must be the kids who left the field trip," the guard said.

"That's right," Sergei admitted.

"Come on down. Be careful now," the guard ordered us.

Next to me, Sergei stayed put.

I hesitated. We had worked so hard to reach the top. "Please, can we stay here for a few minutes longer?"

"Are you kids nuts?" the guard hollered.

"No!" I shouted. How could I make him understand? My request wasn't any crazier than all that had happened to us. It wasn't any crazier than the accident.

"Now!" the guard demanded.

"Come on, Katya," Sergei said. He smiled sweetly at me. "I'll go first." He started climbing down.

I paused, considering. I heard static from the guard's walkie-talkie, and then his boast, "I found the truants. Can you believe it? Ivan Dubko's daughter is climbing the Ferris wheel."

For the first time, I was afraid, but not about what would happen to me. I had been so caught up in my plan that it hadn't occurred to me that my father might get into trouble. I dangled my foot until it touched a lower rung. "Sir!" I shouted breathlessly. "Do you know Ivan Dubko?"

"Yes, I do," the guard said.

"Have I gotten him into trouble?" I asked.

"You can ask him yourself. He was in the office when your guide notified the guards that you two had run away."

"My father's here?" I asked, stunned.

"Yes, at the station," the guard said.

One of Papa's errands must have involved the station. Ever since the guard appeared, I had known that I was going to have to face my father sometime, but the realization that I would have to see him soon made me jittery.

The lone security guard waited patiently at the base. At least, he hadn't called in a squad. Climbing down was less strenuous than climbing up, except that I was scared, and my legs were trembling.

When Sergei jumped off the ladder onto the metal base, the guard lunged for him. For an instant, I thought that the guard was going to handcuff him. Instead, he reached out and shook Sergei's hand.

The guard's plain face broke into a grin. "I always wanted to climb that Ferris wheel."

By the time my feet touched the ground, the guard seemed to have spent his enthusiasm on Sergei. He gazed doubtfully at me.

"My father's sick. Is he really coming?" I asked. I was surprised when I noticed myself batting my eyelashes at him. What was happening to me? Was I turning into a Lyudmila?

"He's on his way," the guard said. He lit a cigarette and took a big drag on it.

"Sit down." He pointed at the grass.

"We did it," Sergei whispered to me and plopped down on the grass.

"Quiet!" the guard ordered us.

I looked up at the yellow Ferris wheel frozen in the sky. Sergei was right. We were the only ones from our whole class who had seen the view from the top. We might be the only people in the whole world who had ever climbed the Ferris wheel. Our climb was something, I told myself. We had defeated time.

Sergei was plucking blades of grass. "That was fun," he whispered.

"No talking," the guard commanded. He lit another cigarette.

Even though Sergei was sitting a few feet away from me, all I could focus on was his presence. His muscled arms. His strong thighs. His hands busily yanking up the grass. I was wondering if Sergei was aware of me when I saw Mokhoyida rushing down the path. Her white shirt had come untucked and flapped underneath her gray jacket. When she reached us, she frowned, breathing heavily. "Thoughtless teenagers! You've gotten us all into trouble. And what you did was dangerous."

We both stood up. Mokhoyida pointed at Sergei. "I'm taking the boy back," she said to the guard. "The girl's father is coming for her."

"I know," the guard said.

Sergei turned to me. He squeezed my hand. "See you at school, Katya."

"Bye, Sergei," I said. Although I was used to having adults angry at me, I doubted that Sergei was, and I was worried about him.

Mokhoyida grabbed Sergei's arm. "Come on, you troublemaker. You should be ashamed of yourself."

Sergei didn't answer. I watched them hurry off together. The guide's finger jabbed at him like a pecking hen as she scolded, but I was glad to see that his face stayed calm.

The guard nodded at me. "Sit."

I sat back down. *Beep, beep, beep.* The dosimeter in my pocket was making a racket. I didn't want to annoy the guard by asking if I could get it out to check if I was sitting in a hot spot. Besides, the thousands of ants that crawled over me didn't seem to think that the ground was dangerous. I started brushing them off.

After the guard had stubbed out his cigarette, he nodded in my direction. "Let's go," he said.

"Where?"

"You ask a lot of questions, don't you?" the guard said.

Never enough, I thought. We began walking until we came to a two-story wooden building. I followed him inside and found myself in some kind of lobby. The carpet curled around the edges. The air smelled sour like the inside of the abandoned apartment. A couple of rickety chairs leaned against a wall. He pulled one towards me. "Sit here," he said.

I sat down. He lit another cigarette, leaned against the wall and stared at me.

"Don't you know that smoking is bad for you?" I asked.

The guard gave out a short bitter laugh. "Like I have to worry about smoking. I work in the Dead Zone." He blew his smoke at me. "We'll all go when it's our time."

A door slammed, and I tensed. *Papa's here. Papa's here*, kept running through my mind. We hadn't argued since his illness, and I was not looking forward to hearing his angry voice now.

But I had to wait twenty more long minutes before I saw him rushing towards me. The building's ceiling was low and made him look huge again.

"Katya, what's the meaning of this?" Papa asked. Underneath his camouflage shirt, I spied a bit of mustard yellow. He had slipped his shirt on over his pajama top.

"I wanted…I'm not sure." My voice faded off, and I touched the treasures in my pocket. How could I explain all this to Papa?

"Comrade." Papa motioned to the security guard. The two men moved a few paces away.

I felt guilty as I watched Papa take out his wallet and hand the guard a few bills.

The security guard started to leave. "Tell her that it was a good trick once, but not to come back."

"Yes, Comrade," Papa said. He turned to me. "I need to call Mama and tell her that you're all right," he said. "Let's go to my room."

"Where is it?" I asked. "How do we get there?"

"I borrowed a Jeep. It's in the parking lot," Papa said.

I followed him outside.

"How did you get here so fast?" I asked him.

"I was collecting my paycheck," Papa said. "I heard that two students had slipped away from a school group. You can imagine my embarrassment when I learned that one was my own daughter."

A beat-up Jeep stood alone in an empty parking lot.

"I'm glad you're O.K., but you still have a lot of explaining to do," Papa said seriously.

As I climbed into the Jeep, I was still wondering how I could explain my actions. I didn't completely understand them myself.

Chapter Thirty-Three

Глава тридцать третья

PAPA'S ROOM AT THE STATION contained a bed, two chairs and a small refrigerator. He had no television to watch on lonely evenings and no soft couch to sit on. The ceiling was so low, I could almost reach up and touch its bumpy surface. Standing in the gloomy space, I felt amazed that I had never once questioned where my father spent his time when he was not with us. In comparison with our apartment, this colorless room was the bare cell of a monk.

While I waited for Papa to call Mama, I studied the narrow bed with its one small pillow the size of a napkin. The thin gray blanket reached just to the bed's edge. This room must be cold during the winter. Yet I had never once heard Papa complain.

Outside, I could hear the occasional sound of heavy boots tramping up and down the hallway. In about five minutes, Papa returned and sat in the other chair.

"I called Principal Goida and explained about my illness. I told him you were upset about my surgery. You weren't thinking clearly." When he had finished, a hint of a smile played on his lips. "Being a liquidator is good for something. I don't think either you or Sergei is going to get disciplined." He turned his gaze on me. "But now, you need to explain what was going on."

It was so odd to be visiting my father's poor home. In this bare room, I felt like he and I were just meeting each other for the first time. Except for the drip of the faucet, all was quiet. "I'm sorry if I embarrassed you, Papa," I said finally.

"But why?" He threw his arms out wide. "Why did you run away?"

I began again haltingly. "I'm sorry, Papa," I said. "I…I had to go back to Yanov."

"So you snuck away to view some dirt hills?" His muscled face grew redder. "With Sergei Rudko? Is he your boyfriend?" he demanded.

I shook my head.

"Tell me, Katya!" Papa demanded. He was glaring at me. "Tell me everything!"

"I had to see for myself. Sergei followed me."

"So you didn't run off into the woods to kiss?" Papa asked. His voice was heavy with suspicion.

I couldn't help wondering. Why had I left the bus trip? Was it to follow Vasyl? Or was Sergei the real reason? "No," I said.

Papa's mouth lost a bit of its clenched look.

"It was all gone. Everything." As I said this last word, tears welled up in my eyes. I reached out to grab his arm. "Are you angry at me?"

His eyes probed mine. "Are you sure that boy didn't touch you?" he demanded.

"Papa," I protested. The feel of Sergei's lips came back to me. Although I longed for Sergei's mouth on mine again, his kisses were my business, not Papa's.

"Then, let's go," Papa said, hugging me close. "Katya, I know you are searching to understand what has happened. But never, ever pull a stunt like this again."

Bumping along in the Jeep, every few minutes, I fingered Sergei's note just to make sure that the Ferris wheel and the kiss hadn't been a dream. We were making our way toward the last checkpoint. When we arrived, we would have to leave the contaminated Jeep and get a ride home with one of Papa's coworkers.

In the distance, I spotted smoke pouring out a chimney. As we drew closer, I saw a cottage nestled in the woods. In front, several cows lazily chewed on green grass. A dog chased his tail. A man hoed a garden. He looked up and shaded his eyes to see us better. He raised his hand in greeting.

"Who is that?" I asked.

"Pavel Pascenko," Papa said. "One of the squatter families."

I had read about these families. They were mostly older peasants. They had hidden during the evacuation until the soldiers left their homes or had snuck through the checkpoints to return afterwards. There were hundreds of them still eking out their living in the Zone.

"Sometimes, I bring him food," Papa explained. He glanced at me. "Do you mind if we stop?"

I appreciated that Papa didn't say the words that I felt hanging between us. *Since I may never see him again.* And at this moment, I felt a surge of hope. All his life, my father had faced physical danger with such courage and determination. I hoped he might find a way to be brave about his illness.

"I wish I had a gift for him," Papa muttered to himself. "A ball of twine. Anything."

I remembered the radioactive doll. "I have something," I said, and reached into my pocket. I offered the baby to Papa.

Papa glanced down at the little doll on the palm of my hand. "Why not?"

"Does he live alone?" I asked.

"He's married. But when I visit him, his wife hides." He rolled down the creaky window. "Pavel Pascenko."

The old man advanced timidly to the Jeep. He wore a faded blue coat buttoned to the top and a tattered beret. Deep wrinkles traveled from the corners of his eyes all the way to his mouth. His bottom lip tilted inward from loss of teeth, and his fingers spread wide out like fleshy fans. I tried to imagine what type of work had molded his hands this way, but gave up.

"Meet my daughter, Katya Dubko," Papa said.

"Hello," the old man said, smiling.

"She has something to give you," Papa explained. "I may not be back for a while. I just stopped to say goodbye."

Pavel Pascenko nodded.

I leaned over Papa and solemnly handed Pavel Pascenko the baby doll.

He accepted it, smiling. "Thank you." He glanced at the doll before slipping it into his pocket. As I caught a final glimpse of the doll, I felt as if I was watching the last bit of my childhood disappear, and I felt sad. But then, I thought, even though I've lost all of my old things, aren't the old ways still inside me? I hoped so.

"Are you thirsty?" Pavel Pascenko said.

Papa looked at me. I realized that I hadn't had anything to drink since I left home that morning. "Yes," I whispered.

Pavel Pascenko smiled. "Come have some milk."

"That would be nice," I said.

"It's radioactive, of course," Papa muttered to me under his breath. "Just pretend to drink it."

We got out of the car and followed Pavel Pascenko to the unpainted wooden cottage. While Papa and I waited on the slanted porch next to the firewood, the old man went inside and returned with three plastic glasses. He dipped the glasses in a bucket by the door. He handed me one glass, Papa the other and sat down on the front step.

"Thank you," I said. I heard a rustling inside the dark cabin.

"How's your wife?" Papa asked.

"She doesn't like strangers," Pavel Pascenko said.

My throat was parched, and the milk looked delicious. Regretfully, I put my cool glass down on the floor. I knew if I drank it that I would be drinking radionuclides. I still wasn't exactly sure what these invisible particles were, but I had all the proof I needed that they were bad for me.

"Will you tell Katya your story, Pavel Paschenko?" Papa encouraged him. "Why you were able to return?"

Pavel Paschenko stared out at his beautiful meadow. When he finally began, his voice sounded unused, like a rusty door. "We left as many spoons as there are souls in the house. All so we could come back."[36] He shrugged. "We hid in the forest with our cow. Then we came back."

"They told us to wash our yards. The very earth?"[37] His childlike blue eyes reflected deep puzzlement. "They closed our well, locked it up, wrapped it in cellophane. Said the water was dirty. How can it be dirty?" He held out his hands as if beseeching someone. "It tastes good. We drink that water every day."[38]

"Pavel Paschenko has told me many times that he's happy to live here," Papa said.

The little man shrugged. "My wife likes to say that people shoot, but it's God who delivers the bullet. Everyone has their own fate."[39]

Papa nodded. "Chernobyl has turned me into a philosopher, too."

Was Papa's illness making him a philosopher?

A cat jumped on the porch and sat down next to the old man. He began stroking the animal's fur.

"I remember it all. Planes, helicopters—there was so much noise. Soldiers. I thought the war's begun. With the Chinese or the Americans.[40]

"Everyone up and left, but they left their dogs and cats. The animals waited for their masters a long time. The hungry animals ate cucumbers. They ate tomatoes. Then the dogs ate the cats. The cats ate their kittens.[41]

"I found this little one in the forest. Half-starved and wild. He and I exchanged glances. 'All right,' I said. 'Let's go home.' But he sat there meowing. 'If you stay here by yourself, the wolves will eat you.' Cats can't understand human language, but then how come he understood me? We've been living together for three winters now."[42] He ruffled the cat's fur.

"What's his name?" I asked.

"Vaska," Pavel Pascenko said. "The police ask: 'What if bandits come?' I say, 'What will they take? My soul? Or my cat? Because those things are all I have."

"He's a pretty cat," I said.

"He's a good mouse catcher," Pavel Pascenko said. "One of the policemen offered me some batteries for my radio if I would give him Vaska. But I said, 'no.' He gave me the batteries anyway."

"So your radio is working?" Papa asked.

"We listen to it next to our kerosene lamp in the evenings,"[43] Pavel Pascenko said.

The man's garden was large and well-cared-for. I saw even rows of tomato plants and corn. Like we did in Yanov, he must grow all his own vegetables. "You have a beautiful garden," I said.

"We live in Paradise," the little man answered simply.

Both Papa's and my gaze turned to the tall grasses swaying in the breeze. The cows wandered lazily across the front yard. Soon, the garden would be loaded with vegetables. My mouth watered, thinking about his tasty homegrown tomatoes.

"Are you ready, Katya?" Papa asked. He stood up.

"Yes," I said. I heard a sound and glanced at the peasant's window. The worn gray curtains fluttered in the breeze.

"Thank you for the *matryoshka*," Pavel Pascenko said. "Where are her other dolls?"

I thought for a minute about the scattered pieces of her mothers now buried under the earth. "She's an orphan," I said.

"We will keep her safe with us," Pavel Pascenko promised.

As I was starting to leave, I heard a noise inside the house. An old woman had pushed back the faded curtains. She opened her mouth in a toothless grin before disappearing into the darkness.

Chapter Thirty-Four

Глава тридцать четвертая

MY MOTHER OPENED THE DOOR as soon as I touched the knob. At first, all I saw was that she was still dressed in the skirt and blouse of her teaching uniform, but then I noticed that her eyes were red and swollen. Before Papa had even followed me inside, she began scolding me.

"Your principal, your teachers, everyone is upset," Mama said.

"It's all right, Natasha," Papa said.

"Didn't Papa call you?" I asked as I wandered inside.

"Thank goodness he called, but Katya, why?" She grabbed my arm. "Why did you run away?" The three of us were huddled together in the small entranceway.

"I'm sorry, Mama," I said. "I had to go back to Yanov."

She eyed me suspiciously. "With Sergei Rudko."

"I don't think her trip was about the boy, Natasha," Papa said.

"We didn't raise you this way, Katya!" Mama snapped.

"Don't fuss at her, Natasha."

When I heard Papa defend me, my reserve broke down, and I began sobbing. It frightened me that I could not stop. I felt like a stream of tears was inside me. Then I realized that I had never cried, not really, since we'd left the Dead Zone four years ago.

My mother relaxed and she put her arms around me. "I know....

I know…"

Mama took one hand. Papa the other. Together, we walked into the living room and sat on the couch.

She stroked my hair. "Katya…Katya…It's all right. You'll be all right."

Afterwards, the three of us sat for a long time. Finally, Papa turned on the television, and Mama got up to make chicken and dumplings.

As if my tears had opened a floodgate of memories, we reminisced about our old life in Yanov while we ate. We talked about Granny Vera, and Papa told me about his grandmother, Granny Vera's mother. Polina Dubko had red hair too. She smoked a corncob pipe, and although she didn't have much schooling, she could calculate math problems in her head.

A knock sounded at the door.

Mama went to open it. With his beret in his hands, Victor Kaletnik walked in. Papa and I were sitting side by side on the couch.

"Hey, Katya," Uncle Victor called to me.

I ran and hugged him. As he rumpled my hair, I peeked over my shoulder at my father.

When Papa stood up, he wasn't smiling at his old friend, but he didn't look sorry to see him either. "Victor," he said simply.

Uncle Victor took a few steps towards Papa. He was at least a foot shorter than Papa and, in comparison with Papa's muscular frame, portly. "I came because I heard about your illness, Ivan."

The two men stared at each other for a few moments as if they were strangers. Then Papa surprised me by opening his arms wide. Uncle Victor hurried over and embraced him. Watching them, I felt as if my broken world was reuniting.

Uncle Victor began patting Papa's back and saying over and over, *stariy druzhe*, my dear old friend.

Papa laughed. "Not so old." He lifted Uncle Victor up and twirled him around before setting him down.

"Still strong as an ox," Uncle Victor beamed up at him.

Papa's face became somber. "I want you to know. This has been hard for me, but our friendship should never have been at stake."

Uncle Victor gripped Papa's arm and gazed into his eyes.

When Papa began speaking again, his voice was halting. "I have had a hard time believing that the authorities are liars... that the tragedy happened for nothing."

Uncle Victor's head bobbed in sympathy. "I understand. Just as you are a loyal friend, you are a loyal citizen."

"Your way is very painful for me, Victor. But I am..." Papa paused, "starting to accept the truth."

Mama motioned to me. As we stepped out of the room, the two men were still talking. When I glanced over my shoulder, it was Papa's cheeks that were wet.

Mama followed me into my room and sat down on the end of my bed. "It is good to see them together again."

I agreed. At first, Mama questioned me about the job Uncle Victor had offered me, but she quickly returned to my eventful day. "So tell me more about Yanov," she said.

At dinner, I had described everything I had seen, but I wasn't ready to share my feelings. "I'm too tired. Tomorrow?" I lay down on the bed and crawled underneath the covers.

She kissed me tenderly. "Don't go running off with a boy ever again."

"No, Mama," I promised. On her way out, she turned off the light.

I gazed at the shadows on the wall and listened to the rise and fall of the men's voices, their laughter, their sighs. They talked until late into the night.

Chapter Thirty-Five

Глава тридцать пятая

IN THE HALLWAY, I WAS RUNNING LATE when Mikhail stopped me. "Katya, is it true that you and Sergei climbed up the Ferris wheel?"

"Yes," I said.

Before I knew it, a crowd of boys and girls formed around me: Natasha Lieven, Valentyna Shabo, Vladislav Tasriov, Theda Shanda, all the kids in my class who I had watched, but never had gotten to know.

"How tall is it?"

"Were you scared?"

"Who caught you?"

"Did they throw you in a jail?"

Sergei was used to being a celebrity for his soccer prowess, but overnight I had become one, too. I had always claimed that I wanted to be alone, and I had even discouraged anyone who tried to be friendly to me. But on this morning, the terrible isolation that had engulfed me since the accident seemed to have lifted. I knew I had done something amazing, and it felt good to have people talking to me at school. It was almost as if I had had a form of radiation sickness. And now I was cured.

I must have attended biology, history and math, but in the day's excitement, I don't remember. Finally, the lunch bell rang.

I hurried to find Lyudmila. I had been too late to catch her at her locker.

"Katya, what got into you two?" Lyudmila cried when she saw me.

"First, tell me how the guide discovered that we had left?" I begged. I wanted to relive every moment of that afternoon.

"No, first you tell me. Did Sergei kiss you?" Lyudmila asked.

I shook my head. "You first," I insisted. I wasn't sure whether I was going to share that kiss with anyone.

Lyudmila put her hands on her hips. "You are so infuriating."

We picked a table on the edge of the crowded lunchroom. For the moment, I wasn't mobbed by curious kids. I ate my chicken sandwich and listened to Lyudmila's story. She said one of the bus drivers had caught a glimpse of us leaving. In front of a group of students, he had alerted Mokhoyida, saying, "I'm pretty sure that I saw a boy and a girl run down that alley." After the guide did roll call, she confirmed that we were missing.

Angelika had told everyone who would listen that she had never liked me. "She's a weird girl, who does dangerous things. She lies all the time. Now, she's trying to steal my boyfriend! Again!"

"I'd never seen Angelika look so furious," Lyudmila said, gleefully. "I told Angelika I don't always understand you either. But you're my friend, and you're not a liar."

"Thanks for sticking up for me," I said. "When did the guide find out where we were?"

"We were going to the car graveyard, where they buried all the cars," Lyudmila said, "when the bus driver got a call on the walkie-talkie. 'They're *what*?' that awful guide said. The two of them put their heads together and conferred. Then, she told the kids nearest her, 'They're climbing the Ferris wheel.'"

"At that point," Lyudmila said with a big grin on her face, "all of us were stunned. You could hear, 'Katya and Sergei are climbing the Ferris wheel,' like the refrain of a song."

I smiled, remembering. Our climb had been like a song. I pulled a pickle out of my lunch bag but left it on the table. My stomach felt too jumpy to eat anything sour.

"When Sergei got back on the bus, he called you a gutsy girl," Lyudmila said. She winked at me. "And here he is."

Footsteps sounded behind me. So suddenly that I didn't have time to prepare, Sergei sat down at the picnic table next to Lyudmila. His blond hair was slicked back. I guessed that he had just finished showering after gym. I wanted to look into his eyes, but didn't dare.

Lyudmila and I exchanged glances. As if she were able to read my mind, she puckered her lips and kissed the air.

I felt my face grow hot.

Sergei set his lunch down on the table. Like all popular kids, he just assumed that he would be welcome. As he was salting the cafeteria's version of chicken paprika, I searched for any trace of our kiss in his handsome face—in the blue flecks in his brown eyes or the high color on his cheeks—- but found none.

"I don't know what your father said to Principal Goida, Katya," Sergei said, looking up at me. "But I just got a warning." He took a bite of his food. "Thank him for me."

"I will," I promised.

"I wish we could have stayed on top of the Ferris wheel for longer," Sergei said.

"Me, too," I admitted.

He gestured towards my plate. "Are you going to eat your pickle, Katya?"

"No," I said. When I handed it to him, his smile was warm. Now, he was remembering our kiss. I was sure of it. I felt myself blushing.

"Why didn't you take me?" Lyudmila demanded.

"I wanted you there," I said. Actually, I had wished our whole class had been with us. Even Angelika, I thought as I spotted her heading toward our table. She was glaring at Sergei. I wondered if they were going out together, but when Sergei glanced in her direction, he didn't seem happy to see her.

Angelika frowned. "I've been looking for you."

Sergei shrugged his broad shoulders. His dark eyes twinkled. "You found me."

"I thought I made it clear," Angelika bent down and whispered loudly into his ear. "I don't want you talking to *her*."

"When was the last time that you climbed a Ferris wheel in the Dead Zone, Angelika?" Sergei asked.

"I'm not stupid enough to return to a buried village," Angelika said.

I thought of those mounds of dirt. My trip home *had* been stupid, and yet...

Lyudmila leaned across the table towards me. "Yeah, Katya. Why did you go back to Yanov?"

"I missed my home," I answered.

Angelika sniffed. "But Yanov is buried."

I shrugged. "I know." I would never admit to her that I hadn't truly believed it until I had seen it with my own eyes.

Angelika pulled on Sergei's arm. "Let's go," she said. Tugging on Sergei's T-shirt, she insisted, "Come sit with me. I have a lot to talk to you about."

"Not now, Angelika," Sergei shook her off impatiently.

Angelika shot me an unhappy look before turning away.

"Hey, Sergei," Lyudmila said. She was twirling her long hair around her finger. "Katya and I are going to a movie this weekend." This was news to me.

"Do you want to go?" Lyudmila played the part of the old village matchmaker effortlessly.

I held my breath as Sergei glanced toward the nearby table where Angelika had sat down. Her sack lunch was untouched in front of her, and she openly studied us.

Sergei turned back and gazed at me. Long after I had given up hope, his face broke into a smile. "Why not?"

I felt a tingle of excitement. The movie theatre would be dark. Sergei and I would sit side by side. When Lyudmila went to get popcorn, hopefully Sergei would kiss me again.

"So what movie should we go to?" Lyudmila asked.

Sergei smiled at me. "Katya, you decide."

"Yeah," Lyudmila said. "What does our hero want to see?"

"The new James Bond movie," I said.

"Did you see the James Bond where…?" Lyudmila started, but I didn't notice what she said. For the first time in a long time, surrounded by friends, and basking in the aftermath of our climb, I felt happy, radiantly happy, once again.

Happiness begets happiness, Granny Vera used to say. I'd learned that she was seldom wrong.

Chapter Thirty-Six

Глава тридцать шестая

WHEN I KNOCKED, Margarita Pikalova cracked the door. Her dark hair was in large rollers, and cold cream covered her creased face. "Katya, I haven't seen you for a while. Come in. Come in."

I followed her inside and was glad to find that the apartment was empty. Hoping that Lyudmila would have gone home, I had chosen to wait until after dinner to stop by.

Margarita stood next to the kitchen counter, wearing only a black slip. A large crystal pendant hung on a chain around her thick neck. "I'm a nervous mess. I have a date tonight."

"Who with?"

"A man I met at the café. He is picking me up in an hour. But I need a cup of coffee. Have a seat." While she boiled some water, I sat on a stool.

"Lyudmila told me about your escapade at the Dead Zone," she said.

"I went back, Margarita. I went back to the boulder where I had seen the *domovyk*," I said.

"Did he appear again?" she asked.

"No." I shook my head. She sat down beside me and looked over at me as if expecting details. But I hadn't come to talk to her about my strange experience. As I watched her sip her coffee, I took a deep breath and told her what I needed to say. "I've got a new job."

"Oh? Where are you working?" she asked.

"For a scientist."

Margarita raised one eyebrow. "What kind of a scientist?"

"He's an engineer, but he's working for an international health organization." I paused, trying to gather the courage to disclose the rest. The fact that I, too, wanted to become a scientist. "He tells me that for something to be true, you have to be able to prove it."

"Can I offer you some soup?" she asked. "I made potato soup last night."

"No," I said. "Papa is going to leave for Kiev tomorrow. I better go home."

"Look at me, child," Margarita said. I stared into her dark eyes. Her usually stringy hair wound tightly around the curlers framing her face. "I thought so." She came around the counter and angled my chin underneath the light. "Your aura has changed."

"You explained that crystals have auras, but you didn't tell me that people have them also," I said.

Her head bobbed knowingly. "Oh, but they do, and yours has changed."

She spoke with such authority that, although I didn't believe her, her words made me nervous. "I hope my parents don't notice."

"I doubt that they will," she said. "Enjoy your new boyfriend, whoever he is."

Remembering the jolt I had felt when Sergei kissed me, I smiled.

"By the way, when does this scientist friend of yours say that people will be able to move back to the Dead Zone?" Margarita asked. She sat back down and started taking the curlers out of her hair.

"He says 400 years." I smiled, hearing Uncle Victor's voice inside my head. *But of course, I am an optimist. Most of my colleagues think it will be 700 years.*

Margarita tapped her long fingernails against the counter. "So hundreds of years from now, some little girl will find your boulder."

"I hope so," I said.

She started humming. "It'll happen."

"Why are you so sure?" I asked, teasingly.

Margarita smiled at me. She walked over to the table and picked up an ordinary ceramic bowl. She set it on the counter in front of us. "Look."

I saw the bowl glazed blue on the outside. It was full of yellow water. The water she used to dye the crystals, to trick people. Disappointed, I was about to tell her that I really needed to go, when she twirled her finger in the bowl and said, "Now concentrate."

The water, wildly spinning around the sides of the bowl, was forming an image.

I thought I recognized it.

She twirled her finger in the water again, and the image became clear. It was the Ferris wheel in Pripyat—the one that had never moved—turning fast and even faster.

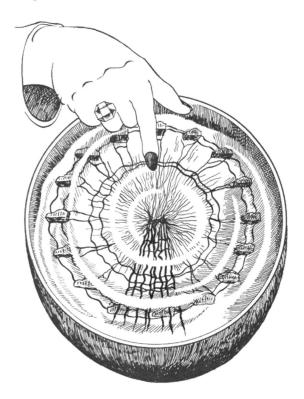

Epilogue

A FEW WEEKS LATER, TATJANA PETROVNA brought us copies of *Nuclear Energy News*. The students on the field trip, about one hundred of them, were lined up in front of the abandoned apartment complex in Pripyat. Most of my classmates were smiling, but not Angelika. Her face was turned in profile as if she were searching for us. Of course, Sergei and I were missing from the group. The headline in big bold letters read: "Dead Zone Safe for School Children."

Another lie!

Although at the time I didn't realize this, the Soviet Union President Mikhail Gorbachev had begun promoting 'glasnost' or political openness throughout the Soviet Union, and everywhere Ukrainians were debating the justice of Soviet domination over our country. Finally, the citizens of Ukraine were beginning to realize that Moscow was destroying their environment and endangering their lives.

A little over a year later—on August 24, 1991—the Ukraine broke away from the Soviet Union. With hindsight, it seems apparent that the government's lies about the Chernobyl disaster played a key role in my country's independence.

Although Ukraine's road to democracy has been marked by struggle, my countrymen know that we can withstand hard times, because we always have. Our national anthem, entitled *She Ne Vmerla Ukrayina*, "Ukraine is yet alive," reflects our perseverance through suffering.

On December 15, 2000, the President of the Ukraine, Leonid Kuchma, shut down Chernobyl Nuclear Power Station forever. American President Bill Clinton called this event, "a triumph for the common good." He added, *Slava Ukrayini*, Glory to Ukraine.

Papa died just two months later. He was forty-two. We weren't allowed to bury him with Granny Vera in Pripyat, so he rests in the new modern cemetery in Slavutich. I visit his grave often. When I drape strings of pink and red plastic flowers over his headstone, I can't help wondering if Papa and Granny Vera are together now.

Just as we decorated Granny Vera's grave, we put Papa's photo on his. After Papa returned from his operation, Mama bought a new camera and snapped his picture. He is dressed in his gym clothes and sitting on our red Moped. He remains my hero.

Slava Ukrayini.

Acknowledgements

Thanks so much to the House of Fiction, including Iris, Tuck, Leslie and Macey.

Shirley Redwine, I am still mourning the Chief's death. Gabrielle Hale, a gifted storyteller. Kat Hunter, a provocative short-story writer, who needs a new non-leaky pen. Brenda Liebling-Goldberg, the female Woody Allen. Georgiana Nelson, master of suspense. Lucie Smith, creator of the incomparable Sue Ann. Angelique Jamail, teller of magical fairy tales. Kala Dunn, the next Flannery O'Connor. Mimi Swartz, a natural. Sarah Warburton, beautiful stories written under the trying circumstances of motherhood.

You guys are such amazing writers, and I miss our laughter.

Most of all, thank you to Justin Cronin, without whom this book could never have been written. I have looked for a teacher all of my writing life, and for a brief time I was lucky to have found the very best. (P.S. Thanks for the titles of both of my last books.)

Lucy Chambers, you are a brilliant editor. Thank you for researching Ukrainian folklore and coming up with the *domovyk*. You may be the only editor in the world who sends happy, upbeat emails. Rue Judd, I will be forever glad that Talmage Boston introduced us. Ellen Cregan, thank you for your wonderful design; and Elaine Atkinson, for your wonderful illustrations. Nora Shire, is there anything you can't do?

To my young readers: Sallie and Alice Chambers, Iris Cronin, Ryan Friedman, Caroline Craddock, Courtney Fontaine, Kristina Chubanova, Chas, Lauren and Jackson Jhin, Franci Williams, Katie Kellner, Marissa and Daniel Leebron, Sam Foshee, Caroline Clutterbuck, Victor Harter, and my own great kids, Elena, Will and Stephen, you guys are the best.

Pam Rosenauer and Quyen Le, I am so grateful to you for always coming through for me. Thank you to Tetyana Keeble and Olena Volkovicher for reading this book, for your many comments and your enthusiasm. I really couldn't have finished the book without Tetyana. You and your BlackBerry were a godsend.

Speaking of people I couldn't do without—Bill, thank you for your cheerful support of my writing time.

Bud Frick, Nancy and Scott Atlas, Nancy Beren, Joanne Herring, Donna Vallone, Dr. Denton Cooley, Kitty Rabinow, B.A. Bentsen, Shafik Rifaat, Carrin Patman, Stanford and Joan Alexander, and Zeina Fares, every writer should have friends like you. Franci Crane, Sis Johnson, Michael Zilkha and Elena Marks, thank you for reading my drafts. Lorraine Wulfe, The River, Literacy Advance, Jonathan Sandys, Suzie and Phil Conway, Courtney and Christopher Sarofim, Gary and Andrea Lynn, and Marsha Kushner, St. John's classes of McNair Johnson, and Carolyn Bell—Thank you for making my last book, *Window Boy*, so much fun.

Thank you also to Oksana Strashna, Kateryna Zhuravska, Natalie A. Jaresko, Irina Trilevich, Natasha Bleyzer, Debbie Hartman, and the late Rimma Kyselytsia, my wonderful Ukrainian guide. Gail Brown, you are always so helpful and resourceful, and I am grateful.

Image of Katya by Tetyana Keeble.

The author and publisher gratefully acknowledge the following publishers for permission to reprint text from the copyrighted material listed below. Quotations are cited using the abbreviations listed before each work.

Reference Books:

JC: *Journey to Chernobyl: Encounters in a Radioactive Zone,* Glenn Alan Cheney (Academy Chicago Publishers, 1995)

TAC: *The Truth About Chernobyl,* Grigori Medvedev (New York, Perseus Books Group, 1991)

WF: Reprinted with permission from *Wormwood Forest, A Natural History of Chernobyl* by Mary Mycio, copyright 2005, (Joseph Henry Press, Washington, D.C.)

VC: Permission to use the excerpts from *Voices from Chernobyl* was granted by Dalkey Archive Press, Champagne, IL., copyright 1997 Svetlana Alexievich

ABL: *ABLAZE, The Story of the Heroes and Victims of Chernobyl,* Piers Paul Read (New York, Random House,1993)

Ukraine, The Bradt Travel Guide, Andrew Evans, (Guilford, CT, The Globe Pequot Press Inc., USA 2005)

Notes

1. VC   p. 168
2. TAC   p. 99
3. TAC   p. 150
4. TAC   p. 150
5. WF   p. 13
6. TAC   p. 186
7. TAC   p.187
8. JC   p. 116
9. VC   p. 132
10. VC   p. 133
11. ABL   p.148
12. TAC   p. 188-89
13. VC   p. 93
14. VC   p. 71
15. VC   p. 71
16. VC   p. 34
17. VC   p. 177
18. VC   p. 264
19. ABL   p. 208
20. ABL   p. 270
21. WF   p. 13
22. ABL   p. 238
23. ABL   p. 270
24. ABL   p. 210
25. TAC   p. 73-77
26. TAC   p. 89
27. TAC   p. 124
28. TAC   p. 83
29. WF   p. 14
30. WF   p. 56
31. WF   p. 25

32. WF   p. 223
33. JC   p. 90
34. VC   p. 34
35. WF   p. 15
36. VC   p. 40
37. VC   p. 29
38. VC   p. 29
39. VC   p. 31
40. VC   p. 37
41. VC   p. 31
42. VC   p. 32
43. VC   p. 41

Glossary

One of the best parts of writing this book was learning about another culture. Here's a glossary of terms which may be unfamiliar.

~ Andrea White

Biological robots – Men and women who cleaned up the power plant grounds after the explosion and carried nuclear fuel to trucks. Robotic machines were used at first, but the high radiation damaged the electronics. Sometimes these workers took in so much radiation that their muscles separated from their bones. Doctors were forbidden to tell them why.

Chertneya – The little devil.

Chernozem – Black Earth is Ukraine's black-colored, highly-fertile soil which produces high agriculture yield

Communist Party – Name of the political party of the USSR.

Comrade – Friend or ally.

Dead Zone – Also called Zone of Alienation, this area has a radius of 30 kilometers (19-mile) and still has radioactive contamination.

Domovyk – A house elf is part of folklore. It protects the house from evil and trouble and alerts the family or a specific individual to impending danger. The elves are known to play tricks on people.

S dnem narodzhennya – Happy Birthday.

ENDEARING AND POLITE TERMS:

Babuska – A Russian word for grandmother or old lady.

Donechka – My little girl.

Kohana – Sweetheart.

Laskavo prosimo – Thank you.

Stariy druzhe – My dear friend.

FOOD:

Borsch – Vegetable soup with cabbage, beetroot and tomato.

Horilka – Alcoholic beverage.

Kutia – Traditional Christmas dish made with poppy seeds, wheat nuts and honey.

Paska loaf – Easter bread.

Salo – Salted and spiced pig fat.

Smaletz – Congealed lard.

Varenniki – Large stuffed dumplings.

Glasnost – An official Soviet government policy emphasizing candor in regard to discussion of social problems.

Gospody – Lord.

Hiroshima – City in Japan where the atomic bomb was dropped Aug. 6, 1945. This action by the United States ended its war with the Japanese.

Lenin, Vladimir Ilyich (1870 – 1924) – First head of the Russian Soviet Socialist Republic (USSR).

Liquidators – Some 600,000 people, military and civilian, went to the Dead Zone to eliminate the contamination by hosing down streets and villages, bulldozing towns, burying topsoil and trees. Then, 90,000 of them constructed the shell, nicknamed the Sarcophagus, that covers the damaged reactor.

Matryoshka – A set of Russian nested dolls decreasing in size (placed inside each other).

MEASUREMENTS:

Dosimeter – Is a device that measures the cumulative dose of radiation received by the instrument at a particular location.

Hectares – One hectare is equal to 2.47 acres. In Ukraine after the explosion, 2.5 million hectares were contaminated.

Kilometer – One kilometer equals 1,000 meters or 0.62137119 mile.

Roentgen – Is a unit that identifies and measures radiation in the air at a particular location. As radiation passes through the human body, radioactive energy accumulates in different organs. The RAD, "radiation absorbed dose," was developed to measure radiation in the body. One dose is equal to one roentgen of gamma radiation. Because doses from different types of radiation do not result in equal damage, the REM, "roentgen equivalent man," was needed to estimate the relative biological damage of different types of radiation.

MONEY:

Grivnas – $1 equals 5.05 grivnas

Kopeika – An old copper coin

Nuclear fatigue – The extreme tiredness that results from intense radiation exposure.

Nuclear tan – Radiation exposure turns the skin a brown color all over the body. The more radiation absorbed, the darker the color. Some people turned black.

Pisanki eggs – Eggs decorated by drawing traditional Easter symbols on them.

Poleise area – A vast, virgin forest west of the Chernobyl plant too contaminated to inhabit.

Pripyat – Town closest to the Chernobyl Nuclear Power Plant. Now a ghost town.

Radiation – Emitted by unstable atoms from many different sources, including sunlight, granite and the human body. It can cause harm when its waves and particles penetrate living tissue, as happened after the explosion.

Radiation sickness or poisoning – Causes damage to organ tissues in the body after a very large dose of radiation exposure is received over a short period of time. It can also result from exposure to a small dose for a long time. The amount absorbed determines how sick the person will be. A dose of 400 roentgens would cause severe nausea, burning sensation in the eyes and chest, headache and nonstop vomiting. Within a few hours, the skin would turn black.

Radioactive patients – Many people who absorbed radiation were radioactive and emitted as much as 20 rems per day from the cesium-137 in their bodies. It is the primary source of radiation in the Zone of Alienation. Water-soluble and toxic in tiny amounts, it can cause cancer from 10 to 30 years after entering the body. The other two radioactive elements are iodine-131 and strontium-90.

Radionuclides – Radioactive elements, which may be naturally-occurring or synthetic. They emit various types of energetic radiation – alpha and beta particles.

Radiophobia –This is a psychological condition whereby every illness from eczema to a cold is ascribed to radiation.

Sarcophagus – After the explosion, a concrete shell was constructed over the damaged reactor to contain the radiation, which was so high the parts were put in place by robots and helicopters and 90,000 liquidators.

Squatters – People who sneaked into the Dead Zone to live or former residents who returned. Some are residents who never left. They hid when others were being evacuated.

Slavutich – A town completed in 1988 and built for the power plant workers after Pripyat was abandoned.

Thyroid - It is a ductless gland that regulates growth. When iodine-131 enters the body, it lodges in this gland.

USSR – In 1922, the Union of Soviet Socialist Republics organized. This Communist government lasted until 1991 when the people in several republics, such as Ukraine, decided they wanted more say in the government.

Zones – After the disaster, the government's Institute of Biophysics divided the contaminated areas into four zones: Alienation or Prohibited, from which the entire population was evacuated; temporary evacuation, in which, against official advice, 1,000 people had returned to live and refused to move; constant control; periodic control in which 84,000 people lived in 176 villages where food had to be brought in. The soil was too contaminated to grow anything.

About the Author

Andrea White was born in Baton Rouge, Louisiana, but has spent most of her life in Houston, Texas. She received her undergraduate and law degrees from the University of Texas. Her first book, *Surviving Antarctica*, was on the reading lists of several states, including the Bluebonnet list. In 2006, she won the Golden Spur award given by the Texas State Reading Association for the best book by a Texas author. She is also the author of *Window Boy*, a middle school novel which Winston Churchill's great-grand-son Jonathan Sandys has praised as "a fantastic introduction into the life of my great-grandfather. It completely encapsulates the principles of 'Never surrender!' and 'Determination' that he lived by."

In addition to writing, Ms. White serves as an active community volunteer. Partnering with the Houston Independent School District Board, she and her husband, Houston's Mayor Bill White, have started the program Expectation Graduation to try to keep more kids in school. The Whites have three children: Will, Elena and Stephen.

The text of *Radiant Girl* is set in Garamond, a typeface attributed to Claude Garamond, who is considered the first independent typefounder. Although he did not invent movable type, he was the first to make type available to printers at an affordable price. In 1541 Garamond was commissioned by François I to cut a sequence of Greek fonts known as the *grecs du roi*. Modern typefaces bearing the Garamond name are not always based on these designs, but they share certain characteristics of timeless beauty and readability.